LOGAN AT SEA

LOGAN AT SEA

TWO FULL NOVELS
"KILLERS AT SEA" AND "LOGAN"

ALAN JOSEPH

CUTTING EDGE

ISBN-13: 978-1-957868-40-0

Published by
Cutting Edge Books
PO Box 8212
Calabasas, CA 91372
www.cuttingedgebooks.com

INTRODUCTION
JON MESSMANN
AT SEA

BY ERIC COMPTON

Jon Joseph Messmann (1920-2004) was a highly-prolific author of action-adventure, westerns, crime-fiction, and romantic-suspense novels. The New York native began his career in the comic book industry, contributing stories and ideas to books like *Captain Marvel Jr.*, *Human Torch*, and *Sub-Mariner* during the Golden Age of Comic Books. After transitioning into the tabloids, Messmann pursued a career of authoring original paperback novels.

Beginning in the 1960s, Messmann began writing installments in the popular, highly successful spy-fiction series *Nick Carter: Killmaster*, the star franchise for Lyle Kenyon Engel's Book Creations. Messmann's talents as a storyteller were some of the most prevalent of the series, leading the author to write a total of 14 novels in the series using the publisher's house pseudonym Nick Carter.

The 1970s proved to be a fertile time for Messmann, a decade in which he developed and authored the vigilante men's action-adventure series *The Revenger*. Messmann also wrote and created a series called *The Handyman*, a globe-trotting action series starring a "President's Man" type of hero, while also authoring a number of gothic and suspenseful romance novels under the pseudonyms "Claudette Nicole" and "Pamela Windsor."

During that time, Messmann used the pseudonym Alan Joseph to write the two excellent adventure novels, *Logan* and *Killers at Sea*. Both books starred a seafaring adventurer named Logan, who was clearly inspired by John D. MacDonald's wildly successful Travis McGee series of nautical private-eye mysteries.

But the real mystery involves the publication history of these two Logan novels.

In 1970, Belmont-Tower published *Logan*, which was followed by the book's supposed sequel, *Killers at Sea*, published by Star Books.

However, even though *Logan* was published first, there are compelling clues within the novel that strongly suggest that Messmann actually wrote the book after *Killers at Sea*.

What comes next could be a SPOILER, so you might want to come back to this introduction after reading the two books.

Okay, now that you've been duly warned, here's why I believe *Killers At Sea* was the first Logan book.

Killers at Sea has all the genre tropes of an origin tale, which are missing from *Logan*. It also provides more (but presumably not all) of the backstory regarding Logan's interest in Sister Mary Angela's charity. But in *Logan*, presented at the first book, Messmann only briefly mentions Sister Mary Angela, as if readers are already familiar with that character, and she needs no introduction. But the real smoking gun is a woman named Julie.

In *Killers at Sea*, Logan meets a woman on the beach named Julie and the two develop an intimate relationship that leads to a rip-roaring adventure for them both.

In the opening pages of *Logan*, he arrives back at his boat with a woman named Julie, who is given no introduction. If this isn't the same woman, why name two female characters the same? The Julie in the *Logan* novel doesn't really say much to reveal her past, and she quickly leaves Logan when bullets start flying. It was as if the Julie chapter of Logan's life had reached its conclusion. And that really only makes sense if *Killers at Sea* actually came first...and *Logan* second.

Why the books were published in the wrong order, and by two different publishers, is something we may never know. But now Cutting Edge Books has set things right in this omnibus edition, bringing the Logan character to you the way I believe Messmann would have wanted it.

Eric Compton lives in the most haunted city in the world, St. Augustine, Florida with his wife, two daughters, three dogs, possibly a deceased lizard, and his alter-ego, *The Paperback Warrior*. His journey into blog super-stardom began in 2013 when he launched the successful *Paperback Warrior* brand (paperbackwarrior.com), a blog focusing on vintage paperbacks of the 20th century in genre fiction like crime-noir, science-fiction, spy and espionage, military, pulp, fantasy, western, and gothic romance. Beginning in 2018, Eric partnered with real life private-detective and retired F.B.I. Special Agent Tom Simon to include additional reviews, interviews, original columns, and more commentary on paperback novels and pulps. *The Paperback Warrior Podcast*, hosted by Eric and Tom, launched in 2019. With nearly 100 episodes, it has become the internet's most popular vintage fiction podcast.

KILLERS AT SEA

CHAPTER ONE

The old man on the beach was dead. Logan put a hand against his cheek. Dry, wrinkled parchment, but warm. He'd been brutally beaten to death. Recently. His eyes shifted from the man's body across the sandy dunes. It was dawn and the surf thundered. Logan had known the old man for years. This morning, as he'd done every time he came to Kingdom Point, he'd come for clams, the big quahogs of the Carolina coast. If the old man had a name, Logan had never heard it. The "old man of the beach" was all anyone ever called him. A harmless, gentle old man. Now he was dead, slain in the soft, gray mist of the early morning.

The knot in Logan's stomach was cold anger, disgust, old pain brought to life. Logan's long, lined face was impassive as he started to go through the old man's pockets. Suddenly, a shot exploded, sending the sea birds screeching, and ripped into his sleeve. Only his eyes changed, blazed. With lightning-fast reaction, he moved. A sand dune to his right beckoned, topped by a thin line of tough railroad vines. He had just rolled behind it when another shot split the air, grazing his ankle as he rolled. He winced at the sharp, searing pain of it and flattened himself down into the sand behind the low dune. Edging upward, he peered out through the vines. Across a dip in the sand, behind the vines of another dune, he glimpsed long, blond hair—the real kind of blond, made yellower by the sun.

"Hold it!" Logan called out. "Listen to me."

The third shot thudded into the dune, showering him with sand.

"Bastard! Stinkin', rotten bastard. I'll kill you," he heard the girl say, words more sobbed than shouted. Another shot whizzed over his head. Keeping down, he called out again.

"Listen, you're making a mistake," he yelled. Another shot whopped into the sand. He rolled over and glanced around. A line of yaupon grew on the other side of the dune, starting left and wandering to circle behind the dune where the girl sat. Staying low, he pulled off his shirt and laid it against the dune-top vines. Almost at once, she fired again. Logan saw the bullet go through the shirtsleeve. He crawled down into the dune and worked his way to the yaupon, crouching behind it. Damnit to hell, he cursed, silently. He'd come to Kingdom Point to see Jennifer, to renew an old moment of peace and quiet. Instead, he was being used as a shooting gallery target by a babe with long blond hair. He crawled alongside the yaupon till he was almost opposite the other dune. He could see her better. He moved on, staying flat on his stomach, moving slowly so as not to disturb the bushes. The girl was intent on the dune where he'd been. Then, suddenly, he heard her voice.

"Why'd you have to kill him?" Logan heard. "I'll get you for that, I swear. You'll have to come out. I'll wait."

There was a choked sob in each word, as though it were torn out from inside her. But now he had circled around behind her and saw that she lay flat on her stomach with the rifle resting on the edge of the sand dune. Her legs were spread apart, her rear a round, full mound, inviting in the tightness of her jeans. He wanted to go up and pat it. But he knew that would get him killed. The girl was near hysteria. As he watched, she fired two more shots off, each shot a kind of curse, accompanied by a deep, choking sob. Logan stood up carefully, lifting himself first to a crouch, then rising to his full height. Moving with the silent grace of a jungle cat, he stepped forward carefully. The girl lay about twenty feet away. He'd crossed a little more than half the distance when she turned. She hadn't heard him, he was sure.

As she whirled, he saw blue eyes blazing and large breasts barely contained by her red-checkered shirt. She rolled on her back and swung the rifle over to fire as he twisted and dived forward. The shot exploded, and he felt the bullet tear past his ribs, grazing his skin. Then he was on top of her, grabbing for the rifle with both hands. He got a trip on the barrel and twisted, but she went with it, clinging to it like a squid to a lobster. He felt the movement of her knee and twisted his body to one side, just in time. She had brought her leg up sharply, trying for his groin.

"Bastard!" she gasped through clenched teeth. She let go with one hand and raked her nails across his face. Logan turned his head away and felt her hands grip his hair and yank. He brought one arm around, letting go of the rifle for a brief instant, and clipped her on the side of her jaw. She went limp, and he seized the rifle again and yanked it out of her hand. As he rose, she half-rolled over and then kicked out, sharply. The blow caught his thigh as he twisted away. He grabbed her leg, twisted and flipped her over on her stomach. She gasped in pain. With one big hand he pressed her face down into the sand and held her there, giving her just enough air to manage a few deep breaths.

"Goddamned little hellcat," he said. "Stop that and listen to me." She tried a backward kick, bringing her leg up sharply. It raked him across the side of his ribs. Tossing away the rifle, he brought his hand down with all his might across her tight, full little ass. She yelled. Yanking her by a handful of her long, blond hair, he pulled her up and tossed her down onto the sand on her back. The sand flew up as she hit, and she lay there, trying to catch her breath.

"I didn't kill the old man, damn it," Logan shouted at her. She lay there, chest heaving, her breasts drawing the red check of her shirt taut with each breath. Her hips, in the tight jeans, were narrow and flowed into long legs. Her lips were full, softly formed, with the lower one thrust out in a half-pout. Her sea-blue eyes glowered at him. She lay there for a long moment as her breath returned, and he stared at her, waiting for her to say something. Then he saw her hands, tensing, pressing into the sand. Another man might have missed it, but not Logan. He'd learned, once, to look for the little things and not forget the things you learned the hard way. When she flung herself up and over, rolling toward the rifle in the sand, he stuck out a foot and caught her in the belly with it, lifting her up and flinging her backward. She doubled up on the sand, hands clutched to her belly and her long blond hair falling down, partially hiding the pain on her face.

"Sonofabitch!" she gasped.

"I told you I didn't kill him," Logan said quietly. He took her by the shoulder and felt the softness of her flesh. Christ, he needed a woman. Even now, with this furious spitfire, he could feel the need. He kept his hand on the girl's shoulder, pressing her back into the sand, pulling her body straight. He knew his big frame almost blotted the sky from her view, and his hand on her shoulder pressed in with the hint of what it could do. But there was no fear in her blazing eyes—only fury.

"I'll tell you once more," he said, his voice menacingly low. "I didn't kill the old man. I came along and found him there."

"You were going through his pockets," she hissed.

"Yes, to find something with his name on it," Logan answered. He let go of her shoulder and stood up. He gazed down at her, thinking how beautifully wild she was.

"I came for some clams," Logan said. "I always do when I stop here at Kingdom Point. Why would I want to kill him?"

The question brought back a flood of pain, and he saw her eyes overflow at once. She got up on one elbow and looked across the spot where the crumpled figure lay behind a rise in the sand.

"Why? Damn, I don't know why," she sobbed. "Why should anyone have to kill him? He never hurt anybody. He never did anything to anyone. He was kind and good."

Logan didn't answer. Her questions were the same as his. He hadn't had any answers then, and he hadn't any now. Only to say that people killed people and right had damned little to do with it. He held out his hand. The girl took it, and he pulled her to her feet. He remembered once hearing that the old man had a girl who lived with him, a niece.

"You the niece?" he asked, crisply. She nodded and wiped her eyes with the back of her hand.

"You can get your rifle now," he said, and she looked up at him, frowning. "Go ahead," he said. "That ought to prove to you I didn't kill him." Her eyes still regarded him distrustfully. "If I killed him why don't I just shut you up, too?" he asked. "Go on, get the rifle. Maybe then you'll believe me."

It was a calculated risk. The girl walked over to the rifle and picked it up. Logan stood watching her and saw the cold hatred go out of her eyes.

"All right, I guess I believe you," she said. She came toward him, and he watched the slow, easy grace of her walk. She was as sensuous as the sea itself, as inviting, as invigorating, and as dangerous.

"What were you doing out here with the rifle?" he asked.

"I got up later than Pops and came out to help him," she answered. "When I found him I ran back to the house, got the rifle and ran all the way back here."

"And saw me beside him starting to go through his pockets," Logan finished. "And you just started shooting."

The girl's eyes on him were steady, her lower lip pushed out a fraction farther. "I guess I just didn't think or care about anything except killing somebody for what happened to Pops," she said. "Who are you, anyway?"

"Logan," he said flatly. "And I just stopped at Kingdom Point to see an old friend. I'm anchored off shore."

She swung around and let her eyes move out across the beach to the rolling surf, now blue and sparkling in the morning sun. The *Sea Urchin* was anchored a few hundred yards below where they stood and about a hundred yards off shore.

"That funny old beat-up one that dropped anchor last night?" she asked, turning to him. Logan was used to the *Sea Urchin* being called that. It was fine with him. He purposely let her peeling, chipped paint hide the powerful, seagoing hull and interior of hand-rubbed Burma teak, Philippine mahogany hull with keel and frames of Yacal and silicon bronze fastenings. The *Urchin*, like her master, preferred to wear old clothes. She could show what she had when it was necessary. That was enough.

"Yes," Logan answered. He saw her take in the powerful muscles of his chest, the width of his shoulders and the rippling movement of his back as he retrieved his shirt. "What's your name?"

"Julie," she said, her voice quiet.

"All right, Julie, I'll take you back," he said. "You can't do anything here. We can call the police."

"The cops!" she sneered, falling into step beside him. "That's a laugh. The only cops here are Chief Redmond and that big ape assistant of his, Luther. They won't do nothin'. Chief Redmond will say some of the rich kids from the other side of the point did it for kicks and that'll be the end of it. Luther will use it as an excuse to come out here to question me with more than his tongue hangin' out."

Logan was surprised at her bitterness. She walked away from the beach and back up across the small hillocks. Cresting the rise, Logan saw the house. It was like some bad joke, a caricature of all old houses ever built. Gray wood, unpainted, weathered, upper floors boarded, it sagged and leaned in all directions at once. There were crumbling towers at the front of the house, one at each end, and a widow's walk circled the roof line, bordering sagging gables. The front door was open, and they walked in through a foyer with dark flowered wallpaper and two sturdy, old chairs. The foyer opened up into a huge living room, cluttered with furniture that was more bits and pieces than whole. A stone fireplace took up most of one wall, and a dark-green, worn sofa filled the space in front of it. On a round table a hurricane lamp stood next to a welter of books. The corners of the room were crammed with oars, crab nets and heavy, wooden clam tubs. A roll-top desk nudged a jumble of boxes and crates at one side, and four heavy, stuffed chairs with faded fabric, were scattered aimlessly around the room. At the far end, a wall of windows stood open. The window sills were lined with cages that looked out toward the sea. A ringed plover occupied one cage, a tern another and a gull a third. Two field mice chattered in a fourth cage. Near the windows was an easel with a canvas on it, and a paint box leaning against it. The room spoke of people who had lived good lives of work, weather and contentment. As Logan watched, the girl walked around the room.

"He taught me so much," she said. "He knew so much. He knew why a particular kind of sponge is the way it is, why the sea birds fly differently when a storm nears, why the ocean and the land constantly borrow life from each other. He taught me to be aware of everything, to wonder at all living things."

She opened the center cage and took out a tern, stroking the feathers. Her lustiness was gone. She was all gentleness and sensitivity.

"He brought this one in with a broken wing and nursed it," she said. "He was going to let it go today."

Released, the tern flew out the window. It circled, wheeled and flew out to sea. Julie turned to the big man, her eyes boring into his. She was once again all earthiness, as though she'd tossed aside the cape she'd worn for a brief moment. She walked to the easel and took down the canvas.

"Who did the painting?" Logan asked.

"He did," she said, her voice small. "He used to like to paint the gray days especially, to find beauty in the things everybody else finds dull and boring."

She turned, anger in her eyes.

"But he wasn't one of those gabby old men, understand?" she said. "He wasn't full of empty words and armchair philosophy. He lived this way because he wanted to. He didn't make excuses and hide behind big words."

"And you?" Logan asked.

"I wouldn't have changed it for anything," she said.

"Not even the loneliness?"

She shrugged. "Loneliness is more inside than outside," she said. As she crossed the room, dismissing the conversation, Logan saw the scuba diving gear half hidden behind the edge of the clam tubs. She moved one of the air tanks, setting it up against the wall.

"Your equipment?" he asked and she nodded.

"I started diving when I was fourteen," she said. "I got interested in it. You could say it's a hobby, I guess. I like it under the water. It's another world. It's like eavesdropping."

Logan smiled. She certainly was unpretentious.

"Why'd you come here to Kingdom Point?" she asked, looking at him sideways.

"Seeing an old friend," Logan replied.

"A girl?"

He nodded. "But not the way you make it sound. She's just an old friend, someone out of the past. I stop to see her whenever I pass this way."

"Who is she?" Julie asked suddenly, bluntly. He was going to tell her it was none of her damned business, but he didn't. That was a mistake, but he suddenly felt sorry for her, for the lost look behind the defiance in her eyes.

"Jennifer Holden," he said and saw surprise flood her face.

"Jennifer Holden, the town librarian?" she asked. He nodded. He'd called Jennifer when he dropped anchor last night, just long enough to tell her he'd be there with clams for lunch. He remembered how wonderfully sweet her voice had sounded, with the bittersweet pain of the past in it. Not that he and

Jennifer had ever been more than friends. But she was still a part of that time and that pain. She was the only one he ever saw any longer, and he often wondered why. Perhaps there was a communication of the wounded between them. Logan brought his mind back to the blond creature watching him, and gave her a small smile.

"Where's your phone, Julie?" he asked. "I'll call the police for you."

"I told you they won't do anything," she said bitterly.

"They can take in the body," Logan said. "Where's the phone?"

"No phone," she snapped. "I'll go into town and tell them. You come, too."

"No, you don't need me," Logan said. "There's nothing more I can do."

"You could help me find who killed Pops," Julie said, glowering up at him. "I'm going to find them, whoever they are."

"Sorry, this is where I get off," Logan said.

"In such a hurry to get to Jennifer Holden?" Julie sneered. "She must have somethin' I didn't notice."

Logan's dark, probing eyes narrowed. "Watch it, doll," he said, a hard note in his voice. She was glowering, sullen with a defiant sexuality. "There's nothing more I could do. Sorry about the old man, really I am."

"You could stay here," she said. "There's plenty of room. You could help me find who killed Pops." She was suddenly all little girl, pleading, anxious. She could change moods like a chameleon changed colors.

"No dice, Julie," Logan said. "Sorry." He turned and started for the door.

"Sorry, my ass," she called to him. "You don't care a god-damned bit." He paused and looked back at her blazing eyes.

"I care, but I'll care alone, in my own way," he said. "And I don't expect you to understand."

"Jennifer will be glad to see you," the girl said. Once more, Logan paused, his big frame filling the doorway.

"Why do you say that?" he asked quietly, frowning at her. She shrugged, a lost, helpless little shrug.

"*I* would be," she murmured, hardly loud enough for him to hear, and his eyes narrowed as he looked at her.

"Thanks," he said, and walked out the door.

"Bastard!" he heard her shout after him. "Don't come back, hear?"

Logan grinned. He didn't intend to. He'd come to Kingdom Point to see Jennifer and the boy. He wasn't getting involved in a murder. It was lousy. It was stinking. But it was done, and he'd have none of it. He and the *Sea Urchin* had other places to go and other things to do. They had their own search, and he knew he could never explain it to Julie. He let thoughts of Jennifer elbow the girl with the long blond hair from his mind. Jennifer would understand his not staying. He started across the soft ground, half sand, when he heard a voice, cold, rough, commanding.

"Hold it," the voice said. "Turn around and go back inside."

Logan saw three men approaching from the right side, just cresting a rise in the ground. One, wearing a cream-color jacket and an ascot, held a snub-nosed .38. The other two, in sport shirts, had the flattened noses and rolling gaits of ex-pugs.

"Sorry, I'm on my way out," Logan said quietly. He started to walk on.

"Take one more step, and you sure will be," the cream jacket said quickly. Ha waved the gun. "Maybe you didn't see this?"

"I saw," Logan commented flatly. He calculated the distance and the odds. They were both bad, and he shrugged and turned back to the house. The three men followed him. Julie turned in surprise as he entered. Her eyes flicked to the three men behind him. Cream jacket stayed close to Logan while the other two fanned out into the room.

"Friends of yours?" Logan asked the girl, but he knew the answer. He shot a glance at the jacketed man. He was the type to get overconfident. Sooner or later he'd put the gun in his pocket. Sooner or later he'd make a mistake. Logan moved to the round table, his hand beside the hurricane lamp. "Look, I don't know what this is all about," he said, putting a note of fear in his voice. "I just want to get back to my boat."

"Shut up," Cream jacket snapped. He focused on Julie and leered as he took in her beauty. "Where'd the old guy put it?" he asked. "We don't have time to play around, baby."

"*You're* the ones who killed him," Julie snarled.

"I don't know what you're talking about." The speaker's glance swept to Logan, then back again to Julie. "One of you better start talking," he said.

"I came here to buy some clams," Logan said. He looked at Julie and saw something leap into her eyes, a glint of triumph.

"Fat chance," she said quickly. Logan's lips tightened. She'd seen the chance to draw him in deeper and had seized it with shrewish glee. Cream jacket's eyes were boring into him, and the man spoke to the others without moving his head. "Watch the girl," he said, and started toward Logan. That was when he made his mistake. Logan watched him drop the gun into his jacket pocket, easy confidence in his face. Logan seemed to be fearful as the tall man approached. Behind him, his hand closed around the brass base of the hurricane lamp. When the man moved within range, Logan smashed the hurricane lamp into his face, bringing it up and around in a hard, fast movement. The glass shattered and the man's face erupted in a dozen separate gushers of red as he screamed in pain. Logan raked the jagged slivers of the lamp back across the already sliced flesh of the face before him, now a dripping mass of red.

"Oh, my God!" the man said as he fell to his knees. Logan raked the side of his neck once more with the broken glass as the man's form fell beside him. "Oh, my God," he screamed as he rolled back and forth on the floor, both hands up to his face. The other two, frozen for a moment at the unexpectedness and savageness of it, gathered themselves and rushed at the big man. Logan flung the remains of the hurricane lamp at the nearest one. He ducked away, but before he straightened up, Logan smashed a looping right to his jaw, and he went crashing backward to the floor. The second one tried a tackle. Logan stepped back and met the man's jaw with his upraised knee. He heard the lower teeth being driven into the upper underside of the mouth and the figure dropped to the floor at his feet. The other one had recovered. As the man rose, Julie dived for the rifle she had stood in the corner. The ex-pug slammed into her waist with a thick arm, driving the breath from her and flinging her back onto the sofa. Logan tried a long-distance right, but he knew he was out of range, and the man easily ducked away from the blow. The one on the floor was still screaming in pain, his cream jacket now a dull red. He was too busy holding his face together even to think about the gun in his pocket. But the ex-pug who'd tried the tackle remembered, and out of the corner of his eye Logan saw him move toward the writhing, blood-soaked figure. The big man moved sideways and kicked him in the head, and the man rolled away in pain. But the yellow-shirted one had dived for the rifle, and Logan saw him grab it up. Diving, he made the space behind the sofa as the rifle fired, the shot slamming through the padding of the sofa just over his head. Another shot followed, and Logan heard the high-pitched ping as it hit the back springs of the sofa. Then the hard click of a hammer hitting an empty chamber resounded. Logan came over the back of the couch like a furious bull. He dived and hit the floor as he saw the other one had gotten the .38 out of the writhing, screaming man on the floor.

"Don't move," he said, but his gun hand wavered nervously. He had them both covered and Logan was too far away to risk diving for the gun. The third one helped the bloody one to his feet. Logan glimpsed his torn, shredded face. It was nothing but raw, hanging flesh. Then the three of them were backing out of the house, through the doorway and out of sight. The one with the gun sent a parting shot at Logan, and the big man fell to one side as he saw the man's finger tighten on the trigger. The slug slammed into the wall behind him. They'd been out of sight only a split second when Julie raced across the floor to the old roll-top desk against the wall. Tearing the top drawer open, she yanked out a box of cartridges and jammed them into the rifle. She ran outside, but Logan had heard the sound of a car engine cough into life, and she was back in an instant, crying through her fury.

"They got away," she sobbed. "They got away," she sobbed. "They got away and they were the ones who killed Pops. I just know it."

"Probably," Logan agreed.

"Now you'll stay and help me, won't you?" she asked, turning eagerly. "We can find them again."

Logan shook his head, his eyes hard. "Maybe you don't go for the local cops, but they get paid for finding killers," he said. "That was a nice try back there, but the answer is still no."

He turned and started for the door.

"You're a no-good, nasty sonofabitch," she shouted after him. He nodded and kept walking.

"You're a bastard," she yelled. Logan's small smile was edged with ice.

"And a coward," she finished. He halted in the doorway once again. He knew what she meant by that last one, and he turned and looked at her. She stood glaring at him, hands on her hips, jean-clad legs spread wide apart, round breasts thrusting against the red-checked shirt. She'd called him a coward, afraid to face what she offered for his help. He let his eyes travel slowly, taking in the lines of her breasts, the softly rounded mound just above her crotch. And then, his face immobile, masking the crying ache of his body, he turned and walked out the door. She didn't know how lucky she was. With some, he'd have taken their challenge fully and then walked away. He didn't like women who tried to lay a claim on him. He and the *Urchin* did *what* they wanted, *when* they wanted and *where* they wanted. It had to be that way, until their search was over. He walked quickly, moving down to the shore and heading for town. The *Sea Urchin* rode easily on the long swells as he strode past the boat. The sight of her made him think of the letter in his cabin, the letter that had caught up to him in Wilmington. His lips tightened grimly. But first things first. Jennifer would be waiting and wondering. He quickened his pace toward town.

The car drew up to the quay in Kingdom Point Harbor and stopped before the sixty-foot, glistening-white, sleek cabin cruiser. The man in the yellow sport shirt with the red stains leaped out and waved frantically up at the deck of the boat. Two figures hurried down the gangplank, the girl in bright orange hip-huggers, bare-mid-riffed with a white halter top. She had the carefully groomed, hard brilliance of a diamond. The man had cold, blue eyes and wore a sailing blazer with gold buttons. He was tall with a face that wore a perpetual sneer. The yellow-shirted one spoke quickly and excitedly, and the man and the girl peered into the rear of the car.

"Christ, get him out of here," the girl said, turning away. "Find a hospital or get the cops—tell them he fell on a glass pitcher on the boat. Just get him away."

"I think Harry's dead," the ex-pug said. "He lost a lot of blood." The girl shuddered. "He's better off. They could never put that face together again," she said.

"Do what Doris said," the man cut in. "You say one joker with a hurricane lamp did it?" The other man nodded solemnly.

"He must be a mean bastard," the tall man commented. "He sure did a job on Harry." He turned away, taking the girl's arm and steering her back aboard the cabin cruiser. Back on the stern deck three other men appeared, dressed as deck hands in blue work shirts.

"What do we do now?" one of them asked. "Christ, Harry dead."

"We lay off the rough stuff for a while," the girl said, crisply, almost angrily. "If Harry hadn't gotten carried away with himself and killed the old man, we might be out of here already."

The girl folded her long legs into a deck chair as the others watched her. She put one beautifully manicured finger up to her finely molded lips.

"Augie said the bastard that turned Harry into sliced hamburger has a boat someplace," she said. "Maybe he was just passing by and maybe not. Maybe he's chummy with Miss Beachcomber. We'll watch the girl and find out."

The tall man nodded to the others. "That's it, then," he said. "You heard Doris. I want her watched day and night. Take turns and use glasses and stay out of sight. Just watch her and report to us."

"If she's got herself a boyfriend, she'll go to him," Doris said. "All we have to do is wait." The girl got to her feet as the others left and stretched. There was a feline grace to her body, a carefully controlled, cool grace. She looked up at the man, her eyes a gray mask.

"With Harry gone, I guess that makes you top man, Varney," she said.

"I guess so," Varney said. The girl started to brush past him when he shot an arm out and caught her by the shoulder, his fingers curling around the softness of her skin. She met his eyes with a slightly bored expression.

"And I'm not Harry, Doris," he said, his voice a controlled hiss. "I won't take what you did to Harry, shoving your ass around but never letting him get to it."

"Don't be crude, Varney," Doris said quietly.

"I'm not being crude, honey. I'm being realistic," he said. "I'm letting you know there's a new set of rules. You and me, baby, or you can cut out."

"This whole operation was my idea," Doris said.

"Sure it was. So sue me, baby. Right now I can train any good-looking chickie to do what you do. Not that I want to. You're good. You're important. But you're going to stop playing the queen."

He put a finger under her chin and lifted her face. Her smile was cold, fixed, deadly.

"What's the difference?" he asked. "We're all the same, Harry, me, you. I'm not that hard to take."

"You're vicious," Doris said.

"And Harry wasn't?" Varney laughed. "It was Harry who killed the old man."

"Harry killed because it was all he knew how to do. Killing was his way of coping with a situation. He was brutal, but you're vicious."

Varney shrugged. "And you're a sweet, little girl scout?" he said. "You're no better than the rest of us. You just like to think so. But you go on and think what you like, honey. Just make sure your gorgeous ass is ready where I want it and when I want it. That's the way it's going to be now."

Doris watched the man go down into the cabin, and she clenched her hands. He knew she wouldn't turn her back on what they had going for them. He knew she had little choice. He'd always wanted her, always watched with amused disdain as she played goddess to Harry's worship. She'd created the image for herself and had held Harry with it, kept him panting in awe of her. It'd been nice, just the way she'd wanted it, and now it was all changed. She had Varney on her back. And all because of some mean, black-hearted sonofabitch who'd ground Harry's face into oblivion. He'd pay for it, she told herself.

CHAPTER TWO

The township of Kingdom Point stretched from the harbor in a huge half-circle with the town merely the hub at the bottom center. The town itself, like the harbor, was crowded, neat, orderly, and clean. It reflected money without shouting it. The money came from the great mansions by the sea and the expensive summer homes that made up most of the township acreage. At the outer perimeter of the town, before the large estate area began, were the older frame houses. They were mostly two-family rentals now, from which the township drew most of its domestic help and labor force. Since the school districts had been consolidated, the town had expanded its library and allowed some new units to be built at the right side of the perimeter. Jennifer and the boy lived in one of these. Logan sat across from her in the neat, modestly furnished living room, his big frame making it seem smaller than it was.

They'd gone through the superficialities, the ordinary questions, and she had apologized for having to go to a staff meeting that evening. Logan told her about the old man on the beach and the girl. Jennifer watched him. She always listened and absorbed and seemed to drink things in with a kind of instant meditation that put people at ease. They were often hurt and angered by her answers. Those eyes didn't prepare them for the penetrating sharpness that was within her. The boy had come home for lunch. He'd grown taller in the six months since Logan had seen him. He had Jennifer's eyes and his father's wide smile. It was after he'd gone off to school that Jennifer brought up the old man and the girl again, leaning back on the couch, her eyes thoughtful. Logan watched the long slenderness of her legs as she crossed them, the long, smooth sweep of her thigh. She had good legs, though perhaps a shade too thin, with narrow hips and a small waist rising up to breasts that were high, softly rounded and small, but terribly appealing somehow.

"I wonder what she'll do," Jennifer said. "She's a strange, wild thing."

"She'll make out," Logan said flatly.

"The old man was her life," Jennifer said. "A woman needs someone to look after." Logan caught the faint pause, and then she hurried on to cover something she hadn't intended to phrase that way.

"There was a boy," she said. "A trucker from Hopkinsville. But he went east and that was that."

"Apparently you learn a lot of things in a library," Logan commented.

"In a town like this you do. You don't even have to ask questions. You just keep your eyes and ears open. She used to come in from time to time and talk to me. She took out books on nature and she'd bring them back with notes on the mistakes in them."

"She'll find another boyfriend and look after him," Logan commented. Jennifer's eyes told him she wasn't willing to see it so simply.

"I do agree with what she said about Chief Redmond," Jennifer said. "Anything like this would be beyond him. He'd try to sweep it under the rug. He doesn't like trouble."

Logan shrugged. "It won't be the first killing swept under a rug," he said. Jennifer turned her deep eyes on him, and he suddenly felt uncomfortable under her penetrating gaze. He let his eyes move over the small, round breasts, the narrow figure.

"You've grown harder, Logan," she commented. "Maybe you ought to stop."

"Stop what?" Logan bristled.

"Doing it all your way. Not caring. Saying to hell with everything."

"I care. You know that, Jen."

"You used to, in your own way. Now I'm not sure anymore. Maybe you're only running now, Logan." Her voice was soft, gentle, her words harsh, wounding.

"You know about running, Jen," he shot back. "When Bob died, you ran all the way here, to the Carolina Coast."

Her smile was rueful. "I guess I deserved that one," she said. "And you're right, of course. I ran, and I made a new life for myself, even with a big part of any woman's life missing."

Her soft eyes flicked over his for an instant, but he said nothing. When her husband had been alive, she and Logan had been casual friends. The world had been different then, a world with love and tenderness. He tried to shut out a laughing face with light-brown hair. Sometimes, if he were fast enough, he could do it. He didn't make it this time. With that penetrating quickness of hers, Jennifer caught the moment of pain in his eyes, and she put a hand on his, a light, soft touch.

"I didn't mean to go back and open hurts," she said. "I'm sorry. It's just that I don't like what I see in you every time we meet. Your eyes grow harder each time."

"Because I'm not sticking myself into the dirty killing of an old man. No thanks. Life's too short, and I've too many things that need finishing."

He didn't tell her of the letter aboard the *Urchin* from Sister Mary Angela in Kenya.

"Even so, you'd have stayed, once," Jennifer said.

"I'd have done a lot of things, once," Logan snapped. He looked at the slender girl in front of him. "Are you asking me to stay for this Julie?" he said, frowning.

Jennifer turned to him. "Oh, no," she said softly. "Oh, no, Logan. If ever I ask you to stay it won't be for Julie. Or for anyone else."

Logan got up. "Will I see you tomorrow?" she asked. "There's a hurricane watch on, have you heard?"

"No, I hadn't," the big man said. "If I'm here, you'll see me."

She walked to the door beside him, terribly small next to his big frame and yet terribly strong in a quiet way. At the door, they kissed without kissing, as they'd done every time he stopped by. Two people, unwilling to risk spoiling something delicate, a sweet, strange bond.

"Keep caring, Logan," she said. "That's important. And be careful of yourself."

He ran his hand down the side of her face, gently, and then he was gone, striding away, not looking back. He walked quickly through the town, past the harbor. He noted a sixty-foot glistening-white cabin cruiser. Even for Kingdom Point harbor it was a spectacular boat, all outside gloss and fancy fittings, built to impress those easily impressed. He hurried on, anxious to get aboard his own boat, away from Kingdom Point, away from the death of the old man. And away from Jennifer. He'd come closer than ever before this time, closer to moving across that line they both held so tenuously. Maybe it was because he hungered for a woman, the taste, touch, and smell of one. Maybe it was because of the girl, Julie. Her throbbing body could make a marble statue hunger. It would have been nice to hide in that thought, but the big man's uncompromising honesty wouldn't permit it. It brushed Jennifer aside and that was lying. But he wondered as he trudged along the beach. Could it ever be more than unspoken, unsurfaced with Jennifer? Once she'd been a thin connection with the past, a necessary reminder to him that once he'd believed in goodness and right and kindness, that once there had been more than the *Urchin* and himself. Maybe that was all she was now. Maybe. Sometime, perhaps, he'd find out. Only the world kept getting in the way, pushing him farther from women like Jennifer, that real world of hate and greed and senseless injustice. Maybe you only see it that way, she had once said to him. Hell, he saw it like it was. Ever since that day long ago he'd seen it like it was. The old man on the beach was dead, wasn't he? He'd been beaten to death, for all his gentleness, for all his kindness, for all his love. Shit, Logan spat out. He didn't just see it that way. It *was* that way.

He found his dinghy on the beach where he'd pulled it up far enough to escape high tide. He pushed it into the sea, the surf hardly more than a gentle ripple now. The air hung, still and heavy, and the sea was glassy calm. The sea birds swooped and circled uncertainly. It was pre-hurricane weather, all right. He tied up alongside the boat, climbed the rope ladder hanging over the starboard side, and then walked the dinghy around to the stern and made it fast on a short line. He went below decks, brought out a bottle of good Kentucky bourbon and made a Logan Special, ice, a touch of grenadine, bitters and bourbon. He sipped it and lounged in the cabin, trying to hold off the bitter, angry cloak that had wrapped itself around him as he thought about the world. The second bourbon didn't make it go away, either. What the hell, he told himself. He took the letter out of the desk drawer against the port wall. He read it again, spreading it out before him. What the hell, he repeated, a few more reminders couldn't hurt now. The memories had started to flood back while he was at Jennifer's. They would keep flooding back until he got very drunk or very angry.

Dear Logan,

I hesitated to write but you insisted with every letter that you wanted me to be honest at all times with you. Every Sister here is writing someone for help. Conditions among the people have grown terribly bad. We need medical supplies, more beds, more plasma. The new government has no funds to spare. You've been so generous in the past that this very letter seems ungrateful. It is not that, please believe me. But who can we turn to if not our old friends? I know you will do whatever you can. May God bless you.

Sister Mary Angela

Sisters of Mercy Mission

He folded the letter neatly and put it back into the desk drawer. It wouldn't be that hard to raise the money. A coat of paint and he could pick up some fishing charters. A visit to the right ports without too many questions asked could bring a job or two. And there were others, with bigger money, but he didn't want to call them. The past would be peering over his shoulder enough as it was. He poured a third Logan Special and drank it quickly, feeling the warm fire of the whiskey inside him. He turned on the radio and heard the marine forecaster's voice.

"Hurricane Phyllis could pose a serious threat," the voice crackled over the set. "The storm is now practically standing still five hundred miles off the coast of South Carolina. Winds are Force twelve at present. We cannot predict future course at this time. All ships at sea are warned to stay tuned for further advisory bulletins. Hurricane Phyllis is at present stationary, we repeat, but she is a wide storm with severe winds around the outer perimeter."

The radio went dead, and Logan turned it off. He'd heard enough for now. Phyllis was standing still and gathering ferocity. If she were still in the same general spot by morning he'd up anchor and try to crawl down the coast going south. Most likely, Phyllis would circle north when she decided to move. He started toward the galley to fry some pork chops but heard the faint sound against the starboard side, a scraping sound. Downing the remains of the bourbon, he picked up a wrench. Moving quickly, silently, he was on deck and across to the rail in seconds. He had the wrench poised in his hand when the head rose up alongside the gunwale, long, wet blond hair hanging in strings.

"It's me," she said, swinging a leg over the rail. She had on cream shorts and the bra top of a black bathing suit. He noticed the way her full breasts pushed out of the little top.

"What the hell do you want?" he growled, feeling the hard, cold anger. If she'd come out to try again to get him to stay, she'd taken the swim for nothing.

"I've got to talk to you," she said, taking deep breaths and putting a helluva strain on that little top. "I yelled from shore, but you must be deaf so I swam out."

"Talk fast. I'm busy," Logan said gruffly. Her legs were full and strong.

"You've got to go to the police station with me," she said. Logan started for her, putting one hand on the back of her neck.

"Have a nice swim back, honey," he said. "We went through this once."

"No, wait, you don't understand," she said, grabbing his hand and clinging to it. "I went there already, but Pops is gone."

Logan took his hand from her neck and frowned at her. Her eyes were serious.

"He was dead, wasn't he?" she asked solemnly.

"Of course he was dead," Logan answered. "Maybe you'd better start at the beginning. You went to the cops. What happened then?"

"I told them about Pops being killed," Julie said. "Then they went back to the beach with me, but Pops wasn't there by the dune. He wasn't anyplace. Chief Redmond and Luther are very suspicious of me. They think I'm out of my skull or I'm trying to be cute, and they want to know where Pops is. You're the only one who saw him there besides me. You've got to go and tell Chief Redmond that he was there—dead."

Logan let a long sigh escape him. "You know you're a pain in the ass," he said.

"I wish somebody else had found Pops, anybody else in the whole world but you," she blurted out angrily.

"That makes two of us, honey," he said flatly.

"Look, I don't want your lousy help," she said. "I just want you to tell those numbskulls what you saw."

Logan's lips drew tight. She didn't want his help, but he knew that one thing led to another. It always did. The three bourbons had only increased his feeling of churning meanness. The past was still kicking around in his head, and she stood there, dripping all over his deck looking like a half-drowned rabbit. "Ah, screw it all," he growled. "Let's go."

He brought the dinghy around and climbed into it after her, rowing to shore with long, powerful strokes as the girl sat silently before him, the wet shorts flattened against the small, round rise of her belly, her young, strong legs extended, almost touching his in the small boat. At the beach, he pulled the dinghy up and saw she had an old battered open-topped jeep standing there. They got in and she leaned forward to release the hand brake. He wondered if she were going to fall out of the bathing suit top. Her breasts, mounds of cream where the deep color of her tan halted, were deliciously inviting. The jeep shot forward and he grabbed the corner post to avoid being pitched out.

"Sorry," she said with satisfaction in her voice. "Why did they take Pops' body?" she asked. "Why?"

"You found that out already," Logan answered. "No body, no cops looking for suspects." It was neat and professional, he added to himself. And it made him stop and pause. Pro's wouldn't go to all this bother without a damn good reason. Maybe killing the old man had been an error on their part, but they definitely suspected something more. Everything that had happened so far pointed to the fact that this wasn't amateur night. The jeep, shuddering to a halt, interrupted his thoughts, and he saw they had stopped before a square white-washed building. Julie slipped on a sweat shirt as she hopped to the ground. Logan followed her inside the building, sparsely furnished, with a large wooden desk in one corner of the receiving room. He saw another room leading off to the right and a corridor to the left. The man got up from behind the desk, a big raw-boned man with a heavy jaw and black hair. His small eyes glittered when he saw Julie.

"I'm back, Luther," the girl said. "Tell the chief, please."

Luther's eyes devoured the girl in one quick glance. Then Luther turned his small, mean, pig's eyes on him. His gray policeman's shirt and silver badge tried its best to make him look natty. It failed. The man rose and walked toward Logan, his arms long and loose.

"What's your name?" he said slowly. Logan forced himself to keep calm. He didn't want any part of this, and he didn't want to make it worse than it was. But Luther's type set the meanness inside him churning faster. The man exuded that special kind of arrogance found in minor authorities with minor minds.

"Logan," the dark-eyed man said, his lips hardly moving, his eyes warning Luther. But Luther had enough trouble reading words. Reading people was far beyond him.

"Well, now, Logan," he drawled. "What are you doing in Kingdom Point?"

"Leaving. As fast as I can," Logan said. "Not that it's any of your damn business."

"Don't get smart with me, mister," Luther growled, squinting his little eyes.

"Don't ask me any dumb questions," Logan said. "I came here because the girl asked me to back up her story. I saw the old man, and he was dead. That's it, pal. You take it from there."

Logan started to turn, but the man raised his voice. "Not so fast there," Luther said. "Chief! Can you come out here?"

Logan felt the angry irritation rising inside him, and he shot Julie a glance. She was watching him. A man emerged from the adjoining room, older than Luther, beefy-faced and red-necked with a paunch covering a powerful body.

"This is the feller Julie told us about," Luther said. "I asked him a question, and he gave me a smart-ass answer."

The police chief's eyebrows lifted a fraction, and he saun-
tered toward Logan. Logan saw the man had experience, if nothing else, the kind of experience which allowed him to read men
on a primitive level at least.

"We don't like smart answers here," he said, his voice quiet.
Logan's irritation was rising close to the exploding point.

"I'm all choked up about that," he said, The beefy-faced man
had cold, blue eyes and they held Logan's hard glance.

"Luther asked you what you were doing here in Kingdom
Point. Julie said you had a boat and you dropped anchor offshore
last night. Now you can answer us or you can get yourself a jail
cell."

"For what reason?" Logan asked, his eyes unmoving.

"I'll think of somethin'," the police chief said. Logan smiled—
a tight, hard smile. He almost laughed. It was going just the way
he thought it would go. Trouble. One thing leading to another.
He wasn't about to drop Jennifer's name into this and his own
stubbornness had taken over. That and his inner anger.

"I'm waiting," Chief Redmond said.

"Don't make it a total loss," Logan answered. "Go screw
yourself while you're at it."

"Damn it, Logan, why can't you just answer?" Julie cut in.
"He's visiting someone here in Kingdom Point, chief. Now can
we get back to what happened to Pops?"

The telephone rang in the other room and the police chief
tore his hard, blue eyes from Logan. I'm waiting for that call," he
said. "But I'll be back. I'm not finished with you."

As the man disappeared, Luther moved to stand in front of
Logan. "Now, suppose you tell us just who you're visiting here in
Kingdom Point," he said, his little eyes glittering.

"Suppose you go to hell," Logan said coldly.

"He's visiting Jennifer Holden," Julie said. "Who cares?"

Logan grimaced, and shot her an angry look. The little bitch
knew he didn't want it tossed around, but she was only interested

in placating the cops. Logan felt his anger start to churn as a slow smile oozed across Luther's face.

"Well, what do you know," he said. "Jennifer Holden." A nasty oil coated every syllable. "Cur little librarian entertaining visiting sailormen," Luther went on. "It's sure a surprising world."

Logan hit him. He caught Luther on the point of the jaw and felt the bone splinter. Luther flew across the room, hit the old desk, catapulted across it, and crashed to the floor on the other side, striking the desk chair. He made a hell of a loud crash as he hit, and Chief Redmond charged into the room seconds later.

"What the hell's going on here?" he barked, one hand on his gun. He looked at the inert form of his patrolman on the floor, the desk chair across the man's back.

"He slipped on something and fell across the desk," Logan said mildly. Chief Redmond took a cup from a paper dispenser, filled it at a water cooler, and threw the water into Luther's face. He did it twice again before Luther blinked his eyes. The chief helped him to his feet.

"Sonofabitch hit me," Luther gasped, putting his head down on the desk.

"Nothing of the sort," Logan smiled pleasantly. "He must have a concussion. I told you he slipped and fell." The big man turned his deep, probing eyes on Julie. "Did you see him slip and fall?" he asked. Juli paused a second and then answered.

"That's what I saw," she said.

"Sonofabitch hit me," Luther repeated, resting one hand against his swelling jaw. "I'm goin' over to Doc Green."

"Two against one," Logan smiled at the police chief. "You'd have trouble making a case."

"You get out of here, the police chief growled. "You go with him, Julie. And don't come back."

"My pleasure," Logan said, his smile thin. He walked outside, conscious of the girl's seething anger as she strode alongside him. When they reached the jeep she exploded into fury.

"Damn you!" she said, eyes ablaze. "What'd you have to go and get everybody mad for? Why couldn't you just answer Luther's questions?"

"I didn't come to answer questions," Logan said.

"Why'd you have to hit him just because he mentioned Jennifer Holden entertaining you?"

"I didn't like the way he said it."

"You're just naturally mean, aren't you?"

"No. I work at it. It's more fun that way."

The night was wrapping itself around the town. Logan followed Julie into the jeep. She swung the car back toward the beach, the headlights stabbing into the darkness. It was black when they reached the dinghy. Logan swung out of the jeep and started to pull the boat toward the water.

"Good luck, Julie," he said.

"What do you mean good luck?" the girl shot back. "You're not just going off, are you?"

"Keep watching, honey," he said, pushing the dinghy into the water.

"After what you did?" she asked. "After fixing it so they won't do anything?"

"Work on Luther," Logan called back. "He'll do whatever you say, doll. Soon as he gets his jaw fixed."

Logan looked back at her, standing at the water's edge. He could feel the throbbing, pulsating rage in her, a rage he could turn into wild passion, he knew. But he kept rowing, just as he'd turned away at the doorway. He had things to do. He'd find another woman easily enough, one without conditions or claims. He was halfway to the *Sea Urchin* when he heard her voice come across the water.

"Bastard," she yelled. He grinned in the dark.

"That's me," he called back and heard the sound of the jeep's engine coughing into life. He reached the *Urchin*, tied the dinghy up at the stern and switched on the radio as he went into the galley. The pork chops were waiting, and he had them frying and crackling in a few minutes. Phyllis, the marine forecaster said, was still more or less in one spot, gathering intensity.

"An extremely dangerous storm," the forecaster said. "Air currents indicate the hurricane will move toward the coast when its forward motion is resumed. The hurricane watch remains in force and all ships are advised to stay tuned for further bulletins."

Logan poured himself a bourbon on the rocks and went on deck. Unless things changed overnight, he'd still weigh anchor in the morning and head down toward the gulf ports.

Logan stretched, finished his drink and went to bed in the aft cabin. Sleep would keep his mind from the throbbing, raw beauty of Julie and the soft magnetism of Jennifer. Maybe he shouldn't have stopped at Kingdom Point this time, he mused idly. Nothing had really gone right this time. His visit with Jennifer had been too full of the things that penetrate and hurt. And memories he kept hidden away.

And the old man on the beach was dead. Logan let sleep wash over him, dulling, numbing sleep that turned off the world for a little while.

The big man slept, naked except for shorts, and the open porthole let the warm, still air into the cabin. But Logan slept like a jungle cat sleeps, with an extra sense constantly tuned to danger, a sudden sound, a footstep, a movement in the air. He didn't know how long he'd been asleep when his eyes snapped open and felt the cold tingling of his skin. He lay still, and then he heard it, the faint scraping sound on the deck above. Swinging from the bed on silent, bare feet, he moved with instant grace, taking the few steps of the companionway in one effortless bound. He halted, crouched, as he saw her moving across the deck on tiptoe toward the forward cabin, leaving little pools of water behind her. He moved forward and kicked out, catching her round little rear with his foot. She yelled as she went sprawling across the deck, and he saw the small oilskin bag roll off to one side.

"Goddamn it, what are you doing here again?" the big man yelled. The girl looked up at him from where she lay on the deck, her blond hair wet, hanging behind her and held by a hair clip, the blouse pressed tight against her skin, outlining the curved peaks of her breasts, the tiny pointed tips.

"I couldn't stay at the house," she said, pushing herself to her feet. "I tried to but I couldn't. Not alone, not with everything reminding me of Pops. And every little noise made me jump. I was afraid those goons might come back. I just had to get away— for a while, anyway. You can take me and drop me off someplace, any place."

"Forget it," Logan said. She moved toward him, her wet clothes clinging to her every curve.

"You owe me that much, damn it," she said.

"I owe you?" Logan frowned. "For what? I went with you to back up your story about the old man."

"And if I hadn't backed *you* up, you'd be in jail now for hitting Luther," she said.

"So we're even. So butt out."

"No. I'm not going back there."

Logan saw her eyes moving over his chest, down the hard-packed muscles of his body, and her eyes smoldered with something that went beyond stubborn defiance. "Please, let me stay," she said. "I won't be any trouble."

"You'll be nothing but trouble," Logan muttered and his hands tightened with the desire to reach out and touch her full, rounded breasts. She was less than an arm's length away, her eyes holding his in the dark of the moonless night. She was a stray cat and a simmering strumpet, a waif and a wanton hellion, all at once. He put a hand out and curled it around the back of her neck. It was thin and soft. He pulled her to him. There was a delicious, wet-hot smell to her. She offered no resistance. Her full lips, parted, beckoned invitingly and he leaned down to them, pressing them open wider with his. His tongue sent its own instant message as it circled her mouth, quickly, with darting movements, and he felt her go rigid. He put one hand on her breast, the wetness of her blouse a thin layer of insulation between his fingers and the warmth of her softness. She shivered, but she didn't pull away, and he felt her shoulder muscles grow tight. Yet she didn't move away, and he pulled back. Her eyes were open, wide, watching him.

"Still want to stay?" he said.

"I'm staying," she answered, her voice hardly more than a whisper.

"I'll throw you off at the first real port we reach."

"I know."

He opened the buttons of the wet blouse and let his hand rest against the warmth of her breast. He heard the sharp, inward sound of her breath.

"I'm not getting involved."

"I heard you."

He moved his hand down on her breast, feeling the deep fullness of her. His mouth was against her cheek.

"You can still go."

"I'm staying. I'm not going back. Not for a while."

Her words were like a final seal on an agreement and he felt his better judgment explode in the whirlpool of his desires. His hand ripped at the brassiere, pulling it down. Her arms encircled him, and she pressed her body against his, pulling his head down her. The big man picked up the girl in his arms, and carried her into the aft cabin.

He flung her on the bed like a sack of wheat and as she rolled, she rolled free of her blouse and came at him with a furious passion, clawing at his shorts, pulling them from him. Her hands were thirsting, grasping, and he came to her with his head buried into her breasts, pressing their soft, warm tips to his lips, pulling gently on them and feeling their pink points rising. She kicked her shorts free, and he felt her young, strong legs clasp themselves around him, the soft warmth of her belly pressing up to him. Logan was caught up in the sweet pain of his exploding needs, but the girl seemed to be aflame with a release of tensions. She wanted little gentleness, little subtlety, and she grabbed and clawed and pressed herself up to the big man's muscular body, twisting her hips so that she could take him in at once. As he moved to her, she clutched at him and, arms tight around his neck, cried out in pure joyous pleasure.

"Oh, yes, yes, Christ, yes!" she gasped as he matched her own frenzy and held her there, just a heartbeat from the peak of peaks, letting her down and bringing her up again until she was crying out in an endless chain of gasps and finally her cries were cries of pleading. "Oh, take me over, damn it, oh, Christ, take me over," Julie screamed in his ear, her body all frenzied passion, reaching for the top, trying desperately to hurry that which only he could hurry and then, with a final explosion of ecstasy, he thrust fully and deeply into her, holding himself against the very inner depths of her, and her cry was a song of towering fulfillment. Beneath his legs, strong and pressing down, her body leaped and flung itself upwards, arching again and again in a seemingly uncontrollable frenzy. Finally, she subsided in a series of quivering motions. He tried to move from her but her legs tightened again, and she moaned, eyes closed. "Oh, no, no, stay with me, oh, God, stay with me," she said. He moved slowly now, like the slow roll of the surf against the sand on a calm day, and she moaned and gasped and shook with small ripples of pleasure. Finally, he felt her legs fall aside, and he turned and lay beside her. He felt her hand stealing down to hold him, and with eyes closed, she turned her face to his ear.

"You're something different, Logan," she breathed. "Christ, you're something different." She fell aside and lay on her back, her full, round breasts moving steadily up and down. Logan raised himself on one elbow to look at her. She was asleep, he saw, her hand limply holding him, spent, exhausted.

He lay back in the contentment of a need fulfilled and a promise of more to come. He would do just what he said, throw her off at the first port they put in. But before that moment, he would drink of her wild, sensuous body again. It had been a day of brutal death, violence, anger, and hurt. Perhaps it was no more fitting that it should come to a close in an explosion of hunger, a meeting that was more frenzy than loving, sex as violent and turbulent as the day had been.

CHAPTER THREE

The new day came in on a blanket of still, thick air with the sun a blurred, diffused red. Logan stirred as the light crept tentatively through the porthole. He turned and looked at the girl beside him. Even asleep, her body had a throbbing lushness to it, and he let his eyes rove over the rounded rise of her belly, the round undersides of her breasts, so full and womanly with such small, pink little-girl tips. She stirred, raised one leg and half-turned in her sleep. Her fleshy opulence seemed to send out its own currents, and he felt himself wanting to move his body against her. He swung silently from the bed. There'd be time for that later. Naked, he went across the cabin and turned on the ship's radio.

On the bed, Julie opened her eyes just enough to see through them and watched the tall man's naked form as he stood at the porthole window and peered out, went to the doorway and glanced up through the opening of the companionway. She let her eyes roam across his figure, the powerful pectoral muscles, the easy grace of him, the maddeningly stirring maleness of him. She felt him against her as he'd been last night, felt him moving inside her, felt his lips pulling on her breasts and her body began to stir and ache at once. She was no worldly sophisticate, no creature of infinite experience, but she didn't have to be to know that she'd never be made love to again like this man had made love to her. He was a strange one, this Logan. Hard, immovable, living in his own world. But, she mused, her mind stirring to sudden life, perhaps she could be part of that world.

She could understand a man like him. The years of lonely living with Pops and the sea and the sand had given her the gift to understand the lone things of the world and this big man was one of them. She smiled. Maybe she'd even have a surprise or two for him. The sound of the marine forecaster on the radio interrupted her thoughts, and she listened to the words crackling into the air.

"Hurricane Phyllis is moving toward the Carolina coast at a very slow rate but is expected to pick up speed. Phyllis has become an exceedingly dangerous storm with Force ten winds around the outer perimeter and one hundred and fifty mile winds at the center. All shipping is advised to stay in port or to head for shelter until the course of the hurricane can be more exactly charted."

"Damn," Logan muttered, shutting off the radio. If Phyllis hit directly, Kingdom Point hadn't the kind of protection needed. Bayville would be better, but it was always so damned crowded there that getting in was uncertain. He knew just the place, a little cove with high protective walls and a narrow entrance. But it was a day's trip north and he wanted to go south. He'd wait a little longer. If Phyllis changed direction he might still be able to stick to his original plan of crawling southward along the coast. He walked back to the bed and saw Julie watching him. He put on his shorts and trousers as he took in her loveliness. She stretched, moving her lush body with soft grace, inviting him. He grinned. All in time, honey, he said to himself. Right now he wanted to check over the *Urchin* and see that everything was tight and in place. Even if Phyllis didn't hit them directly, they'd be sideswiped and that would be bad enough.

"You'll find breakfast in the galley," he said. "I like my eggs sunny-side up. Bacon and coffee."

When he walked from the cabin, she swung her legs over the side of the bed. He went out into the morning sun and the still air. As he started to put away loose equipment, leaving out two deck chairs, stowing away ropes and snap-shut canvas covers, he smelled the bracing aroma of coffee and bacon. Soon Julie appeared with the breakfast tray. He quickly noted that her breasts moved freely under the blouse, unconfined, swaying and pressing their little tips against the thin fabric. She wore the shorts again, tight and provocative on her firm little seat.

They sat down to eat.

"Do you like anyone or anything?" Julie asked. Logan's smile was hard, his dark eyes moving across the water.

"Lots of things," he said. "People are at the bottom of the list, though."

"You didn't seem to have much trouble last night," she snapped.

"That's another game, sweetie, and you know it." His eyes probed into her, a small frown on his brow.

"You got another name beside Julie?" he asked.

"Banntry," she said.

"Julie Banntry," he said, turning the name over in his mind. "How'd you hook up with the old man, Julie Banntry?"

"My mother was sick, back in Towerville, across the state," Julie said. "She sent me to him for the summer. I was twelve. She died while I was here, and I stayed on."

"Nobody else to take you in?"

"Nobody that wanted me," she said, suddenly all waif again. "My relatives all had too many kids. They didn't need another twelve-year-old around. We're alike, Logan, you know that? We've learned to be loners, to go our own way."

Logan grunted and his eyes narrowed. He could see where she was heading. Like all women, she calculated constantly. Only it wasn't really calculation with them. It was part of them, built into them.

"And that's the way it's going to stay, honey," he growled and saw the small flicker of annoyance in her eyes. "You won't have any trouble finding someone to want you now."

"Who are you, Logan?" she asked. "I've seen a lot of sea bums, but you're not one of them. And this boat, it's a lot different when you're on it. Who're you hiding from?"

"Not a who, a what. I hide from being bothered."

"Like having to help someone."

"That's right," he said, standing up. "Wash the dishes and put them away. Then come on deck, and I'll give you something else to do." He watched her go below and knew that her submissive obedience was a strain on her. He'd seen her flaring temper, sampled her chameleonlike swift changes of mood already. She was utterly female, from the smoldering lush beauty of her to the pathetic appeal she could exude. And female in her inability to read signs, to think that anyone could be beyond her reach. He smiled inwardly. What the hell, it'd be fun for a few days, anyhow.

A sleek, glistening-white motor cruiser moved out of Kingdom Point harbor. A girl stood on the forward deck, in tailored white slacks and a black jersey top, every blond hair in place, sparkling with her own light. She was listening to the tall man in the brass-buttoned navy-blue jacket. She seemed to be ignoring him.

"Damn it, Doris," he said. "The boys watched her swim out to her boyfriend's boat last night. What have you got against moving in?"

The girl turned and fastened the man with a cool, steady gaze. "You growing deaf, Varney?" she said. "I told you last night, we should wait till they make their move and then act. We've been too quick with the rough stuff right along."

"Waiting bothers me, Doris," Varney said. "You know that." He turned to her. "Waiting for anything bothers me." He smiled, a thin, knife-edged smile. The girl ignored the remark.

"I'd think you'd be happy to let me get at her boyfriend," Varney went on, the edge still in his voice. "After all, if it hadn't been for him you'd still have Harry here in my place."

Doris gave Varney a smile that dripped with venom. "That's why I don't want to see anything go wrong," she said.

"Nothing will go wrong, baby," Varney said, his eyes hard. The gleaming-white motor cruiser, clear of the small harbor, gathered speed and sent showers of spray cascading into the air as she turned left and moved along the beachfront. Varney, lifting binoculars to his eyes, saw the paint-chipped hull of the *Sea Urchin* looming just ahead.

"They've weighed anchor!" he exclaimed excitedly. "They're trying to get away."

"They don't seem in much of a hurry," Doris commented acidly as she watched the other boat drifting lazily in the gentle swells.

"Tony," the man called to the helmsman. "Swing on her port side. Keep her between you and the beach."

Aboard the *Sea Urchin*, Logan watched the glistening-white cruiser coming up at full speed, and his eyes narrowed as the hair on the back of his neck rose—his own personal alarm bell that had never been wrong. He'd weighed anchor to put a few hundred yards more water between himself and the beach. He'd planned to drop anchor again, but now he didn't. He saw the other craft start to swing out to come alongside him on the port side. Sweeping his glance along the rail he saw the five men lining up, saw the carbines in the hands of two of them. A little farther on, he picked out the shapely figure in white slacks and black jersey top. A blue-jacketed man stood beside her.

"Something wrong?" Julie said, coming on deck and looking up at Logan's narrowed, hard eyes watching the approaching boat.

"Yes, I think so," he said. "Anyone see you swim aboard last night?"

"Not that I know of," she answered.

"No, not that you know of," he said. "I never should've let you stay."

"Make sense," she snapped, anger flaring in her voice.

"Maybe they'll make sense for you," he shot back, nodding to the approaching cruiser. "They're not out for a sail. They're coming for us. I can tell by the way she's moving."

Slow realization started to move into her round blue eyes. "You mean the goons who killed Pops?" she gasped. "The ones who came to the house yesterday?"

He shrugged. "I've got no friends with fancy motor cruisers around here. Maybe you have."

She looked out at the oncoming boat, fear in her eyes. With startling abruptness, Logan turned and moved into the pilot house, taking the few steps to it in one bound. She followed and saw him flip a switch on the instrument panel. The dull throb of the boat's engines flooded the air, deep, powerful.

"The engines are idling now," he said. "Get over here and stay by this wheel. If I tell you to hit the switch, you flip it over to full, understand?" She nodded. "And hold the wheel just where she is, with the top of it lined up with that little arrow on the compass."

Logan glanced out to see the white cruiser slow to a halt as she swung around to come alongside him. "Just do what I told you to do when I say so," he said. He stepped out of the pilot house and went to the rail. Inside his cabin he had a big Colt Python .357 Magnum. He decided to leave it there for the moment. The gleaming cruiser had come to a dead halt alongside them with perhaps ten feet or so between them. Logan moved to the *Urchin's* rail. The tall man with the blue jacket called out, and Logan let his eyes travel over the man's cold face, then move to the girl. He took in her curving breasts, the nice long line of her thighs beneath the tight white slacks and the cool interest in her eyes. How large a role did she play in this, he wondered. Sweeping the men again, he saw the two ex-pugs that had been at the house. Cream jacket was missing, he noted with grim pleasure.

"We don't want any more trouble," the tall man called. "Just hand it over, and you can go your way."

"I'm going my way, cousin," Logan said. "And I don't know what the hell you want."

"Either you or blondie in there knows," the man said. "Are you going to play ball or do we come aboard?"

Logan's eyes scanned the five men at the rail. One of the two with carbines stood at the near end of the line.

"You want to come aboard?" he said. "I'll give you a line."

He picked up one end of a mooring line and tossed it with a quick motion at the man with the carbine. The man, reacting automatically, almost dropped the rifle as he reached out to grab the rope that flew at him.

"Hold onto it," Logan called and the man, tucking the rifle under his arm, curled the rope around his wrist. Logan hissed through clenched teeth, not turning toward the pilot house.

"Hit that switch," he said and paused a second to see Julie throw the switch out of the corner of his eye and then grab the wheel with both hands. He yanked the rope hard and suddenly and saw the man pitch forward, hit the rail and go over in a head-long plunge from the cruiser. He hit the water as the full force of the *Urchin's* wake swept over him, engulfing him in a cascade of swirling water, pulling him under and turning him over and over. It had all taken not much more than a second and Logan flattened himself on the deck as the initial surprise aboard the cruiser gave way to a burst of rifle fire. But the *Sea Urchin's* powerful engines had taken hold to send the boat leaping forward, and the shots flew harmlessly overhead. Logan got to his feet and ran to the pilot house where Julie sat at the wheel, fingers clenched around it, eyes wide with determination mixed with fear. He took the wheel from her and looked back to see the cruiser had gathered speed and was giving chase. He slowed somewhat and adjusted the synchrometer readings to assure himself maximum power. He let the cruiser come up on him and then shot the

Urchin forward in a burst of raw power that threw her wake up onto the white vessel's foredeck. Julie, pressed against the far wall of the pilot house, saw Logan's small grin.

"Jesus, what have you got in this thing, airplane engines?" she asked. Logan chuckled.

"Just a little extra power," he answered. He knew that aboard the white motor cruiser the same question was being asked. Logan cut back again on the power and once more the other vessel moved closer but this time, as she closed in, he spun the wheel and the *Urchin* turned in a tight circle. He saw the white craft try to follow suit and only succeed in swinging wide in a clumsy arc. He kept the *Urchin* in the tight circle and watched the figures aboard the other vessel rush to the starboard side. Then he heard the sharp, staccato sound of a submachine gun and he felt the thud of the bullets as they slammed into the bottom section of the pilot house, just below the line of the windows, sending up slivers of wood.

"Goddamn it!" Logan cursed. He spun the wheel and pulled the *Urchin* out of her tight circle, sending her straight at the cruiser's white side. He saw the man at the wheel, unnerved and outmaneuvered already, come apart and frantically spin his wheel to port. The long, sleek vessel heeled precariously as she swung about, sending those on the deck stumbling and sliding along the rail. Logan let the *Urchin* drive past the stern of the cruiser while it yawed and floundered, lost headway and direction. By the time she swung back Logan had put plenty of water between them. But the machine gun had added a new element to the game. He could outmaneuver them easily, and keep a lead on the straightaway. But he couldn't do battle, not just himself and Julie against a submachine gun and God knows what else. He peered back to see that the white vessel had gathered herself and had taken up the pursuit. Julie poked her head out of the pilot house window and saw the sleek white vessel roaring after them.

"What do you want to do?" she asked.

"Throw you overboard," he snapped.

"So they saw me come aboard last night," the girl answered angrily. "That doesn't mean anything."

"It does to them," Logan said. "And are you sure it doesn't to you?" Julie's lips tightened. She hesitated a brief moment before answering. He wondered if it was just anger or something more.

"It meant I wanted to get away," she said. "Maybe you'd like me to save you the trouble and just jump overboard?" Her sarcasm was defensive.

"Use either side, honey," Logan snapped. He saw the blaze of anger in her blue eyes.

"You never stop being a bastard do you, Logan?"

"I did last night," he growled. "And now look." He peered back at the pursuing boat to see she had gained a little, not enough to worry about.

"Can you outrun them?" Julie asked.

"Not enough to lose them," he said. "I'm going to put in at Bayville."

"Bayville?" she exploded incredulously. "They'll come right in after us."

"I know," he said. "But in a harbor jammed full of boats all they'll be able to do is sit there and watch us. As soon as that damned hurricane decides which way it's going, I'll decide what we do next. Now shut up and let me move this boat."

Julie lapsed into silence, and went out onto the deck. Logan checked the pursuing vessel, gunning the *Urchin* just enough to keep the distance the same between them. They'd be in Bayville in an hour or two. Damn, he swore to himself. He should have sent her away last night. But he hadn't, and now his pursuers were convinced he either had or knew about whatever it was they were after. He looked down at Julie on the deck, the wind pressing her blouse tight against the soft contours of her full breasts. She glanced up at him, and he saw the glint of smug satisfaction in her eyes. Damn her, he swore under his breath. In the same way she got to you with her swift changes of mood, she pulled you into her problems, and she'd managed to pull him in deeper, perhaps too deeply to turn aside now. And she was pleased with herself for it. He felt the cold anger building inside him, a cold anger at her, at the bastards chasing him in the white boat, at the world in general. He didn't want any part of this. He had things to do, things important to him. And this wasn't one of them. So if he was in too deep, he'd cut his way out as quickly and as ruthlessly as he could.

He looked back at the other craft, and he thought about the girl he'd seen on her. Where did she fit in, he wondered. She had a cool, disdainful air to her, even in the few seconds he'd watched her. He eased off on the throttle as Bayville harbor came into sight. Casting a glance behind, he saw that the motor cruiser continued racing toward them at full speed. His faint smile was cold, and he steered for the harbor mouth. The other craft had closed the distance by the time he reached the harbor, but now they were already in full view of the quays and piers jutting out from the curved shoreline. There'd be no room to find docking space, but that didn't matter. He moved slowly into the harbor, keeping one eye on the sleek cruiser as she nosed in after him. He saw a spot at the outside edge of the boats moored offshore, in a direct line from the harbor mouth. He swung the *Sea Urchin* around and dropped anchor. The long, white cruiser reversed engines, moved to the right and found a spot almost directly opposite them but on the other side of the harbor channel. Logan went into the aft cabin and took out the big Colt Python .357 Magnum, stuck it into his belt, got a pair of field glasses, and went up on deck. He trained them on the cruiser and made a fast count of those aboard. He came up with seven, besides the girl and the cold-faced man in the navy-blue blazer. Allowing for one or two more possibly below decks that made at least ten. But there had been two more, he smiled grimly. He put down the glasses and saw Julie watching him.

"Now what?" she said. "We just wait around?"

"We just wait around," he said. He went below and turned on the weather forecast. Phyllis was still moving very slowly directly toward the coast, and Logan's lips tightened grimly. There was still time for decisions, at least twenty-four hours. He opened a bottle of bourbon and took out two glasses.

"Relax, Julie," he said, handing her a glass. "We might as well enjoy ourselves." He saw her eyes darken, and he knew she got the message. It was mid-afternoon and the pre-hurricane stillness in the air continued. The harbor, without the winds of the open sea, was hot and Logan took off his shirt as he relaxed on the deck, aware that they were no doubt watching from the cruiser. He lifted a glass high, gestured toward the other vessel, and downed the drink.

Aboard the white boat, Varney cursed and put down his binoculars. "The bastard," he swore. Doris's lips formed a slow smile. "He's a cool one, all right," she said. "And that little old boat is something more than it looks. But you found that out, didn't you, Varney?"

The man turned to her and his eyes glittered. "Don't give me any of that superior shit you used to hand Harry," he growled. "You've got as much to lose as any of us. If that damned hurricane hits before we get the stuff and get out of here, God knows what'll happen."

Doris's eyes held their cool, infuriating disdain that she knew stabbed deeply. "You wanted to play it your way, remember, darling?" she said. "I said to hang back until they made their move. But you had to go chasing out after them."

"How do we know she didn't bring the stuff to the boat when she swam out last night?" Varney asked angrily. Doris shrugged. "Maybe she did. But we could have followed them till we got the right spot to move in. Now he's got us boxed in here where we can't make a move. Not your kind of move, anyway."

"What do you mean by that?" Varney asked quickly. Doris leaned on the rail, and her eyes narrowed as she looked across the harbor channel at the *Sea Urchin*. A faint smile touched her patrician features.

"He's cute, mean, and dangerously competent," she said. She turned to the cold-faced man. "Which all means he's a smart cookie. And, if he's as smart as I think he is, he can be made to listen to reason. I think I could get him to cooperate."

The tall man's eyes grew small as he turned her words over in his mind. He smiled slowly. "You going to try waving it in front of him like you did with Harry?" he said. "Suppose he wants you to come across first?"

"That's my problem, Varney," Doris said, not bothering to conceal the hatred in her eyes. "You want the stuff. I think I can get it for us. That's all."

"That's right, baby," Varney said. "I don't think you can do it, but it's worth a try. I'll have Augie row you over."

Varney turned and walked forward along the deck. Doris looked out across the water again. The girl might pose a problem, she mused. But then perhaps she wouldn't. She remembered the big man's eyes as they flicked over her. She waited, watching the dinghy being lowered into the water, and then went down the single-curved ladder at the side of the boat.

Logan saw the rowboat moving toward the *Urchin* as the afternoon turned to dusk. He didn't move. "We're going to have company," he said to the girl. She got up at once and looked over the rail. Logan went to his cabin, opened a drawer and took out a double-edged knife with a weighted handle. He put it into his belt next to the big Colt Python. When he went back on deck the rowboat was alongside, and he heard the girl call out. He looked down at her and saw the beauty that lay behind the cool, contained facade she wore.

"I want to come aboard," she called up to him. "I think we ought to talk."

Logan lowered a rope ladder, and she reached out and started to climb up. He stopped her halfway up. The man had begun to climb up after her, holding the boat's line in his hand.

"Just you, honey," Logan growled. She halted, looked down at the man and spoke to him.

"It's all right, Augie," she said. "Just wait for me."

She climbed up the rest of the way, and Logan let her clamber over the rail by herself.

"Thanks for the help," she glared at him. He looked down at the man in the rowboat. "Move over to the port side," he said and watched as the man rowed around the *Urchin*. On the port side he was away from the eyes of the harbor and of the white cruiser. Logan took the knife from his belt, raised it and threw it with speed, strength, and accuracy. It hurtled silently through the air and hit the man in the rowboat at the top of his breastbone, going in at an angle to pierce his neck. He uttered a short, strangled cry, half rose, hands clutched to his neck, and then toppled forward and over the side of the rowboat. Logan looked at the girl and saw her eyes darken with surprise and shock.

"What was that for?" she asked, brows knitted in a deep frown.

"Cutting down the odds," Logan smiled pleasantly. Her eyes held his for a long moment, and then she shook her head. There was almost a tint of admiration in her voice as she spoke.

"You are a mean, no-good hard-nose, aren't you?" she said. "You're the one that sliced up Harry with the hurricane lamp, aren't you?"

"Harry killed the old man on the beach, didn't he?" Logan countered. Doris smiled.

"I guess neither of us likes to answer questions, do we?" she said. Logan shrugged. "Depends on the questions."

"May we go below?" the girl asked. "I'm Doris. And you?"

"Logan," the big man said, starting down into the cabin. He saw Julie move to follow and heard Doris speak, cool contempt in her voice.

"Not you, dearie," she said. "This is private."

Logan smiled inwardly. He didn't know what her game was, but he wanted to ler her try it out, anyway. "Stay on deck," he said to Julie and saw her about to explode. Only the cold, icy command in his eyes held her, and she subsided into a silent, seething rage. Logan went below and pulled the cabin door shut after Doris. She glanced around the cabin with cool, appreciative eyes.

"This funny little boat is quite something, isn't she?" she said, taking in the rosewood paneling and the Burma teak cabin floor. She turned her eyes on Logan.

"And I think maybe you're quite something," she said.

"Thanks," he said flatly. "But you didn't come here to admire my boat. Get on with it, honey."

Doris sat down on the edge of the bed and studied the big man's hard, lined face, handsome with a driving, dangerous recklessness to it. He radiated an electricity that was more than pure animal magnetism, and she was glad she'd come. She didn't see this man with the lush little creature on deck. Not for more than a few nights.

"I came because I thought perhaps you were a reasonable man," she said. "I thought perhaps you'd be interested in an offer."

"Maybe," he said. "But first you tell me what this is all about."

"Stop playing games, Logan," the girl said tartly. "You know what it's all about."

"You make believe I don't and tell me," he said. "Start from the beginning. I don't like coming in at the middle of anything."

Doris's lips pursed, and her eyes held Logan's coldly.

"The old man found something very important to us," she said. "It fell from a small private plane flying low across the beach. The old man was seen picking it up. He took it and hid it someplace. We didn't know who he was or where he lived, but we figured he might come back to the beach. Harry waited for him and got carried away questioning him."

A small smile flickered across Logan's face. The girl's story had fitted into what he suspected already. Her breasts, pointed peaks pushing toward him, held his attention for a moment. Her cool, contained disdain was infuriatingly tantalizing. With her every movement and glance she seemed to dare one to pierce her outer shell. The very perfection of her features added to the superior attitude that cloaked her.

"What's your offer?" he asked blandly.

"A thousand dollars," she said. "You give us what you have of ours, get your thousand and everybody's happy."

Logan smiled. "I don't need a thousand dollars," he said. "Try something else. Or raise the ante."

Doris leaned back on her elbows on the bed and saw the big man's eyes drink in her figure. His powerful shoulders rippled as he moved toward her and she felt the overwhelming strength of him, the maleness of him. She started to get up but a big hand pushed her back down. The hand stayed on her chest, holding her on the bed.

"I'm not for sale," she said.

"I didn't say you were," he answered. "Don't you ever do anything because you feel like it?"

"I only feel like it on special occasions with special people."

"All flash and no fire, eh?"

"I didn't say that," she answered, and saw his big form bending over her, saw his face coming down to blot out her vision and then his lips were on hers, forcing her mouth open roughly and she felt his tongue caressing her. Doris felt her hands move involuntarily and a surging desire coursed through her body.

"This is a special occasion of a sort," Logan said to her, moving his lips from hers. She scooted up on the bed, putting more distance between them. The moment of feeling had passed from her eyes. They were cold and contained again, and Logan permitted himself a small smile.

"Okay, you're not for sale, but I am," he said. Her contained disdain had aroused an angry desire in him. But it was more than that. She was one of those responsible for the old man's death. And it was nothing to her, a passing incident. Death was nothing, brutality no more. She took pride in being able to avoid giving out. To make her come across would be to defeat her, to strike back for the old man in the only way that would reach this beautiful, unprincipled little bitch. He had wanted no part of this whole damned thing, but he was in it and he'd hit back at every one of them where it would hurt the most.

"You want to buy what I can tell you?" he asked, pulling her toward him savagely. "You know the price."

Doris's eyes held his for a long moment and then suddenly she was smiling. Maybe this could work out in more ways than one, she told herself. This big bastard could take care of Varney for her. He might even fit in with a new set-up. She'd give him something to come back for.

"What about your girlfriend on deck?" she asked, starting to pull off the black jersey. Logan got up and went out of the cabin, bounding up onto the deck. Julie stood in the fading light of the dusk. He lowered the dinghy and pulled it around to the side.

"Go ashore for a few hours," he said.

"Go to hell," she retorted, arms folded across her breasts. He grabbed her arm and shoved her to the rail.

"Now listen here, doll. You got me into this damned thing in the first place. Now you do as I say and let me handle it my way."

"I know what you want to handle," she snapped angrily. "How could you? She's one of them, the ones who killed Pops. How can you even touch her?"

"I do things my way," he said. "You wouldn't understand."

"I understand you're the rottenest, lowest, stinkin' thing I've ever seen," Julie yelled at him. She was starting to say more when

Logan scooped her up in one quick motion and tossed her over the side. He saw her hit the water with a resounding splash a few feet from the dinghy, and he pulled up the rope ladder on the boat's side.

"Bastard!" she yelled as she came up for air. "Rotten bastard!" He grinned for a moment as he turned after seeing her start to pull herself into the dinghy. Her fury had more in it than just anger because Doris was part of the group that had killed the old man. Part of it was plain, ordinary female jealousy. They were all jealous, even when they had no right to be.

He went down to the cabin and saw the girl sitting on the bed, clad only in white lace panties and a half-bra. Her eyes mirrored reluctance, anger, and a creeping hunger. He tore off his clothes and pulled her to him and felt her grow rigid. He pressed his lips to hers, tore the bra from her and let his hands curl around her curving, upturned breasts. Her nipples, brownish and large, sprang erect at his touch and he felt her quiver, still fighting within herself. He moved back and grinned at her and she saw it for what it was—a grin of victory—and she cried out and clawed at him. He slapped her, hard, knocking her halfway across the bed and then he was onto her, his lips pulling her breasts up into his mouth, first one, then the other, and she was crying out and protesting and opening her legs for him. Doris felt this big man's hardness against her and she grabbed his head with her hands. "Oh, God, yes, yes," she cried out, a half-scream. "Oh, God, yes!" She knew, as he moved slowly into her and she screamed in ecstasy, that she had held back too long. She felt the world moving sideways and then turning, and she was floating on a bed of unbearably sweet pain, her own body a thing beyond her command, moving beneath him, answering, wanting, craving.

Logan held the girl tightly and felt the surge of triumph as her body came to life under his savage assault. There was a wild and angry satisfaction in making love to this cold, amoral creature, in feeling his ability to make her react beyond her controlled desires.

And she was beyond her carefully held control now, far beyond tossing and thrusting beneath him and crying out in long, gasping sounds, trying to free herself of the tyranny of ecstasy. She was beautiful, immaculately beautiful, with breasts that turned up at the brownish tips and quivered as he made love to her with increasing savagery. He increased his savage thrusts and she tried to hold back that last moment of capitulation, to salvage victory, and he felt her fists close to pound against his back. But he knew that if she did that, it would all have been for nothing. He would have sacrificed the very meaning of it all on the altar of pleasure. He drew back slowly, and moved forward again, alternating his every movement, using every skill at his command and suddenly he felt her body stiffen and from the depths of her there came a shriek, a wracking, shuddering shriek, and she arched her beautiful body upwards and lifted him with her.

And then it was over and she fell back onto the bed, her breath coming hard and fast. He moved from her to see her eyes on him, staring, almost dazed, unblinking. She forced them to close for a long minute and when she opened them the cool disdain was back in them. But it was tinged with something new—respect. He tossed her the white lace panties and watched her slip them on. The half-bra was torn and useless, and he let his eyes feast on the beauty of her breasts as she moved from the bed and put on the slacks. She faced him, slipping the black jersey over her head and she made no effort to disguise the victory in her eyes.

Doris studied him for a moment before saying anything. He was more than she'd expected, more in every way, and he offered more possibilities than had first entered her mind.

"After this is over I want you to look me up, Logan," she said. "We could go places together. I could use you."

"For those special occasions?" he asked and saw her eyes harden. "No, for a lot more than you ever dreamed about," she snapped. "Play ball with me, Logan. It'll be worth your while." Logan felt a sudden, overwhelming sadness. She was so gorgeous, so promising. Nothing that beautiful should be that rotten. He felt the sadness turn into the deep, furious anger at the way of the world, the same anger that had been there from the start.

"Now where is the stuff, Logan?" Doris asked, all crisp and contained once again.

"The old man hid it," Logan answered mildly.

"I told *you* that," Doris said with annoyance.

"So you did," Logan said, giving her a boyish smile. "That's all I know, honey."

The small frown on Doris's brow deepened, a slow realization creeping into her eyes.

"Now wait a minute," she said. "We made a deal."

"That we did," he smiled again at her cheerfully. "I said if you wanted to buy what I had to tell you, you knew the price. You bought it. I told you I didn't know anything. I was only passing along the beach when I found the old man."

Doris stood looking at him, her jaw muscles twitching, her eyes burning with a wild rage. Logan smiled again.

"You ought to believe people more, honey," he said. "Live and learn, eh?"

"I'll kill you," she hissed. She dived headlong across the bed, reaching for the chair where he'd put the big Colt Python on top of his trousers. The inside of the boat wasn't that wide, and she had her fingers around the butt of the gun when he landed on her. She wasn't wasting breath and energy calling him names. She swung her arm over her head to elude his grasping hand. He got his fingers around her wrist as she tried to bring the gun down and felt her furious strength. She got a knee free and brought it up against his groin, and he felt the moment's wave of pain. But he held onto her wrist and rolled back across the bed with her, flipping her over and landing her on the edge of the mattress. The arena was the same and so was the struggle, essentially. He brought her arm down hard against the wooden edge of the bed, and she cried out in pain. The Colt fell to the floor of the cabin.

He yanked her up and threw her off the end of the bed. He had one big hand around her neck, pulling her out of the cabin and up the few steps to the deck. She was cursing at him now, cursing through clenched teeth as he sent her sprawling across the deck.

"Now you tell your friends that I don't know anything about this and I'm not part of it and to stay out of my hair or you haven't seen anything yet, honey," he said.

"You haven't seen anything," she hissed, getting to her feet. "You'll pay for this, you will. You can count on it."

"I always tremble like this," Logan said grimly. "Start swimming, doll."

She turned, went to the rail and dived off. It was a nice dive and her white slacks were ghostly in the dark. She cut through the water cleanly and he stood watching as her head, a blond spot in the blackness, emerged. Then, as he watched, he saw the white slacks float away on their own and, she struck out for the cruiser. It wasn't very far to swim. Besides, she could make it or she wouldn't have jumped. She wasn't the kind for gestures. He turned and went down to the cabin. He wished he felt quite as secure and confident as he'd sounded to Doris. He lay down on the bed and then, too restless to sleep, went back on deck. Taking a length of wire, he strung it around the rail of the ship, from bow to stern. Then he took out a half dozen small brass bells and hung them from the wire. It was a simple but effective alarm that had proven itself often. Leaving only the mast light on, he went back to the cabin and switched on the marine forecast. The urgent tone of the forecaster's voice told him the bad news even before he heard the words. Phyllis was still moving slowly but still heading toward the mainland and the coast. Logan said a small prayer that the hurricane would continue its slow forward movement. But you never knew with hurricanes. She could decide to pick up speed at any moment and sweep onto them like an avenging angel. The air had grown thicker and the stillness continued ominously.

Logan tried to lie still, but his skin crawled with inner tension. Then he heard the tinkle of bells. He reached over and picked up the Colt Python and moved silently to the top step of the companionway. The long blond tresses glowed softly in the dark as she moved along the rail, pulling the dinghy to the stern. He watched her tie the small boat up and then returned to the cabin. He heard her moving softly down the steps and into the forward cabin, and he smiled. Perhaps some day she might understand.

In the forward cabin, Julie Banntry undressed and lay awake, rubbing her hands down the length of her naked body, fighting down her desire to go to where Logan slept. She didn't understand him. Maybe he was all the things she'd called him. Maybe he wasn't. But whatever he was, he was beyond her. But she needed him. She could make him happy, and she felt herself stir as she thought of how he had made love to her. Pops was gone, and she had her own plans for a new life, a new world. But it was no good without someone to share it with. Anger swept over her as she thought of him with that bitch from the white cruiser. Why did he have to touch her? He must have had some good reason. But whatever it was, he'd forget about her. She'd see to that. In the morning she'd make him forget. She closed her eyes and let the gentle roll of the boat put her to sleep.

Logan still lay awake, letting certain conclusions crystallize in his mind. He was involved up to his eyeballs now. He didn't want to be, but he was. And he'd get the most out of it. Doris and her playmates weren't so determined over a set of bubble gum wrappers. Whatever they were after was valuable, very valuable. Valuable enough perhaps to provide the answer to Sister Mary Angela's letter still lying in the desk drawer. The old man had found something and had hidden it, perhaps to give himself time to think about what he should do. But they hadn't given him any time. They'd gotten to him, and perhaps he'd been stubborn. As

Doris had said, "Harry got carried away" and the old man had been killed. That much was easy enough to reconstruct. But what had he found and where had he hidden it? In the old monstrosity of a house? If so, he'd have Julie go through the place with him. She was angry, he knew. And hurt. And jealous. And God knows what else. But he could handle her, spitfire that she was.

But time was running out. Doris and her friends would be getting desperate. They heard the weather reports just as he did, and they'd know that when the hurricane came, all bets would be off. And with the damn storm moving so close already he couldn't move freely, either. There would be tomorrow and that would be it. If he was to move, it had to be tomorrow. Phyllis wouldn't hold off much longer, and when she came she would descend with screaming winds and mountainous seas. He and the *Urchin* had to be somewhere else before that happened. He'd been sucked into this, maneuvered, trapped, and boxed into it. That was more than enough. He wasn't adding a hurricane to it. He forced his eyes shut and turned off his mind.

CHAPTER FOUR

I t was hardly dawn, still dark with only the hint of light in the sky, when Logan heard her soft footsteps and woke at once. He lay still in the cabin and felt her move to the side of the bed and stand there, looking down at his hard-framed nakedness. Then she crawled onto the bed beside him and pressed her full breasts against his chest. He felt the lush softness of her. As she moved her breasts against him, he stirred and raised his arm to press it against the small of her back. Julie looked up at Logan and moved up to crush her lips against his. Whatever had happened last night, she would make him forget her, forget ever having had her, forget everything but what she could do to him. She moved from his lips, letting her mouth caress his cheek, down along the side of his neck and across the broad muscles of his chest. She moved her lips in a wet, sensuous path, down across his flat stomach and then, with a gasp of hunger, still further until she was making little sounds of pleasure and desire. He felt the wild flood of desire course through his body and he rose up under her to turn her over and find her rounded breasts with his mouth. Their small pink tips sprang erect, tiny, pink, as sweetly sensuous and vernal as she was. The frenzied passion of the day before was gone from her and her desires were less edged with frantic release. A full, deep, complete, and surging emotion had replaced that, even more fulfilling and more complete. She was all over his body, holding him, kissing him, stroking and straining against him.

"Oh, Logan, Logan," she said. "God, Logan, more, more." He was holding her breasts cupped in his hands, moving his lips on one, then the other, pulling and drawing them up into his mouth. Her hips twisted in desire, and she pulled at him with her hands on his buttocks. He came over to press down upon her, and she cried out and opened her full thighs in the eternal invitation of woman, and he moved to find her warm, welcoming wetness. Julie's torso rose and twisted under him as she cried out, her body urging itself on, pursuing that moment of moments, that eternal goal never reached often enough. Her hands bruising his body as she pulled them up and down along his sides, digging deeply into his skin, she began to gasp in rhythm with his movements, each gasp a grace note of ecstatic pleasure. Her lips formed words that came out only as a gasp, and suddenly she was clutched to him, her legs lifted up high around his back, moving pistonlike up and down, hanging onto him. With almost startling suddenness she let go of him and her shoulders fell back onto the bed. Then it was he who thrust deeply, over and over and her gasps rose faster and faster until there was no sound but the silent paean of pleasure beyond pleasure, of raptures never scaled before.

Julie fell limply, and Logan, staying with her, laid his body across hers, and she smiled through closed eyes. "Oh, God, Logan, it was no accident the first time," she breathed. "You're something different, all right." She opened her eyes and looked at the big man. "What is it with you?" she asked, questioning herself as much as him. "How do you make it come like you do, like it never happened before and never will again?"

He moved to lay beside her and his smile was rueful.

"Maybe because I feel just that way about it," he said. "Maybe because it's the only real thing in this damned world, the only thing nobody can change or ruin or louse up."

Her eyes were thoughtful. "Maybe it is," she said.

"Take me with you, Logan," she said and suddenly she was the waif again, that lost quality in her eyes and her voice, and he was silently amazed at how she could change from throbbing woman to little girl.

"To the first real port, remember?" he said. "You just had to get away for a little while. There were too many reminders, and you were afraid."

"I know that's what I said."

"But I meant what I said, Julie."

"I did, too, but it's different now. I know I could make it with you. I know your kind of person. And I'm not like most girls."

Logan smiled at her. "You're right there," he said. "But it's still no."

"We could try, Logan. We could try."

"It wouldn't work."

"You don't know that. There's nothing to lose. Maybe you'll be surprised."

"I don't like surprises," he grinned and ran a big hand through the long, blond hair, soft, light almost hiding his fingers in its denseness. It would be fun, he knew, for a while. For him, anyway. She was a lusty animal, a vessel of pleasure for those who could take it and not be overwhelmed by her. But it would be that and only that to him while she would want something more. It was there in her eyes already, just as she wanted him to explain his rejection of her. But she wouldn't be able to understand the only explanations he could give. She wouldn't understand that you could die and still live, that a world could shatter so completely that it left only a cold and consuming rage. She wouldn't understand that kind of a hurt, a hurt that made you see so clearly you had to look away. She hadn't lived enough yet, or loved enough. She hadn't looked deeply enough into mirrors yet. She would hate him for the uncompromising honesty he lived by. But that was the one thing he had now, the one thing he lived by, the honesty of his own hardness, of following his own trail in his own way. And no one would take that from him. Not now, not until he gave up enough of it to rejoin the world.

Besides, Julie was all emotion, a creature of the senses, not the mind. Her understanding came from her heart, not her head; her truths were felt, not reasoned. And that was all to the good, a kind of wisdom all its own and greater than most learned wisdom. But for him it would not be enough, he knew. If ever he turned to another again he would need the understanding of the mind as well as the compassion of the heart. Not a little of one and more of the other but both in full measure. And so he pushed her down on the bed and kissed her.

"It's still no, and let's drop it now," he said. "And if we don't figure out how to get rid of our friends on the cruiser you may not need to think about it again." He got to his feet and disappeared for a moment to snap on the radio. He was back beside Julie's naked warmth as the marine forecaster's voice flooded into the cabin.

"Hurricane Phyllis has picked up speed and is heading toward the Carolina coast," the announcer intoned. "It is unlikely she will change course substantially now. Her forward motion, however, is still unstable. Urgent warnings are out for all shipping. This is an extremely dangerous storm. Coastal areas should expect tides of fifteen feet or more and extreme flooding."

Logan got up and snapped off the radio. He looked at Julie and saw her face was clouded. She was standing by the porthole, looking out at the gray daylight. She reached for her clothes, frowning.

"I've got to go back to the house," she said. "I've got to get some things." Logan watched her as she dressed and saw the strange urgency in her eyes. The marine forecast had upset her deeply.

"The house is far enough back to avoid flooding, I think," he said. "And you can't do a damn thing about the wind and the waves and the rain."

"I still have to go back," she said.

"What's so important there?" Logan asked her.

"Just some things I want," she snapped. "Personal things." Evasiveness laced her irritation and Logan eyed her speculatively. She was pacing the cabin, glancing out the porthole at almost every turn.

"Some sentimental things from the old man?" he tossed out.

"Yes, that's it," she said quickly. "You think the hurricane will really hit us?" she asked him, worry in her eyes.

"You heard the man," Logan answered. He didn't want to be here then. He'd get away, head up north to that sheltered cove. This overcrowded harbor would be a graveyard for boats torn loose from their moorings. But Julie's sudden concern still bothered him. He didn't like the smell of it, and he pressed further.

"You and the old man were really close, weren't you?" he said. She nodded as she poked her head out the porthole and looked up at the sky. The first faint puffy wind was already making itself felt, blowing away the still hanging air.

"Our friends aboard the cruiser say they saw the old man find what they're after," he said casually. Julie shrugged.

"They must have seen somebody else, that's all," she replied.

"If he had found something valuable he'd have told you about it, I'd think," Logan went on. "You and he being so close and everything, no?"

"That's right," she said and suddenly there was a tinge of wariness in her voice. He didn't like it. If the scheming little bitch had been lying to him all along he'd make her sorry for it in more ways than one. He decided to press again. If his suspicions were wrong, he would have bought his answer at a damn high price. He took her by the shoulders and turned her to face him.

"Forget the house," he said. "I've been thinking about what you said. Maybe you're right about trying it, you and me. I think I can give our friends the slip. There's still time, before that damned hurricane stops us. I'm willing to give it a try."

Hope and excitement leaped into her eyes, and he felt like a heel. But then she answered.

"I can be back in a few hours," she said. "I'll go ashore and hire a car or even a cab. I can drive to Kingdom Point in just a little over an hour. I'll be back before the morning's over."

He'd gotten his answer. She wanted what he offered, all right, but something else was suddenly even more important. And the hurricane somehow figured into it. It hadn't changed her desires, just shifted around the order of priorities. She'd been willing to go off with him—hungry to—but the hurricane had loomed up to scare her. But why? If the old man had confided in her, if she knew more than she'd let on, why was the hurricane so important? If she knew what was hidden and where it was in the old house, it'd still be there, even if it was amid the rubble. The old place was back far enough to be blown down but not washed away to sea. He stepped back and smiled at her.

"If you really want to go back I guess that's it," he said. "I'll just have to wait for you. Take the dinghy. And hurry."

Her arms flew around his neck, and her lips were open and hot against his mouth. "I will," she said. "You damn well know I will."

He went on deck with her and watched her as she clambered into the dinghy, waving as she rowed off toward the docks. He stayed there till she was lost amid the welter of hulls and masts crowding the dockside. His eyes swept the small-boat owners hurriedly adding line, some letting out more mooring line, others battening down everything they could. He knew that those aboard the white cruiser had seen Julie row to shore, but he was betting they wouldn't move after her. Not so long as he hadn't gone with her. He let his eyes scan the sky. Gray, fast moving low clouds were starting to scud by and the wind was growing puffier. He turned and went below, his mouth a thin, hard line. Damn it, he cursed to himself. Time was really running out. He snapped on the weather for the latest storm advisory. They gave

Phyllis six hours to reach the coastline. Six hours and less for the gales at the perimeter of the storm. Six hours, maybe seven. Or maybe five. It wasn't much time, but it was all he had, and he had to make do with it. He cursed the blond-haired vixen for having pulled him into this in the first place. He could try to cut out now on his own and head north for that cove. But the cruiser would be after him, and he couldn't fight and steer alone, even with the automatic pilot. Besides, he had come too far to turn back now.

He took his clothes off and rolled his shirt, trousers and a towel inside a protective oilskin covering. Putting on a belt, he tied the package to it and crawled to the forward hatchway. He pushed the hatch cover up only enough to squeeze out, keeping beneath the level of the gunwale. They would have a constant watch on the *Urchin,* he was certain. But the tide had swung the bow of the boat away from the cruiser and four compass points of the port bow were out of visual range. Pushing his way across the forward deck on his stomach, almost to the bow, he reached the side of the ship. Then he slipped over the gunwale and lowered himself into the water, disappearing beneath the surface. Swimming with long, powerful strokes, he moved underwater, keeping himself in a line with the bulk of the boat. When he surfaced for a brief moment, drinking deeply of the air, he was but a tiny, bobbing spot on the water. He dived again and swam on underwater, surfacing only when his lungs were about to give out. Finally he was at the docks and pulled himself out of the water. He crouched in the shadow of a big, fifty-foot, flush-deck pleasure cruiser and unrolled the package at his waist. He dried himself with the towel, put on his clothes, and in minutes was rushing past the grim-faced, worried hordes of yachtsmen trying to prepare for the hurricane. Police cars were cruising the harbor streets with loudspeakers blaring hurricane warnings and storekeepers were attempting to shore up windows. His eyes caught a sign, *Cars For Hire,* and he hurried to the small streetfront office. The lone occupant of the office was a glum-faced, balding man.

Logan noted the black '67 Lincoln with commercial plates at the curb just outside the door.

"I want to get to Kingdom Point," he said to the man who looked up from behind the desk.

"Forget it," the man grunted. "You're the second one that's come in here wanting to go to Kingdom Point. There was a girl, little while ago."

"Where did she go?"

"I showed her where to get the bus that runs between here and the Point," he said. "She caught it. Last one running today, too."

"I'll go for anything within reason," Logan offered. The man shook his head. "I'm not risking that run now, especially back. It's all along the coastal road. I told her the same thing."

Logan grimaced. He didn't like what he had to do, but time and nature were riding him hard. He glanced out into the street, saw no one near. He whirled, striking out with a karate chop that caught the balding man on the neck. He slipped under the desk noiselessly. Logan yanked open a door. It was a broom closet. He pulled the man inside it. He found some rope and tied the man hand and foot and stuffed a makeshift gag into his mouth. Logan checked the bonds. With a little effort they'd work loose—about an hour's worth of effort.

"Sorry about this," he muttered, patting the unconscious figure on the head. He took the car keys. Seconds later he was inside the black Lincoln, heading north out of Bayville for the coastal road to Kingdom Point. His eyes swept the sky as he roared down the flat road, and he felt the pull of the gusts of wind against the car. The grayness had deepened and the low-flying clouds were hurrying. The road ran within easy view of the sea. He saw that the tides had already started to rise, and the breakers swept in with increasing speed. Traffic on the road was light, and he held the heavy car near the top of its speed, taking the gentle curves without slowing. With every glance at the sea the tide seemed to rise, the waves beginning to take on an angry hiss as they tumbled after each other. He was glad to see the low, flat buildings of Kingdom Point come into view. He threaded his way through the town, past the harbor and beyond to where the sand of the beachfront loomed before him. The road began to curve inland there and he pulled to the side and leaped from the car. A gust caught him as he started to trot along the sand. He saw the old, crumbled towers of the monstrous house rise up over the crest of sea-oats, the hardy grass screening the lower portion of it from him. He slowed and crouched. He looked for a sign of the girl inside the house. He waited, frowning at the silence. The line of windows facing the sea were open. Whatever she'd come for, she hadn't yet taken the time to close the old place. He shifted position, crawling to the side for a better view. But the empty silence persisted. "Damn!" he exploded, finally, crossing the short distance to the old house at a run. He burst in through the open door, halting in the disheveled, cluttered living room. She wasn't there. He called her name. There was no answer. But she'd been there. He saw the blouse lying on the sofa, the shorts beside it. He glanced across the rest of the room and then he saw it—the empty spot where the scuba gear had been. Eyes narrowed, he ran from the house. Between the house and the Point there was only sandy beachfront. He turned and ran north, crossing to the hard-packed sand of the beach to make better time. The wind had strengthened to a steady blow now, and the sea had risen to cover most of what ordinarily was uncovered even at high tide. The surf came rolling in hard now, each wave a curled lip of white edging the gray face of the sea behind it. And then, ahead, he saw rocks and a small inlet carved into the rock, interrupting the stretch of sandy beach. The rock rose to form a protective wall around the inlet. He clambered up it and made his way down the other side. She had to be in the waters of the inlet someplace. He stripped to his shorts, laid his clothes behind a heavy boulder, and dived into the gray, cold water. He struck out sharply, diving, and staying close to the rock, seeing it move down to become encrusted with coral.

The gathering turbulence of the surface water disappeared as he dived deeper. Then he saw her, a flash of bare legs moving close to the coral and rock. She had the air tank strapped on, and she moved slowly. Logan swam closer, moving out from the rocks. She was intent on her search, concentrating on it as she moved from rock to rock and coral to coral. She had a long pole in her right hand, and she paused at each crevice and hole to poke inside it with the pole. Without scuba gear Logan's lungs were beginning to burn, and he struck out for the surface, breaking into the air a second before they burst. He drank deeply of the air and glanced at the gray, threatening skies. The water pushed him twenty feet toward the shore in seconds, and he dived again, this time staying in the center of the little inlet. She was still intent on her search now farther along the small curve of the inlet He watched from a distance, fighting back the demand by his lungs that he surface. But she was still poking the pole into crevices when he had to kick upwards again and gasp in air. This time he drank quickly and surface-dived at once. Julie had reached a point past the center of the curve where the staghorn coral grew thick and a myriad of dark gaps clustered together. Finally she pulled at the pole and then turned, lifting a small bag from the end of the pole. It was tied at the top by a drawstring. Logan swam away quickly, striking out for the surface. He burst into the air and got a mouthful of spray, shook it out and headed for the shore, the force of the water strong enough to fling him against the rocks with bruising, scraping pain. He pulled himself out and pressed his body behind a wind-smoothed boulder.

Julie surfaced a few moments later, a dark shape fighting against the force of the water. She came ashore only a few yards from where he crouched, and he watched her slip off the air tank and rest for a moment. The little bag was tied to her wrist, and she unwound it and started to pull the drawstring open. Logan stepped from behind the boulder.

"I'll take that, Julie," he said. She gaped at him as he moved over to where she sat.

"I can explain, Logan," she said, finding her voice.

"You knew all the time," he said. "It was all an act."

"No, Logan, no it wasn't, I swear it," she said, her voice tense, tight.

"You were so upset because the old man had been killed."

"That's right, I was. Terribly upset. They didn't have to do that. I never expected anything like that."

"But you knew his death was tied into this, whatever it is," Logan countered. "I'll buy that you were shattered by it. But you knew there was a reason. You knew that all the time."

Logan felt a sadness, a hollow, empty sadness, the kind that would turn into black meanness inside him, as he fixed Julie with his deep, probing eyes. Lusty, throbbing creature, lost waif, peppery spitfire and now conniving, scheming, lying, little bitch.

"You touch all the bases, don't you?" he commented grimly.

"What do you mean?" she asked.

"You wouldn't understand," he answered. "Give me the bag."

She held back. "Will you give it back to me? Promise?" she bargained. It was a mistake. Logan wrapped his hand around the rubbery wetness of the scuba suit at her neck.

"I promise I'll twist your damn head off if you give me any more trouble," he growled. She lifted her hand and gave him the bag. She'd seen that cold hardness in his eyes once before, when he'd used the hurricane lamp on the man's face. He let her sink back onto the rocks and loosened the drawstring on the little leather sack. He dumped the contents out into his cupped palm.

"Diamonds," he said, looking at Julie. "But you knew, of course." Her sullen silence was his answer. He poured the gems back into the bag and drew the drawstring tight again. These were not raw stones but all cut and polished gems.

"You've got about fifteen seconds to tell me the truth," Logan growled. "Let's start with what I know. It was this bag of diamonds that was dropped from the low-flying plane and picked up by the old man. Take it from there."

Her eyes held his, unblinking, sad.

"Pops came home and told me what he'd found," she said. "He wanted to think about what he should do. But he hadn't wanted to bring them back to keep in the house. He was afraid someone might come looking for them and find them there. So he told me he'd hidden them, during low tide, in one of the coral crevices in the inlet, a deep one where they'd stay safe. That night we talked about right and wrong and what it would mean to be rich and not worry about tomorrow and have a lot of nice things. When Pops went to bed that night he said he didn't care much about himself, that he had the kind of riches he wanted right here. But he was thinking about what the diamonds would do for me. And the next morning they killed him."

Logan nodded. It fitted this time. The old man had no doubt been stubborn and Harry had gotten "carried away."

"I wasn't going to keep the diamonds," Julie said, getting to her feet and putting her hands on Logan's chest. "I only decided that after they killed Pops. There was nothing left for me after that, not here, not anywhere, and keeping the diamonds would at least mean he hadn't died for nothing."

"Would it?" Logan asked. "Some people would say just the opposite. Some people would say that turning them in to the cops would be the only way to show the old man hadn't died for nothing."

The stubborn thrust of her jaw grew harder.

"He would have wanted me to keep them," she said. "He would have."

"Trying to convince yourself, Julie?" Logan asked. Stubborn anger crept into her eyes. He could fit the rest of the pieces together easily now, even to the sudden fear at the news of the coming hurricane.

"You didn't want to get away from memories of the old man," he said to her. "You just wanted to get away so you could lay low safely until things cooled down. Then you'd sneak back to the inlet here and get the stuff."

She didn't answer, but she looked away, her jaw a stubborn line. It had been the hurricane that wrecked her plans. She knew that when it struck, its howling, driving fury would force churning seas into every hole and crevice in the rocks, sweeping each one clean. Her little cache would be swept away and lost forever. And as he thought of the coming storm, he turned to clamber up the rocks. Julie's arms flew around his neck.

"This hasn't changed anything, Logan," she said, anxious fear in her voice. "Only made it better for us, don't you see? I was going to tell you, later, as a surprise."

"I told you I don't like surprises," he growled and pulled away from her. "Come on."

"What are you going to do with the diamonds?" she asked.

"Nothing for now," he said. "Take them with me. There's no time for anything except getting back to the boat and finding a safe spot. And you're going with me."

He saw the pleased little glint appear in her eyes and he reached out and pulled her up to him.

"It's not for the reasons you're thinking," he said, his hand pressing hard into the soft flesh between her neck and shoulder. "If the *Urchin* and I don't make it out of this damn thing safely it'll be because of you, and you're not going to make it either then. Get that straight, Julie girl?"

"What about the things you said? ... About giving it a try?" she asked, her eyes wide.

"Bait, honey, just bait. In the same class as your story about having to get away from memories."

He let go of her and gave her a shove backwards. "Pick up the air tank and bring it along," he growled. "It might come in handy." He put on his clothes, pushed the little sack into his pocket and started up over the edge of the rocks.

"My clothes are at the house," she called after him.

"We'll pick them up. It's on the way. Your jeep still there?" She nodded. They'd use it to return to Bayville. He walked with long, hard strides, with an occasional glance to make sure the girl was close behind. They strode along the edge of the water. The sea was gray, unrelieved under a gray sky, rolling, crashing grayness, sending gray-white scud flying from the tops of the waves. The wind carried an occasional gust of rain and flung it at the two hurrying figures. Logan's grim-lipped estimate was two to three hours, not more, before the hurricane broke in full fury on them.

When they reached the old house the rain was starting to move in more forcefully, in steady, slanting sheets. Julie crossed the threshhold of the open door first, and Logan came in close behind her. He had just stepped into the huge, cluttered room when the blow struck him. With a moment of instinctive warning, he had started to duck away, but it still caught him hard enough to send him falling forward to his knees. Another blow followed it—again glancing off his head—but the room was spinning and he heard voice, and then screaming that grew dim. He a voice, a tight, hard voice, and then the girl's shook his head and kicked out with one leg, feeling his foot strike flesh and bone and hearing a cursed cry of pain. He rolled over, shook his head and the room came into focus. He got a glimpse of Doris and two men holding Julie. Then a shoe caught him in the side. Now it was his turn to gasp in pain. He rolled away, felt hands grabbing at him. He struck out with both hands, wrapping his arms around a leg and pulling. The leg's owner went over, and Logan got to one knee when another blow descended, catching him across the back of the neck. He pitched forward onto his face again. Somebody was using a billy. Darkness came over him in a wave, and he somersaulted forward, kicking both heels up and catching someone in the face. An arm tried to grab him as he landed on his back. He got hold of it, twisted and heard a satisfying groan. A foot kicked him in the side of the temple and once again the grayness descended. If only he could get on his feet. But they were all over him, not giving him a chance to spring back from that first sudden blow. He swung furiously, fighting from instinct more than anything else, bringing his blows up from the floor, rolling and kicking, punching out in all directions, feeling some land, some miss, using the powerful muscles to battle back. He heard a man cursing, shook the grayness off long enough to see two men tackle him and bring him crashing to the floor. He glimpsed others coming in and then the cold, unyielding butt of a revolver crashed down on his skull. He shook his head, but the darkness continued to wrap around him. Then there was nothing but silence and sudden sleep.

When Logan woke he felt the hard pull of the ropes tied around his wrists. He was sitting up, propped against the worn sofa, his back against the bottom portion of it, his wrists bound together in his lap. He let his eyes focus before raising his head to see the others standing in the room. Doris was nearest to him, beside the tall, cold-faced man. The man had the little sack in his hand and swung it casually by the drawstring. Julie, her wrists bound together as his were, sat against the opposite wall, still clad in the top part of her scuba suit. Doris saw Logan's head come up and turned toward him, her eyes cold.

"So you didn't know anything?" she hissed and walked over to Logan. She kicked him in the face with her pointed shoe. He turned to take the blow on the cheek and felt the trickle of blood instantly flow down his face. His legs were stretched out in front of him. He moved one, curling it around Doris's ankle and pulling hard. She went down backwards, her head hitting the wooden floor with a resounding thud. Varney quickly picked her up. She put her hand to the back of her head and winced in pain. Logan saw the others in the room, eight of them, and three starting for him.

"No," Varney said. "There's no time for that."

"Work him over, boys," Doris said. "Work him over till the bastard's face looks like Harry's did."

"I said no," Varney spoke up. "We'll fix them up and get out of here." As if to add emphasis to his words, the wind tore a shutter from the window and sent it clattering along the side of the house.

"Damn it, Varney," she snapped. "Maybe you better just do what I say without arguing all the time. You argued about coming here, too."

The man's eyes narrowed. "Shut up, Doris," he said. "So you were right. But I'm still running this show."

There was trouble simmering just below the surface. Maybe it could be fanned. Maybe a fight amongst them would give him a break, a chance. All maybes but what the hell, he had nothing to lose at this point. He shot Julie a glance which told her to keep her mouth shut. He hoped she got the message. Her eyes were sullen, defiant. The rest of the men watched Varney and Doris.

"You better listen to Doris," Logan said. "It seems Doris gives good advice."

Varney turned to look at Logan. "She thought things were too damned quiet on your boat after the girl left," he said. "We didn't see you anywhere, not even stirring around below decks."

"And so Doris said you'd better get the hell back here to the house," Logan finished. "I told you, Doris is smart. She gives everyone good advice. You ought to know the offer she gave me."

Varney turned to face Logan more fully.

"What offer?" he said.

"She offered me a big piece of your operation," Logan said, smiling up at Varney. "In fact, she said she could use me as a replacement."

"Varney! Are you going to listen to that lying sonofabitch?"

It was Doris, her voice sharp and commanding. The tall man looked at her, a slow, icy look. "Shut up, Doris," he said softly. "Let's hear what he has to say."

Doris was white-faced, her eyes blazing. "He's lying, don't you see that?"

"Am I, Doris?" Logan laughed, his mind racing on. He thought of the diamonds in the sack, all cut and polished, finished pieces. He threw out an educated guess.

"That's why I knew you've got a fancy operation," he said. "An operation that needs Doris to front it. That's why I know I could be fitted into it."

Varney was looking at Doris as he spoke to Logan.

"Who were you thinking of replacing with him, Doris?" he said. "You weren't going to use him to go into the jewelers and buy the pieces, were you? No, that's your job. And you weren't thinking about him bringing the pieces back to them after he switched stones, were you? No, not that, either. You have to carry through on that. Who were you going to replace with him, baby?"

"Nobody," Doris said, but there was fear in her eyes, fear that revealed guilt. Varney saw it, too. With a suddenness that surprised Logan, he struck Doris across the face. It made her head twist, and she staggered backwards.

"He's lying," Doris gasped out. "Look, Varney, believe me." Her eyes were wide and fearful and she moved to the tall cold-faced man. "You wanted something from me, Varney," she said. "You'll get it. Everything you wanted. He's lying, I tell you."

Logan was seeing the whole picture, now, putting it together. It was a smooth, sophisticated operation, all right. Varney's few questions had revealed it in broad strokes. Doris was sent into jewelry stores in rich, swank communities with a good check to purchase a particular piece on approval of a nonexistent husband or boyfriend. It was a common enough practice. They took a few days, maybe a week, to switch the diamonds in the piece with fakes, probably undetectable by the ordinary jeweler's glasses. Then she brought the piece back, saying it was not liked by the husband, got her check back and they took off with the real stones.

Logan looked up to see Varney staring coldly at him. The old house suddenly creaked and groaned in a hard gust of wind. "Let's get out of here, Varney," Doris said. "Just kill them and let's go."

"We'll do it the way I said we would," Varney answered. "Plain old murders bring cops and cops bring questions and questions bring searches. That's why we ditched the old man, remember?" He gestured to three of the others. The men pulled Julie to her feet and threw her down beside Logan. "We'll let the hurricane do the dirty work for us," Varney smiled. The others seized Logan and rolled him against Julie, back to back, and tied ropes around them both, binding them together, pinning their arms tight in front of each of them. In a few moments they were tightly bound, unable to move more than their toes.

"Get them down to the water," Varney said. "If they're ever found when the hurricane blows over it'll look like whatever they tried to do just went wrong someplace. People do all sorts of crazy things at times like this."

Four of the men half lifted, half dragged them out into the rain and the wind, dragged them across the wet sand. He could see Doris walking along beside him, and he saw the racing clouds overhead, all dark gray, moving with the impatience of waiting death. The taste of salt water mingled with the rain now. They were at the edge of the rising, roaring sea. The men threw them forward, into the leading edge of the sea, and a wave immediately flung itself over them. When it had receded, he saw the others walking away. Only Doris hung back for a moment, cold victory in her eyes, a special victory only he and she knew about. The wind rose, curled around them and threw the sea over them. Their bodies shook in the force of the breaking waves and he heard Julie coughing out salt water.

"Use your breath as if you were swimming," Logan called. The water broke over them again and they were half in the sea, now, being moved by the swirling surf. Julie coughed and sputtered, and he felt the movement of her back muscles.

"Watch your breath," he called again. "Try to time it with the waves."

"It's no use," Julie coughed. "I'm sorry, Logan, I am."

"That makes two of us," Logan answered bitterly. The sea struck him in the face, but he held his breath as the water flowed over and around him and then receded. But another wave followed at once and he had chance for only a short breath. It wouldn't take long, he knew. They'd be engulfed in a matter of minutes, swept in on the fierce, roaring waters and then out again. Goddamn it, Logan swore. No, it wouldn't end this way. Not without a final try. He wasn't ready to cash it all in yet. There were too many unfinished things to do—one especially. His anger at the world exploded, and it took in the girl strapped against him, the vicious amoral creature from the white cruiser, and himself. He twisted and pulled his arms, crying out in pain, but the wet ropes refused to budge. A huge wave came in, and he felt himself lifted, sent swirling and rolling by it, his body riding up over Julie's, and then her body across his as the sea rolled them along. As the waters receded he yelled. "Roll over. Dig your feet in. Push and roll."

"What?" Julie sputtered back.

"Roll, damn it," Logan yelled again. He pushed his feet in against the wet sand as the waves struck him again, and he rolled over the girl. "Now you do it," he yelled, and he felt her push her body and rise, rolling over with him.

"Keep it up," he yelled. "Keep going. All the way to the house."

The girl rolled over him again and then he rolled over her and they rolled and tumbled together like some unearthly insect and finally she gasped out in pain.

"I can't, Logan," she said. "I can't anymore."

He kicked out savagely, as hard as his bonds would permit him, and rolled over her. He pulled at her with his powerful shoulder muscles. "Come on, damn you," he yelled. "Come on."

He felt her back arch and she came over again. The old house loomed up in the driving rain. "Just a little farther," Logan called to her. Once more he pressed his shoulders up and started her over. She was crying as she came over and crashed to the ground. His body rolled over hers, and she continued crying, great, gasping sobs of pain and weariness as they reached the doorway and pushed their way inside. His own body ached and throbbed, but the cold, bitter anger inside him carried him on. Julie screamed in pain as he rolled over her on the wood of the floor and came to rest against the doorway leading to the kitchen. He saw the handle of the bread knife hanging off the edge of the shelf and kicked at the wood of the kitchen cabinet. The knife shivered, and he kicked again. It fell to the floor. He rolled, pulling Julie with him, and got his hands on the handle. Turning back, he lay on his side and pressed the knife against the ropes that encircled them, sawing it back and forth, each motion traveling no more than an inch. But the knife was sharp and it cut through the cord, little by little, the strands parting with agonizing slowness. Logan listened to the old house shudder as the wind rose still higher, and he wondered if he were not already too late. But he continued to saw against the rope, cursing under his breath with every movement of the bread knife and then, suddenly, it came apart in a small shower of twine. The ropes binding them together loosened and he struggled free, kicking himself away from Julie. The knife still in his hands, the angle too sharp to reach the ropes binding his own wrist, he moved to the girl and cut her wrist bonds. She sat up, breathing hard, her face still echoing the pain of her body, and untied his wrist ropes.

He was on his feet instantly, pulling her up. With one hand he scooped up the air tank as he ran into the living room. "My clothes," Julie cried.

"No time," Logan answered. Outside, the wind and the rain struck them with an angry hand, pushing them against the house. The jeep was around at the rear, and he threw the air tank in the back and leaped in. The winds were a raging gale now, and he peered through the driving rain at the low-flying clouds as he sent the jeep roaring away from the old house. Another hour and a half, perhaps, before Hurricane Phyllis hit with all her fury.

His eyes were bitter and cold as they roared through the gale winds of the perimeter of the storm. He was seeing the harbor at Bayville in his mind, thinking about the *Sea Urchin* as she waited there for them. He saw the ships straining at their moorings, saw the carnage of those too tightly tied to the docks, and he pressed the gas pedal to the floor. They roared away from the sand and onto the road to Kingdom Point. He looked over at Julie huddled in the front seat, but the terror and fear in her didn't touch him at all. The hurricane of bitter anger raging inside him could match anything that happened outside. They would pay, the girl, the cold-faced man, the whole lot of them. And if the *Urchin* were lost, Julie would pay, too.

CHAPTER FIVE

ogan kept the gas pedal to the floor as they careened through the deserted streets of Kingdom Point, and he briefly wondered if Jennifer and the boy had found safe shelter. He sent the jeep spinning onto the coastal road to Bayville. His fingers were cramped and stiff from gripping the wheel so tightly. He glanced at Julie, and saw her swaying despite her grip on the edge of the seat.

"You'll fall out sitting up here," he said. "Get down on the floor and wedge yourself against the seat." Julie, fear making her obedient, slid down to crouch on the floor, braced against the bottom of the seat. The wind and the rain tore at the jeep as Logan sent the small, open vehicle roaring along the road. But it was not the wind or the rain that reached the deadliest hands for them. The sea sent its fury rolling inland to obliterate the road in spots with a frenzy of leaping waves. He took a curve, skidding through it, when suddenly there was no road in front of him, only the sea, straining further inland. He peered ahead and saw the road where the land rose. Taking aim at the road on the other side of the raging sea, he sent the jeep ahead, hoping there were no unseen curves beneath the sea. A wave crashed against the side of the jeep, sending it skittering sideways and out of control. As his shoulder muscles cried out in protest, he fought the wheel and felt the tires cling to the road while the sea smashed into them again, waist-high, dousing Julie completely where she sat on the floor. But the vehicle continued to move forward as he kept her going in reckless, unstinting speed until the ground rose and

ALAN JOSEPH

carried them up beyond the sea's reach. They sped along a stretch of road where only the wind and the rain grabbed at them, and then down into another sea-covered portion. With every passing minute the wind heightened and the sea took away more sections of the road. But with every minute they drew closer to Bayville. Finally Logan saw the tall tower of the church through the grayness and the rain.

Once more they roared through a ghost town of rain-swept streets and boarded storefronts, skidding to a halt at the edge of the harbor. The wind had whipped the harbor into a churning froth and the smaller boats foolishly made tight to the docks were already being lifted over and smashed against the quays. Dimly, through the downpour, he could see the *Urchin*. He was grateful she was farthest out in the harbor, free of the danger from boats torn loose of their moorings and driven toward shore. And the white cruiser was still there, straining hard at its anchor line. But he knew it would be, as he knew they'd be aboard, huddled inside, trying to sit out the storm. He felt Julie's eyes on him and turned to the girl.

"We can't go out there," she said. "Nobody can. It would be suicide. A boat would be turned over in seconds. A swimmer would be broken to pieces against the docks."

"Put on your air tank," Logan answered flatly. Even the pelting rain could not hide the sullen anger of her eyes.

"Dive in and down," Logan said. "With your scuba gear you can get far enough below the surface turbulence."

"Then what?"

"Take a visual bearing on the white cruiser now," he commanded. "Look at it and swim out to it underwater. When you get there, hang onto the anchor line and wait for me."

Julie saw the cold determination in the big man's rain-soaked face, the unswerving line of his jaw. There was no fear of failure there, no concession to reason in those eyes.

"What are you going to do?" she asked.

"Pay back our friends," he growled. "Get those stones back."

"They're not that important to me, Logan," Julie said.

"Who the hell cares about you?" he shot back. "They are to me now. They've tried to kill me three times. They'll keep trying if I let them. It's too late to turn back now. I'm finishing it once and for all."

He pushed Julie forward and lifted the air tank up, strapping it onto her back, holding her against a fierce gust of wind that pushed her sideways. He moved to the edge of the nearest dock as a wave smashed against it and threw its spray fifteen feet into the air. They huddled together for a moment as the front of the dock exploded in a shower of flying bits of wood.

"All right—now!" he yelled in her ear, running forward with her, throwing her into the churning waters. He knelt for a moment, watching her black-suited form disappear under the surface. Then he was engulfed in a cascade of water that knocked him down and carried him back along the dock. He felt himself crash into the side edge of the pier and felt his body shake from the force of the blow. But he crawled forward as the wave spent itself, waited for a moment to see another huge wave gathering itself, and then ran for the end of the dock. He went off in a running dive, beating the towering wave by seconds, knifing through the water, striking out downwards, fighting his way to the calmer depths below. Somewhere ahead of him Julie was swimming toward the cruiser. He leveled off and struck out in the same direction. He swam with powerful strokes, making as much headway as he could while his lungs held out. He'd have to surface for air and each time he'd lose some of the precious distance he'd make. He kept swimming, fighting off the protest of his lungs until his chest felt as though it would burst. Finally he struck out for the surface, buffeted by the water as he neared the top. He was flung up and into the air, gulping in great draughts of oxygen as the waves swept him backwards, lifting him in huge watery hands. Gauging, waiting, he let himself be scooped up by a wave and then, as it rose, he surfaced-dived and avoided being swept away by the crest. But he had lost precious distance, and he struck out below the surface again, covering what he'd lost and half again as much before he had to come up again. Time and again the exhausting procedure was repeated and time and again the surface fury swept away half of what he'd gained below.

But he managed to avoid being tossed to his death on a breaking crest each time, and each time he swam a little further underwater until he saw the cruiser's hull ahead. He made out the dark figure of Julie, clinging to the anchor line in her scuba suit. He passed behind her and went around to the starboard side of the vessel, now fighting against the churning water. He moved about fifty feet beyond the cruiser before surfacing. As he burst onto the surface he was immediately seized and swept along by the fury of the water toward the white-hulled cruiser. The vessel was tossing and heaving in the waves, and he saw they'd left the side ladder out. He'd counted on that kind of sloppy seamanship from them, and he smiled. Another high, driving wave lifted him up. He rode it high and then down into the trough, then up again. He saw it was no good. He'd be on the crest when he reached the cruiser. He surface-dived into the rising crest, knifing through it as it broke over him and found himself out on the back side of it, being seized by another wave immediately. This one, with the few seconds difference in time, carried him down into its trough as it rolled beneath the cruiser. He reached out, getting his hand onto the ladder along the boat's side, tightening his grip on it at once, and feeling the wave pulling his arms out of their sockets as it tore at him. But he clung to the ladder, and the boat carried him up and out of the sea's grip for a moment as it rose on still another wave. He locked a leg around the ladder and started to climb up. The wind helped push him over the rail, onto the deck. He felt himself sliding along the wet deck, coming to rest against the side of the cabin. Grabbing a door handle, he pulled himself to his feet. The motor cruiser was pitching terribly, but he got the door open and fell into the enclosed corridor. He lay there on the floor and let his breath come back. Finally, he got to his feet, pressing close to the outside wall of the cabin as the cruiser rolled violently. He peered into a window and saw a man with curly black hair, holding a whiskey bottle in one hand, trying to gauge the roll of the ship as he lifted the bottle to his lips.

Logan moved fast, flinging open the door and diving into the room. Tackling the man, they both went flying into a corner of the cabin as the vessel rolled hard to port. The bottle rolled from the man's grip to the floor and Logan seized it, smashed it apart against the wall molding and held the jagged end to the man's throat. Stark fear was in the man's eyes. The ship rolled, and the glass nicked his throat. "Where are the diamonds?" Logan growled at him.

"Varney has them, in the main stateroom, amidships," the man blurted out. Logan pulled him to his feet, spun him around and got an arm across his neck. He pushed him out the door and onto the deck. The man tried to twist away, but Logan's grip was viselike.

"I can't swim!" he screamed. Logan put his shoulder into the man's back and pushed. The man hit the rail and went over, his scream lost in the howl of the wind. Logan took a moment to glance at the sky and feel the wind slam him back against the cabin. Phyllis was on them with fury—but not quite full yet. He gave himself another fifteen minutes Moving back into the inside corridor, he made his way along it, passing cabin windows quickly, glimpsing the men inside them. The main stateroom of the cruiser had curtained windows. Varney was in there, the man had said. But who else? And how many? He'd passed cabins with four or five men inside them. That still left at least three besides Varney and Doris. But there was no time for caution any longer. There never had been. He stepped back and hit the door with a shattering dive. It flew open, and he pitched into the room. Doris was there, and Varney, and a third man, one of the two ex-pugs.

Doris looked at the soaked, wild-eyed figure in open-mouthed astonishment. The ex-pug, slow to react normally, was even slower now. Logan took him out with one roundhouse punch that caught him on the jaw. He crashed back against the table in the center of the room and fell to the floor. Varney reacted fast, pulling a .38 from his jacket pocket. He fired just as the boat pitched sharply, this time to starboard, and the shot went into the corner of the cabin. Logan dived for him, catching him at the knees and bringing him down. His second shot hit the ceiling as he fell. Logan had an arm on his throat, pressing hard. Varney's eyes started to bulge.

"The diamonds! Where are they?" Logan spat out. Varney moved his left hand, slapping it against his trouser pocket. Logan crossed a short right to his jaw, and the man's eyes rolled upward and closed. He pulled at the trouser pocket and yanked out the little sack. A sound behind him made him dive forward flat, across Varney's limp form, and a wooden chair smashed into his back. The ship pitched again, and he rolled over, tossing the chair aside to see Doris, fighting to keep her balance and stay on her feet. But Doris was the least of the problems. Varney's two shots had brought the others. They tumbled into the stateroom from the port door. Logan saw there was a starboard door. He dived for it, yanked it open as another shot rang out, splintering the wood less than an inch from his head as he raced through the doorway. Tying the sack around his wrist with the drawstring as he ran, he dived over the rail of the cruiser, the wind catching his body and tossing him into the sea. He landed on his back and took a deep breath as he was flung sideways, then turned in a somersault. He came out of the somersault, found a moment between waves, and surface-dived. Once more he fought his way below the turbulence which reached deeper now.

Julie's dark shape emerged as he swam to the anchor line. He moved to her, handed her the little sack and waved her forward, pointing in the direction of the *Sea Urchin*. She nodded, and he clung to her back as she started off, letting her pull him along, conserving his breath and strength. They'd made up a little less than halfway to the *Urchin* when he felt his breath going and left the girl to strike out for the surface. He came out and once more was flung about helplessly. His legs were hardly more than hanging appendages, with little muscle strength left in them, his arms aching and ready to fall off. He concentrated on getting in enough air for another dive, and he let himself be tossed by the angry waves. He knew that he survived only because the water was harbor water, angry hurricane driven, but still harbor water, broken up by the mouth of the area. Outside there was the real fury of the sea, the real pounding of the water driven unchecked across hundreds of miles. He gathered his little remaining strength and surface-dived again, taking in a glimpse of the *Urchin's* position as he did. Getting below the turbulence took more time and used up more strength, but he kept going. The *Urchin's* hull loomed up before him and he saw Julie clinging to the anchor line. He motioned to her to follow him, and he grasped the line and pulled himself up it. As he broke into the air he wrapped both legs around the anchor line and pulled himself up it. The sea and the wind tore at him, trying to dislodge him, but he clung to it like a spider clinging to the strands of its web. He inched his way up to the bow of the *Urchin,* each moment's progress a battle to hang on against the waves that swept over him, pulling and tearing at him. At the bow of the boat he grasped the gunwale and let the wave that burst over him catapult him onto the deck. He untied a line wound around a cleat and threw it to Julie as she clung to the anchor rope. She could never pull herself up it as he had, he knew. She grabbed the line and swung free with the sea pulling at her, pushing her out. Bracing himself against the wooden rail, Logan began to pull her in, his back muscles tearing and screaming in pain. But he pulled and finally she was against the hull, being slammed into it by the waves. She had slipped off the air tank. He pulled her up. As her blond hair came level with the top of the gunwale, he grabbed her, and they both toppled to the deck as the boat pitched to port. She lay there, her breath coming in great gasps.

"Into the pilot house," he said to her. She shook her head and lay there. "I can't move," she said. Logan kicked her in the rump, turning her over. "Into the pilot house," he yelled again. "Crawl in and stay there."

Logan crawled to the small forward mast where a rail held a small hand axe. He took the axe and crawled back to the anchor line. Five hard blows severed the line, and the boat immediately rose on the crest of a wave and went scooting forward. Logan crawled and stumbled his way to the pilot house, falling into the protected dryness of the cabin. Fighting off the nausea of exhaustion, he pulled himself up on the wheel seat and switched on the engines. Julie, huddled in a corner, watched him with disbelieving eyes.

CHAPTER SIX

Aboard the white cruiser as it pitched and rolled dangerously, Varney and Doris made their way to the deck, clinging to a lifeline they'd rigged up and tied around themselves. The other men held onto the line from inside the cabin.

"Shut up, Doris," Varney said to the girl as she continued to loose a string of curses. "I didn't expect to see the crazy bastard any more than you did. So we'll get the stuff back from him when the storm's over. He can't go anywhere till then."

Doris peered through the rain and the wind and the spray of the leaping sea, and her eyes darkened in disbelief.

"No?" she cried out. "He can't go anywhere, you goddamned fool? Look out there."

Varney peered through the rain. "He's moving!" the man exclaimed, awe in his voice. "He's heading out to sea."

Doris's face was a mask of fury. "Get the engines started," she screamed at Varney. "Follow him. He's not going to get away." She turned and looked out at the *Sea Urchin* moving slowly toward the mouth of the harbor. He wasn't going to win, she told herself through gritted teeth. The big, mean, no-good bastard wasn't going to win. She remembered his body against hers, his complete and utter victory over her in bed, and the way she had wanted and hated him all at once. And she remembered how he'd laughed at her afterwards.

"Goddamn it, get going," she screamed. Varney watched the other boat in transfixed awe.

"It's suicide," Varney protested. "Going out there is suicide."

"You sniveling sonofabitch," Doris shouted at him. "If he can do it so can we. He's not about to commit suicide, not that big bastard. He's too mean to do that."

Varney looked at Doris's hate-filled face. Then he turned and called into the cabin. "We're going after him," he said. "Get started. Make it fast." He turned to look at the girl again. She'd been right about damn near everything so far in this messed-up affair. Maybe she was right about this. The white-hulled cruiser shuddered to life and one of the men went forward to cut the anchor line. The vessel turned, rolling terribly as she did, and her propellers churned the water as she took after the *Sea Urchin*.

Aboard the *Urchin*, Julie peered through the rain smeared glass of the pilot-house windows and saw the motor cruiser swing around to follow after them.

"They're coming," she cried out to Logan as he wrestled with the ship's wheel. "They're coming after us."

He smiled, a slow smile of satisfaction. "I figured as much," he said quietly, and Julie shook her head. Logan steered the boat through the harbor's mouth and into the sea. There'd be no chance to reach the cove up to the north, but there was another only a few miles down. It was high-walled, protected, but with a narrow entrance. It would have to do. There was nothing else. The first wave of the open sea caught the boat, lifting it up and plunging it down, down, down into a trough so deep Julie saw nothing but walls of water all around them. She screamed in terror, but they rose again. They were still there, still afloat. Logan was turning and twisting the wheel, meeting each roaring wave with the bow, heading out into the wild fury of the hurricane. He would have to turn for the cove, he knew, but he would head in at an angle for it. Gray-green mountains of water rose to tower over them and sweep them up in a rush. A powerful wave caught them four points off the starboard bow, and Julie felt the boat shudder and seem to halt for a moment. She heeled over but came back at once, and Logan sent her forward again.

And now Julie began to realize the power and seaworthiness of the *Urchin,* the strength and balance built into her. A tremendous wave caught them, carried them up and sideways and half around. They were struck amidships. Julie crashed against the back wall of the pilot house. A window shattered. The boat quivered and her seams cried out but she came back and Logan managed to head her into the wind again. Julie glanced back and she saw the white shape against the gray water, pitching and rolling from side to side.

Aboard the cruiser, Varney stood ashen-faced beside Doris. He heard the sea slam into the boat, heard the sound of wood being pounded to pieces. A wave swept over the entire vessel, and he saw the port rail break away and fall into the furious waters. The man stood beside the girl at the pilot-house window, and two helmsmen struggled with the wheel. The boat was a bucking bronco, nosing into the sea and shuddering each time, coming up to be slammed sideways. One of the doors to the enclosed cabin was flung open and a man fell inside.

"She's leaking below decks," he gasped. "The port side has sprung. Turn back."

"No!" Doris screamed. "Not till he does."

"Turn back," Varney said to the helmsman. The man started to turn the wheel when a mountain of roaring water swept over them and the sound of splintering wood and crashing glass fought through the storm. The white hull shuddered and wallowed and the sounds of men screaming carried into the cabin. A figure burst in again. "The seams have split," he yelled. We're going down."

Varney turned to Doris. He hit her in the jaw, and she flew across the cabin and into the man at the wheel, bounced off him and fell to the floor. She lay there, dazed.

"Bitch!" Varney spat at her. He grabbed at the ship's wheel with the helmsman, frantically spinning it. But the cruiser hardly responded as the hole widened and the water poured through the seams. She was heeling fast, her stern already under water on the port side.

"They're sinking," Julie cried out inside the *Urchin's* cabin. "Their boat's coming apart."

Logan nodded, and Julie stared at him. "You know that would happen, didn't you?" she said. "You knew they'd follow you and their boat could never take these seas. You figured to get them all at once this way."

Logan didn't answer, but he glanced back at the white hull. It was going down, starting to turn on its side. He watched a huge wave lift them up and pass and then they were in a wide trough.

He spun the wheel and they turned before the next one caught them. He headed back toward the coastline, angling the *Urchin* for the little cove south of Bayville. They were alone in the raging storm now, driving before a sea of destruction. He kept checking in back of him, letting the boat ride the waves as they caught up to him and rolled on with gargantuan power. The *Urchin's* seams were shuddering, too, he felt, but she'd been built for seaworthiness, constructed to withstand the elements. She was no thin-skinned pleasure boat designed and built for smooth water. But a hurricane was something beyond ordinary power. She could stand a lot, but hurricanes had taken down huge liners. It would have taken them but for the fact that they could ride over most of the waves. It war only every sixth or seventh one that really smashed into them.

"Are we going to make it?" Julie asked, her voice tremulous. Logan shrugged. The line of the shore was coming into view and the fury of the storm had them in its grip. He gunned the engines to ride a towering wave and then slacked power to let it carry them down into its trough. He felt his body clammy with cold perspiration, his muscles tiring fast. His shoulders ached from holding the wheel against the sea's efforts to wrestle it from him. The rain slackened slightly as the eye of the hurricane was approaching. There'd be a few minutes' relative calm before the back of the storm delivered the one-two punch that was part of a hurricane's deadliness. The little cove jutted out from the coastline, high walls of rock surrounding it. But the tide was so high that the rocks that jutted out toward the center from each side were below water. He maneuvered the *Urchin,* angling the bow for the far line of the rocks. A wave lifted them and flung them sideways on its back, and then another, like the coils of some monstrous sea serpent rising up beneath them. Logan kept the bow pointed toward the far end of the rocks. Suddenly the rain stopped, and he could see more clearly. They were nearing the center of the entrance. He pushed the throttle to full and sent the boat churning forward. The sea seized them, lifting and pushing them sideways again. Logan's lips were a tight line, and Julie saw the tension in his face. The rocks stretched out from both sides, somewhere beneath that churning, foam-flecked water. He had to be exactly in center to make it, even on the calmest of days. It was like threading a needle with the boat the thread. It would take more than skill, now, he knew. It would take luck. It would take a smile from fate, a reward for having fought a good fight.

They were moving toward the line of rocks on the top of the thrusting waves, almost broadside. Suddenly Logan saw that they were too far off center. He gunned the powerful engines, but the propellers caught only part of the sea as a wave lifted them on its head. He held his breath.

"Get ready to jump," he said to Julie. "Get by the door." The line of the rocks was just ahead, and he was helpless to do anything but hold the wheel and keep her from slipping further off center. They were abreast of the rocks, and then they were in the little cove, past the line of the rocks. The tide had risen high enough to sweep them over the rocks. Ordinarily, their position would have sent them crashing into oblivion. Inside the cove, he headed the *Urchin* for the left edge, behind the sheltering wall. He cut the engines just enough to maintain headway against the pitch of the water.

"Hold the wheel where she is," he told Julie and brushed past her to the deck. He had an emergency anchor which he dragged to the bow and dropped over the side. It was smaller than the regular one, but it would hold in the shelter of the cove. He felt the anchor line grow taut as the anchor caught on the bottom, and he went back to the pilot-house. He cut off the engines and stood quietly, leaning against the wheel, his head bowed low. The thunder of the sea crashing against the rocks outside the little cove was a kind of victory hymn. But he didn't really feel victorious. He felt terribly tired and strangely sad and still angry.

He looked across at the girl whose long blond hair was still tight and wet against her head. She had nearly cost him his boat and his life. He turned, opened the door of the pilot-house and stumbled down to the aft cabin. He flung himself on the bed, face down, and his body shuddered with complete exhaustion. His stomach was a tight knot and everything was suddenly all so very far away, almost as in a dream. His eyes closed, and he was wrapped quickly in the blanket of complete exhaustion.

Julie stayed in the pilot-house for a moment longer then slowly went below. She passed the inert form stretched face down across the bed and went into the forward cabin. She took off the top of the scuba suit and lay down, pressing her breasts into the softness of the bed. She turned over and ran her hands down her body and smiled. It was unbelievable but she was here, alive. Every muscle burned with pain, but she was alive. And Logan was alive with her. And the diamonds were in their hands. She closed her eyes. In the morning, she'd make him see. In the morning, he would feel differently.

The wind still howled and the sea still crashed against the rocks beyond the cove. But the terror was gone from it now. She and the big man were together, alive. They'd made it. He'd realize it meant something more than just their survival. She was still smiling as she fell off to sleep.

CHAPTER SEVEN

The sun was shining warmly when Julie opened her eyes in the morning. She lay still and listened to the gentle slap of the water against the hull. Yesterday's fury and terror was dreamlike, only she knew better. She got up, naked, and peered out of the porthole at the soft blue of the water. She shivered as she thought of the gray, angry awesomeness of the sea yesterday. But then that was the sea, always its own master, gentle lover and screaming killer. She smiled as she thought of the man in the aft cabin. It was a description that fitted him, too. She thought of how he had made love to her, and she thought of the coldness of his smile as the white cruiser disintegrated in the pounding seas. But loving or cruel, he was something special, something she would make hers.

On silent bare feet she crept into the cabin. During the night sometime he'd stripped off his shorts, and he lay naked on the bed, his powerful frame a thing of lithe beauty. His torso had twisted so that he lay half on his side. She went over to him, pressing her fingers into his back, massaging the rippling muscles with her hands. Logan stirred and felt the strength of the girl's fingers as they moved up and down his back. Then they crept across his ribcage, and he turned on his back to see her, her long blond hair now dry and full framing her face like a halo. Her full lips were half open as she ran her hands across his chest, and he watched her breasts rise and fall in a steady rhythm. There was something different in her touch this time. She moved her body against his and he felt his skin come alive. He reached down and pulled her across his body and took her deep, rounded breasts and stroked them.

"Oh, Logan, Logan," Julie cried out, the throbbing, sensuous Julie. He leaned down and took one full breast in his mouth, pulling at it, holding it, moving his tongue across it, and her body was working itself up and down in frenzied pleasure. She pressed her breast deeper into his mouth, wanting to have it all, wanting to become part of him and when he pulled away she cried out and clutched him to her. He rolled over on her and caressed the full-fleshed curves of her body, cupping the deep breasts, playing on the slight convexity of her belly. "I want you, Logan, I want you," she breathed, her breasts against his chest. He moved his hand across her torso and held her with a gentle motion. Her body began to move, slowly at first, undulating rhythmically. Logan held her tighter and her breath came in gasps. She cried out, and he bore down on her as her cries grew louder. She was clutching at him, now, and her lips moving across his chest and shoulders as he carried her higher and higher. And then, as it seemed she would reach new peaks of ecstasy, he pulled away from her and rolled to the side.

"Oh, my God, no!" she screamed and sprang upon him, a feverish, pleading, wanting tigress, and he grinned at her and came to her again, carrying her up once more, only now it was all the greater for the interruption. Her body was building its own crescendo and once again she heard the thunder of the seas crashing against the rocks—only now the hurricane was all inside her, whirling and roaring. "Logan, Logan, oh my God, Logan," she gasped and sank down upon the bed. He moved in her, and she came instantly alive again, wanting more. He gave her more, and it was like no other time. There was more of everything, more of her hunger, more of his own desires. She had to give all that was in her, holding nothing back, for to her, it was a beginning. He wanted to give all he could to her, for he knew it was an ending.

The throbbing, sensuous creature he'd seen that first day on the beach was beyond stopping until finally, with steady, mounting ecstasy, he made the sea stop moving for an instant and the sun explode inside her quivering body. Then she fell back and lay still, spent, satisfied. He moved beside her and let his eyes feast on her beauty, the complete womanly magnificence of her body. They lay side by side for a spell, their bodies touching, the lingering warmth of their passions translated into tactile sensations. She turned and lifted herself onto his chest. Her eyes were clear.

"Oh, Logan, it's so perfect," she said to him. "Just the two of us, together. It was meant to be that way. That's why we lived through yesterday."

Logan smiled. The throbbing sensuous creature had given way to the wide-eyed romantic girl.

"Yesterday isn't finished," he said. "Don't cast it away so quickly."

"Oh but it is," she said, pulling herself up on one elbow, her breasts just barely touching his skin, their rounded undersides lightly resting against his chest. God, he could take her again, he realized. But there had to be an end to it. There had to be or she'd win in her own way.

"All the bad part of yesterday is done with, Logan," she said. "Only the good things are left."

"Like what?"

"You. Me."

"And the diamonds," he finished for her. She nodded. "Julie, honey," he said softly. "It's still the first real port for you. That's still where you get off."

She frowned and threw herself down on his chest again.

"Not anymore, Logan, there's no need for that now," she said, the eager, happy child again, simple and terribly appealing, shifting from one flashing mood to another like quicksilver. "We can do what we want, go where we want, have whatever we want," she said, getting up on her elbow again, using her beauty with complete naturalness, fighting with it without even knowing she was.

"I do that now, Julie," he reminded her. "It still wouldn't work. I told you that once already."

"But it will work, Logan," she pouted. "Especially now."

"But the diamonds are going back, honey," he said. "To the police."

Her eyes darkened, and her pout grew more pronounced.

"No," she said, the edge of stubbornness creeping into ther voice. "Not after all that's happened. It just wouldn't be right. We've earned them."

Logan grinned at her. She could supply her own excuses with the same speed that she could change moods.

"You know better than that," he said. She put her hands on his chest, all eager sincerity.

"They probably couldn't even be traced back to anyone, Logan," she countered. "It'd be just a big waste of everything. They'll rot away in some lockbox."

"Diamonds don't rot away," he grinned at her. "And these certainly won't. Once the police learn how the operation worked they'll send a bulletin to all jewelers. The jewelers will have their major pieces analyzed and the ones with the phony stones will come forward. It'll work out."

She was watching him with a frown, her eyes angry and defiant. He swung himself from the bed.

"I'll make breakfast," he said. "We can take our time sailing back to Kingdom Point."

"You shouldn't have made love to me then," she said crossly.

"Why not? Didn't you want to?" he asked, his voice cold. She leaped from the bed and went to the porthole and glared out of it. He put on his trousers and went into the galley. When he'd finishing making bacon and eggs she appeared, wearing an old shirt of his and the bottom of her bathing suit. Her eyes were a hard blue, piercing, angry.

"You never did give a damn, really, did you?" she said accusingly.

"Drop it, Julie," he answered. "Don't end it this way. You wouldn't understand, and I'm not explaining so leave it where it is."

"No, you don't understand," she said, and suddenly her voice was soft, hurt. "I don't have anything now," she went on. "Nothing and nobody. Not Pops, probably not even the house."

"You've got a lot, Julie," he said. "You've got yourself. You've got you. You're a beautiful girl. You're young and healthy. You've got the whole world to pick from."

"I don't want the whole world. I want you, Logan," she sobbed. Of all her shifting, changing moods this was her most powerful, the lost waif, the homeless stray. "Take the diamonds back but let me stay," she sobbed. "Please, Logan."

Logan's lips were grim. He felt the anger inside him bubbling to the surface. She'd done it to him once before. She wouldn't do it again. He'd sampled her sudden shifts. And he'd sampled her duplicity. He had a long memory.

"We made a deal," he said. "That's it."

He turned away from her. Damn but she was a deadly combination, throbbing beauty and helpless appeal. He took a cup and poured himself some coffee. He had just put it to his lips when he heard her voice, hard now, cold and angry.

"All right, I want the diamonds, Logan," he heard her say. "Give them to me."

He glanced at her and saw the heavy barrel of his Colt Python pointing at his stomach. It didn't move. It didn't waver or shake or wander. She held it steady as a rock. His lips tightened. She'd taken it from his cabin after he'd gone to the galley.

"This won't work, either, Julie," he said, looking deeply into her eyes. He saw only angry impatience.

"It'll work," she said grimly. "First in Mexico, then maybe South America. Like you said, diamonds don't rot, and they do bring a nice piece of change on the open market."

She motioned with the Colt. "Get them," she said. She carefully kept her distance from him. He turned and went into the cabin and took the little sack out of the draw. "Throw them to me," she said. He threw them.

"You don't know what you want to be, do you?" he said to her.

"Maybe not," she shot back. "But I don't want to be poor, and I don't want to be alone. These will help take care of both those things."

"No they won't, Julie," Logan said. "What about the old man? Will this do right by him?"

"You leave him out of this, damn you," she shouted back at him, but he knew he'd drawn blood.

"Start the engines," she commanded. "Get this tub as close to shore as it'll go. Bring it in until it scrapes bottom. Make it fast, Logan. I've got places to go."

Logan's smile was grim, with a ruefulness in it she ignored. It was an error. It was never wise to ignore anything Logan did. He started the *Urchin's* powerful engines and slowly moved the boat toward the shore. He got in pretty close before he felt the soft scrape of a sandy bottom against the hull. He switched off the engines and looked down at the water. It was clear and he could see bottom, not more than four and a half feet down. He walked out of the pilot-house onto the deck. Julie was amidships, one foot on the gunwale, still holding the Colt on him. She had the little sack in her other hand.

"Don't try coming after me, Logan," she warned him. "I'll use this thing."

"I won't," he said quietly. She lifted herself onto the gunwale and jumped overboard. She hit the water and got her footing on the bottom to wade onto the beach. She turned at the edge of the water to look at him. Logan walked into the pilot-house, put the boat's engines in reverse and slowly pulled her from the soft, sandy bottom. He swung the *Urchin* around slowly, and he was stern to the beach when he heard her cry out.

"Logan!" she screamed as it was all there in that one word, fury, astonishment, towering disappointment. He looked back at her. She was standing there, the little sack open, holding the fifteen little pebbles he had put into it in her hand. He waved a hand to her as he started to sail away.

"Logan! Come back, Logan," she called. "Logan, I'm sorry. Please come back."

Her voice carried the bitter disappointment and the real fear that was in her. He heard her sob. "I'm sorry, Logan," she cried. "Please, wait. Please, Logan."

It wasn't an act, that lost waif part of her, no more than the throbbing sexuality was an act. It was there, a part of her, and it came across the water to him. He wondered if the house were still standing. And he wondered how alone she really would be. She wasn't one of the crowd, he knew. She never had been. Her world had fallen in on her, had died with the old man on the beach. Damn it, he swore to himself. She could get to you.

"Logan, please," her cry followed after him and then there was a long moment of silence. He was going to look back when she called out again.

"You bastard, Logan," she called. "You sonofabitch! Don't you ever come back, you hear me?"

Logan grinned, and he shoved the *Urchin's* throttle to full speed. He was still grinning as he roared toward the mouth of the cove. She'd make it. Whenever it got too bad the hellcat would take over. He looked back as he went through the narrow entranceway to the cove. She was striding along the beach, walking toward Bayville and Kingdom Point, swinging the little sack vigorously as she went. He put his head back and laughed as he headed out to sea. When he had changed course for Bayville he put on the automatic pilot and went into the galley. Taking down a tin can, he poured the diamonds into his hand and looked at them. They did owe him something. They owed something to the spirit of hope and goodness. An old man had been killed because of them. He took two and put them aside. The rest he'd turn over to the police with a note, unsigned. They'd take it from there and work backwards to piece it all together. But he put the two he'd laid aside into a drawer of the little wall desk in the cabin. Then he took out a piece of notepaper and began to write on it.

> *Dear Sister Mary Angela,*
>
>   *A separate little package is being mailed to you. It will contain two small objects you can convert into dollars, about fifteen hundred dollars I'd guess. Believe it or not, they were found on a beach. It's time they did someone some good. With everlasting gratitude for that which you did for me.*
>
>

As always,

Logan

He put the note into an envelope and placed it in the pocket of his jacket. He'd mail that in Bayville, along with the little package. His eyes held both a cold fire and a sadness. The old man on the beach was dead and the world cared nothing about it. But maybe something good had been salvaged out of it, the life of a child somewhere else, a new hope for someone without medicine. But he wondered if the day would come when he wouldn't always have to salvage good out of the debris of life. Maybe it would, sometime. Meanwhile, he steered his own course, and searched for that moment, the something that would make it all meaningful again. And he paused to enjoy all the way stations of pleasure. That's what kept him going. That and the search.

THE END

LOGAN

CHAPTER ONE

H e helped the girl up the short gangway and onto the boat. She walked with that extracarefulness of someone who knows she's had too much to drink. On the deck, he spun her around and she came to him with lips open, her mouth waiting for his. His hand found her breasts under the scoop-necked satin blouse. They were small but so soft, so very soft, and suddenly she was not a girl he'd met at a bar a few hours ago but Venus, Aphrodite, Helen of Troy.

"Here, out on the deck?" he heard her murmur and he stepped back.

"Go below," he said. "The light switch for the cabin is on the right. I'll take in the gangway and be right down."

He watched her start down the companionway, her firm, young rear wriggling in the too-tight black skirt. He hurried to pull in the gangway, and he had just set it on the deck when the scream split the night, pure terror, and loud as hell. He was down the few steps into the cabin in one bound. The girl was in the doorway, her hand still on the light switch, her body shaking, her eyes riveted on the cabin floor. Logan followed her eyes.

"Jesus Christ!" he said. Eyes, protruding and huge, stared up at him with the sightless stare of death. The girl's neck was twisted horribly, with a harsh red-blue ugly line creasing her throat. She wore only a slip and one lifeless breast had spilled out one side. Logan looked at the girl by the door.

"I'm going to be sick," she said.

"Not here you're not," he growled. He grabbed her and half-lifted, half-flung her up onto the deck and saw her fall against the rail. He turned back to the staring, twisted thing on the cabin floor. He knelt down and touched the girl's head, moving it a little, holding her by the chin with his big, powerful hands. He got up and went out on the deck. The girl from the bar had finished being sick and she was edging toward the rail near the quay, looking at Logan with wide, frightened eyes.

Logan put the short gangway back in place. "Go on, get off," he told her, grimly. She scrambled up and over onto the quay, shooting him glances that were half-apology, half-fear. Logan pushed back the peaked cap on his head and watched her disappear into the night. He wasn't surprised when two sets of headlights pierced the dark, and he saw the cars turning at the top of the hill to start slowly down the narrow quay. He wasn't surprised to see they were police cruisers. Nor was he at all surprised to see them stop in front of the *Sea Urchin*. It figured. His mind was racing, thinking of the man he'd thrown off the boat the night before. He wanted to think more about that, to replay it in his mind, but the police sergeant was talking to him.

"May we come aboard, *señor*?" the sergeant was saying. Logan smiled thinly. The Panamanian police, like most cops in Latin American countries, always started off polite. They also politely ignored a bushel of legal, civil and moral rights when they got going.

Logan indicated the cabin. "In there," he said. The sergeant told two of his men to have a look. He stayed on the deck and surveyed Logan.

"May I see your papers, captain?" he smiled. "Passport, licenses, whatever you have."

Logan handed him a cluster of glassine-covered cards and papers. One of the cops called the sergeant, his voice excited, shocked. The sergeant glanced into the cabin and turned to Logan, a subtle grimness settling onto his face.

"Who is she, *señor*?" he asked, looking balefully at the tall American with the lean, hard face.

"Goldilocks. Little Bo-peep. Ophelia. You give her a name," Logan said, matching the cop's baleful stare. "You seemed to know she was there. That's more than I did."

He felt the angry rage gathering inside him, the frustrated, churning rage of a man who knows he's been trapped. He could predict the coming sequence of questions and answers, all leading to the same, inexorable ending. It added a further edge to his already reckless temper.

"You did not know she was in the cabin of your boat," the sergeant said, patiently. "You do not expect me to believe that, do you, *señor*?"

"I don't give a shit what you believe," Logan said. "I never saw her until just now. Why don't you ask whoever told you she was here about her?"

"A phone call, what you *americanos* call a *tip*," the officer said. Logan nodded, bitterness in his eyes. He had figured that much the minute he saw their headlights swing into the quay. The sergeant returned Logan's papers.

"You have a lot of papers, *Señor* Logan, a lot of licenses," he said. "But none of them tell me what you do for a living."

"We hire out, the *Urchin* and me," Logan said. "When we feel like, where we feel like and how we feel like."

"Perhaps you hire out to murder young, blonde *señoritas*?"

"No," Logan answered, his voice hard, flat. "We do that for the fun of it."

He had the satisfaction of seeing cold anger move into the sergeant's otherwise impassive face.

"You refuse to tell us anything about the girl, eh?" he said.

"I don't *know* anything about her."

"And of course you would like it if we just forgot about the *señorita* and just went on our way," the sergeant said, a resigned smile on his face.

"No, I'd like you to take her with you," Logan said. "If nobody calls for her in thirty days she's yours."

The sergeant's face turned to stone and he nodded toward the police car. "Let us go, *Señor* Logan," he said. "We shall let you try your humor on the inspector."

Logan walked to the police car and slid into the back seat. The sergeant moved in beside him while one of the policemen took the wheel. As they moved slowly away, Logan saw the other two cops take up positions at the gangway of the *Sea Urchin*. They would wait for the coroner's wagon and then impound his boat, as they were going to impound him. He stared out the window, his mind racing, bitter thoughts tumbling over each other in their haste to sort themselves out. He was alone, in this little hole in Panama, being taken in for the murder of some chickie he'd never seen in his life. But it didn't just happen. It had been carefully set up. Once again, he was seeing the man who'd come to the *Urchin* the night before. *There* was the connection. He laughed grimly, inwardly. Some connection. He could just see the sergeant's face if he tried to tell him about the man last night. But the bastard had been real enough. Tall, thin, well-dressed, speaking English with just the trace of a South American accent. Logan replayed it in his mind, seeking something that would help him in his present spot.

The man had said he wanted to hire him and the *Urchin*. It was for a task of some delicacy and he'd promised a big chunk of loot, ten thousand dollars worth of chunk. Logan recalled how his temper had started to rise.

"All that for something delicate?" he had frowned. "You mean dangerous, not delicate. The answer is the same, anyway. No, I'm not interested."

"The people I represent will not take no for an answer," the man had said. He was an errand boy, for all his silk suit and smooth manners, Logan realized. And he was talking down to him. Nobody should talk down to anybody, ever, Logan felt. It was one of his mottos, along with enjoy.

"This'll be a new experience for them," Logan said. "Now get the hell off my boat."

"We have ways of persuading you, my friend," the man had said, putting menace into his voice. Logan put shoulder into his blow. It caught the man flush on the jaw and he went flying into the *Urchin's* rail, bounced off and rolled across the deck. He started to get up, his hand gropingly trying to reach into his inside jacket pocket. Logan clipped him again and he flipped over to hit the deck with a resounding thud. Logan picked him up as though he were a child, lifted him across the gangway and flung him onto the quay, watching his body roll across the stones to hit up against the building wall on the other side.

"How's that for persuasion, pal?" Logan had tossed after him. He recalled how he'd taken in the gangway and gone down to the cabin, fixed a good shot of Tennessee sippin' whiskey and stretched out on the bunk. He'd had the same trouble many times. People and money. He didn't go for either, except on his terms.

His thoughts snapped off as the police car rolled to a halt. There was a why to all this. He'd be finding out, he was certain. But he wasn't so sure he'd like it when be did.

CHAPTER TWO

The inspector had been called from a party, not a very good party but nonetheless a party, and he didn't like the interruption. He disliked the vermin he normally had to deal with but this one, at least, was different. Murder itself lifted this one out of the ordinary. He was meaner, too. The sergeant's briefing had told him that. Logan returned the inspector's stare under a fluorescent fight tube in the ceiling that brought a glaring brightness to the lone chair on which he sat, the small table, the dingy gray of the walls. It heightened all the contrasts, making Logan's dark eyes darker, the inspector's white suit whiter. The room, what he presumed to be the interrogation room of the jail, was thoroughly inhibiting. Logan didn't consider himself an authority on much of anything, except perhaps women and boats, certainly not jails. But this one, he guessed, would set some sort of record for unrelieved drabness. The inspector wore an air of weariness which, Logan interpreted, cloaked active hostility. Behind the inspector, in a comer of the room, stood a gray-shirted jailer who oozed evil from every pore of his body but mostly from his eyes. Logan had seen eyes like those before, always on men who enjoyed other people's pain. He saw the man's tongue move across thick lips as the jailer's eyes flicked up and down his lean, hard-packed frame. The bastard was already estimating how much pain this new one could stand, Logan knew, and once again he could predict the script. Yet it had to be played out. It had been written, the characters cast into it, all by someone else, someone who knew that each of them would play their roles, the inspector, the jailer and himself. Last night he had thrown a man off the *Urchin* and now he was paying for it.

The inspector had read the sergeant's report, conferred with his man, looked at Logan's papers and was now fastening the tall American with a world-weary eye.

"The truth, *Señor* Logan," he said. "It would save everyone a lot of time and trouble."

"It would," Logan agreed, his face expressionless. "I never saw the girl before she was dumped on my boat. That's the truth, all of it." He got up. "Feel free to call me if you find out who she was," he said. "It was nice meeting you."

He started for the door. The gray-shirted jailer was across the room instantly, blocking his way to the door, a puzzled, uncertain frown on his face.

"All right, Soyez," Logan heard the inspector say, "sit down, captain."

Logan shrugged, cast Soyez a wide grin, watching the man's frown deepen, and then turned away and sat down again.

"You have a quixotic sense of humor, I see, *amigo*," the inspector commented. "A luxury, I would say, for a man in your position."

"Everybody needs a few luxuries," Logan said, and his eyes grew cold. "You wanted the truth and you got it. So bug off and let me get the hell out of here."

"You must think we are exceptionally gullible," the inspector said, his eyes half-closed.

"No, exceptionally stupid," Logan shot back and saw the inspector's eyes narrow still further. "If that excuse for a cop had examined the body he'd have noticed that rigor mortis had already set in. She was killed at least six hours before your boys arrived."

"A mere detail," the inspector countered. "What is to say you did not kill her six hours before?"

"And leave her lying around the cabin?" Logan snorted. "That could draw flies."

The inspector's eyes widened enough for Logan to see them grow hard.

"I do not know if you killed her," the inspector said. "But she was found on your boat. This means either you or someone you know did kill her aboard your boat. In either case, you are not telling us the truth. The sergeant and I are of one mind on that."

"One mind," Logan echoed. "And each of you got half of it."

The man's eyes registered no change. Only his voice grew deadlier.

"I shall let you meditate overnight on this," he said. "We have found that a night of meditation in the care of jailer Soyez invariably produces a change of attitude."

The inspector rose. "You have nothing further to say, I take it," he said.

"I do," Logan said. "Go screw yourself."

Logan got up and started for the narrow doorway that led into the rear of the jail. The man, Soyez, fell into step behind him. He could feel the man's excitement. He had already sized him up. With room to move, he would be easy enough to take. In close quarters, his raw strength would be rough, very rough. Soyez prodded Logan into the adjoining room and Logan felt his temper rise. That was good. He would need anger to hold out. He walked into the room and heard the door close behind him. Four empty cells lined the far wall. An old desk stood just off-center. A wooden chair on casters yawned emptily in front of it. A lone, green-shaded light bulb hung from the ceiling. The place smelled of urine and stale vomit and he saw a parade of big, fat *cucarachas* leisurely moving across the floor. He felt his right wrist seized, suddenly, and the coldness of metal. Soyez yanked Logan forward to one of the cells and clamped the other handcuff onto one of the bars. His smile was a sneer of triumph and he rested a heavy hand on the butt of his Police .38 and surveyed his prisoner.

"It would be so much easier to shoot you and simply say you tried to escape," he mused aloud. "But the inspector doesn't like that. He wants truth, confessions, trials."

"Confessions and trials, not truth," Logan muttered. The jailer's sneer had become a vicious grimace. "Outside the front door are two guards," he said. "But in here there will be only the two of us. By morning, you will confess."

The man was too insensitive to read the icy determination in Logan's eyes, the inflexible will reflected in his jaw. Soyez went to the desk, rolled aside the chair and opened a drawer to pull out a round, thick, hard-rubber truncheon. He turned to Logan, slapping it into his beefy palm. It made a dull, flat, menacing sound. Soyez knew the value of terror. Only Logan wasn't terrorized. The jailer advanced and raised his arm. When he brought it down in a sudden arc, Logan raised his free arm instinctively. Too late, he saw the man change direction with his blow and sweep in under his upraised arm. The truncheon slammed across his belly. Logan felt more than saw the second blow land across the back of his neck, knocking him forward to his knees. The handcuff around the cell bar slid down with him as he fell forward. Again the rubber truncheon came down, this time across the base of his spine and he felt himself cry out as the sharp slivers of pain shot up through his body. He swung his free arm around, caught one of the cell bars and started to pull himself up, kicking out blindly at the same time, only to hear the jailer's harsh laugh. The time, the truncheon landed hard against the backs of his knees and he felt himself collapse.

The truncheon came down again, and again, and now the man was beating a steady tattoo with it. Logan cast out with his one free arm but it was no more than a blind, futile gesture. Soyez used the truncheon skillfully, hitting those places where few marks would show. As the rubber truncheon landed hard against the small of his back, Logan steeled himself against waves of pain. He turned each agonizing blow into a hymn of revenge, fighting off the waves of nausea, concentrating on the murderous fury inside himself. He wondered how many men Soyez had beaten to death. I'm going to kill this sick, sadistic bastard, Logan told himself over and over, repeating the promise with each new blow. And then, suddenly, the blows stopped. He heard the jailer's voice.

"Only a beginning, my friend, only a sample."

Logan felt himself being uncuffed and flung into the cell. He was on the floor of the jail cell and heard the cell door clank shut behind him. He lay there, face down, thoughts moving through his mind, separate, disconnected bits of semiconsciousness. The stone floor was cold and the perspiration on his face gathered there in little droplets.

He let his eyes open into slits, taking a long moment to focus and adjust. He could see across the floor, through the cell bars, to where Soyez sat with his feet up on the desk. He saw the man lift up the rubber truncheon, push away from the desk and send himself and the little chair on casters rolling back across the floor to the opposite wall. The lean, hard man on the cell floor remained motionless but was forming a plan. He felt surging, icy fury gather, fill his pain-wracked body with new strength.

He lay there and waited and watched Soyez roll himself in the chair toward the cell. Then the man rose, pushing the chair away, and Logan saw the jailer's feet grow larger as he approached the cell, heard the sound of the man's voice calling to him. He remained motionless, as if dead. Soyez called again and then Logan heard the cell door being opened. He felt the man's big, beefy hands turning him over on his back, and he kept his body completely limp, holding his breath. On his back, seeing only through slitted eyes, he saw the blurred shape of the jailer bend down. As the man bent closer, Logan erupted, bringing his knee up sharply, feeling it smash up between the man's legs. Soyez let out a howl of pain, grabbed at himself, and Logan brought him down and was on him instantly, smashing a fist into the thick lips. The jailer tried to get an arm up but Logan drove his own forearm hard into the man's throat, hearing the sharp gasp of pain that followed. He brought his knee down again into the man's groin, smashed into Soyez's neck and then locked his fingers onto the jailer's throat. He clung there, pressing his body down hard onto the heavier man, digging his fingers deeply into the thick neck. Soyez flung his body about, trying to dislodge the lighter man, but Logan was fastened onto him like a limpet on a rock, unshakeable, his hands tightening slowly around the man's throat. Soyez's eyes grew wide with fear. His heaving motions grew more frantic, but Logan held his position and tightened his hands. His fingers were like steel claws, and Soyez was breathing in harsh, rasping draughts, clawing with his own hands at Logan's wrists. But he had already been robbed of strength and his motions grew weaker and weaker.

The struggle was fought in silence, and only the heaving, rolling, twisting movements of the battlers attested to its savagery. Logan thought briefly of all those who had come before him, of all the poor slobs Soyez had beaten, and he pressed down for the final few seconds. The man's heavy body suddenly went limp, the harsh breathing ended, and it was over. Logan unlocked his fingers with an effort, slowly massaging them.

He reached down and picked up the lifeless form and dragged it to the chair. Then he rolled the chair and its limp occupant over to the cell door. He took the keys from the dead jailer's pocket, entered the cell and slammed the door shut. Reaching out through the bars he locked the cell door from the outside. He took the keys and shoved them back into Soyez's pocket. Then, bracing himself on one leg, he pushed his foot through the space between the bars and sent the chair rolling on its casters across the floor to crash into the desk. Soyez's form toppled from the chair as it smashed into the desk and crumpled onto the floor, half-under the desk. Logan turned, lay down on the narrow cot at one side of the cell and went to sleep.

CHAPTER THREE

The commotion in the morning was almost worth the price of admission. The two outside guards found Soyez first when they came in to check their carbines before going off duty. They called the inspector, got him out of bed, and he rushed down to the jail. And there his jailer was, very, very dead, the keys to the cells in his pocket and Logan locked inside the cell. No one had come in or out, the guards swore, and Soyez had been clearly strangled to death. Logan stayed on the cot and only glanced up when the white suit of the inspector pressed against the cell bars.

"Of course, you know nothing about this, either," the man said, his lips pursed.

"Right again," Logan said from the cot. "I'm a heavy sleeper."

The inspector's eyes were narrowed, speculative, the eyes of a man who knows he's been had but doesn't know how.

"The man is dead, strangled to death, and there you are locked inside your cell some twenty-five feet away from his body," the inspector mused aloud. "It is what you call an *airtight alibi*, no?"

"It'll do," Logan said. He watched the inspector turn and stroll out of the room, past the men taking out Soyez's body in a canvas sack. The inspector returned fifteen minutes later. He unlocked the cell door.

"You have a visitor," he said, and hidden in his tone was a note of surprised respect.

"Oh, yeah?"

"You may speak to him out here." The inspector called to the adjoining room, "*Señor* Alvarez, in here, please." The inspector left the two men alone.

Logan's lean, lined face stayed impassive as he watched his visitor enter, a tall man, expensively clothed in a blue-gray silk suit, light blue shirt and diamond tie clip. The man reeked of confidence. He had olive skin, long sideburns and a straight nose.

"*Buenos días,*" the man called Alvarez said. "You are not surprised to see me?"

"Not really," Logan said. "I just don't know whether to break you in half now or later. Where's your messenger boy?"

Alvarez smiled. "I decided to come myself," he said. "But let us not be unfriendly. We only did what we had to do. Your uncooperative attitude forced us to take steps."

"That was nothing. I can be a lot more uncooperative."

"So it seems," Alvarez smiled again. "The inspector told me of the most unusual death of his jailer. More and more I become pleased at selecting you and your boat, *Señor* Logan."

"Got to hell."

"You are no fool," Alvarez continued, his voice growing less charming. "You know, Soyez will be replaced by another of his kind. There will be more beatings. You could rot away here. You might even hang." He paused and smiled. "For the murder of the girl, of course."

Logan permitted himself a small grin.

"On the other hand," Alvarez went on, "I can have you out of here in five minutes and your boat released at once."

"You confessing to the chickie's murder?"

"Let us say I will provide information as to who the girl is and who killed her."

"Providing I agree to do that delicate job your boy spoke of."

"That is correct."

"Your boy offered me ten thousand," Logan said. "I want half of it in advance, certified check only."

Alvarez shook his head. "You are a most unique man, Logan," he said. "But I came prepared, suspecting as much."

"And that girl I had with me last night," Logan said. "I want her back aboard tonight. Straighten it out with her and tell her I'm waiting. Her name is Julie. Now let's get the hell out of this flea's paradise. You can tell me the rest on the boat."

"You boys go all the way to set up a frame, don't you?" Logan commented as he and Alvarez sat down on the *Urchin's* deck chairs. Logan had already scanned his boat with the eyes of a man who knows every inch of his woman and can instantly tell whether she's been touched or not.

"Do not feel too flattered," Alvarez answered. "We did not kill her. Her boy friend did that. We only borrowed her."

"Suppose you tell me what I do to earn my ten thousand?" Logan poured bonded bourbon for each, and Alvarez lifted his glass. *"Gracias,"* he said. "Your job is really very simple. You are merely to take someone someplace."

Logan's eyes told Alvarez he didn't believe anyone shelled out ten thousand for anything simple. "Cut the sales pitch or you can forget our agreement," he growled. "Just who the hell are you? Let's start with that."

"I represent the government of Peru," Alvarez said. "We are having a problem with a very dangerous, left-wing revolutionary group. They are active in the jungle mountains near the coast where it is difficult to pin them down. They have been led by a man of mystery named Panico. He is personally known to only a few people but he has been made into a legendary figure, a symbol of the revolutionary movement. Recently, some of our troops did engage a guerrilla force in pitched battle. We have reason to believe this Panico was killed in that encounter. But the revolutionary forces have denied this. They claim he is alive."

"Understandable," Logan said. "The death of a leader is often the death of a movement."

"Precisely," Alvarez went on. "We believe they have buried him in a little, remote village inland from the coast. We want you to take someone who knows Panico to the cemetery in that village. There, you will dig up the body and positive identification will be made, one way or another. It is very important to us that we know."

"Why the *Urchin* and me?" Logan asked. 'Why not just send someone else to do your grave-digging?"

"The guerrilla forces are thick in that area. They have people who would instantly spot and kill our men. But your boat is exactly the kind of tub that could conceivably be traveling up the Río Tinina to pick up hides or bark. You could get to the village with our agent."

"And after the body is identified as this Panico, or as somebody else, what then?"

"You bring our agent back, that is all."

"And Panico?"

"He stays. We only need him identified," Alvarez finished.

"That ten thousand," Logan said. "I want the whole thing in advance." He didn't say that because he felt that something about the whole story smelled. He didn't have to.

"Impossible!" Alvarez bristled. "Then there would be nothing to stop you from sailing away with our money."

"That's right. But I won't, and you know it."

Alvarez muttered under his breath but drew out four checks for twenty-five hundred each. Logan noted, as he stuffed them into his pocket, that both bore bank certification stamps.

"Where do I pick up your man? And when?"

"At the entrance to the harbor there is a red buoy," the Peruvian said. Logan nodded. "I know it," he added.

"At four o'clock this morning our agent will approach the buoy in a rowboat. A flashlight will signal with four flashes. You will answer with two sets of flashes. The rest of your instructions will come from our agent."

"Four o'clock, the red buoy," Logan repeated. Alvarez rose and handed him a slip of paper with a phone number written on it. "I can be reached at this number should you have any further questions," he said. He paused on the gangway and looked back at Logan.

"Tell me," he said. "How did you kill the inspector's man and lock yourself inside the cell?"

"I didn't kill him," Logan said. "Soyez ate some bad tortillas. Make sure the girl, Julie, is here tonight," Logan added. "Or your man's going to have a long wait around that red buoy."

He went down inside the forward cabin, stripping off his trousers and shirt as he went. The *Sea Urchin*, contrary to Alvarez's opinion, was both spacious and comfortable inside and he enjoyed the luxury of a shower. He still hurt plenty from where the big bastard had worked him over with that truncheon but that would pass. Purely physical pain always passes. It was the other kind that never went away, and for a moment the tall, lean man's eyes grew haunted. He stepped from the shower, towel in hand, and continued to dry himself as he reached into the pocket of his trousers and drew out the four checks. Wrapping the towel about his groin he sat down and pulled out the small writing board of the little desk built into the forward section of the cabin. He put three checks in an envelope and sent them to an account in his name in Key West. Then, the other check before him, he took out a sheet of notepaper. His dark probing eyes softened as he began to write, slowly, gracefully:

Sister Mary Angela
Mission of Mercy Sisters
Nairobi, Kenya

Dear Sister:

For you, to use as you need. Like all the others, it comes to you with the same thanks and the same memories. They stay with me, always just below the surface. Be sure to let me know if you transfer elsewhere.

With gratitude ... Logan

He put the check in with the letter, sealed the envelope, and thought briefly of the close link, as Henry James had put it, "between the things that help and the things that hurt." He shut out the flood of memories that threatened to engulf him and quickly dressed. On the quay, he strolled past fishermen bringing in their catch, tradesmen with pushcarts of fruit and vegetables, early-afternoon whores and a sprinkling of tourists. At the far end of the quay, beside a telephone booth, was a mailbox. He dropped both envelopes inside and turned, looking up at the sky. The air was heavy, thick and humid. It was the kind of weather that made seamen uncomfortable. It refused to point in any direction. It could just sit there or it could build up to vicious thunder squalls. He went back to the *Urchin* and checked out every compartment, every special piece of gear he had aboard, every spare part he kept in the spacious below-deck storage compartment. It was a procedure he undertook before any job. It made him feel better. The *Urchin* had cabins both forward and aft. He decided to give his passenger the aft one and he straightened it up. The night he had spent in jail had left him with a lot of rest to make up and he decided to take some of it. He went into the fore section and stretched out on one of the wall bunks. The heat and his own tired body let him go to sleep almost at once and when he finally woke it was nearly dark. He went up onto the deck, feeling refreshed but more unsatisfied than ever. He expected the girl. His lips tightened. If Alvarez thought he had been bluffing, he would find out how mistaken he'd been. He returned to the cabin for a moment, opened up a small liquor cabinet and made himself a Logan Special—bourbon, ice, dash of grenadine and bitters. He took it back on deck with him and sat down. Where the hell was the girl? He thought of Alvarez and how he still owed him plenty for framing him into taking that beating. It would serve Alvarez right if he just took off into the night. The Peruvian hadn't given him the whole truth, anyway. He could feel that in his bones. Two girls, young and long-legged, walked past along the quay and Logan watched their smooth, provocative legs moving along, slender stems going up into firm thighs that disappeared beneath their skirts, mockingly. Damn! Logan muttered and went below to fix himself another drink.

He came back on deck, feeling his mood growing blacker with every passing second. And then, walking beside the phone booth at the far end of the quay, passing beneath the lamplight, he saw her coming, black skirt and scoop-necked blouse. He waited, watching her as she neared and saw her pause at the gangway, then step onto it. His eyes lingered on the firm, young flesh of her thighs as she crossed the gangway and he passed the drink to her as she came aboard. She took it and pulled at it quickly, eager for its instant assurance. She was, as he'd remembered, young and eager and bouncy, despite her uncertainty. She took another long pull at the drink.

"Everything's all right, they told me," she said, getting a smile out. He cupped her chin in her hand.

"Everything's fine," he said, grinning at her. "Sit down."

He made her another drink, and one for himself, bringing them on deck.

"What was it all about?" she asked, hesitantly.

"Just somebody playing a joke on me," he answered, thinking how the answer wasn't really a lie. "Some people have a strange sense of humor."

"I'll say," she replied, draining her drink. They talked a while longer and laughed and he felt the desire stirring inside him as his eyes fastened on her small but upturned breasts, watching the way they moved under the satin blouse. The incompleteness of the night before had left its mark on the girl, too, he saw in her eyes as they searched his hungrily. Logan reached out a hand and put it on her arm. It acted like a door flung open, and in seconds she was in his arms, her warm, open mouth pressing upon his, lips working, tongue sending out messages of its own. His hands found her breasts, as soft as he'd remembered, and she thrust herself against him.

"I wanted to come back," she murmured. "You're something different. Something about you stays with a girl."

His answer was to send his tongue slowly revolving inside her mouth, and she moaned. He stopped, put his arm around her and led her below deck. He'd decided on the forward cabin this time, where the layout was different, and there would be no reminders. He turned off the lights and switched on the blowers. Cool air burst through the cabin. In the dim light, he saw her whip off her blouse, then her skirt. Pushing her back onto the bed, small but large enough for his purposes, he undid her bra and the soft breasts seemed to reach up for his lips. He lowered his head onto them, rolling his face in their softness, and then let his tongue trace small circles around their tips, first one and then the other, feeling each little tip rise under his touch. The girl was making small, eager sounds as he let his lips travel down over her body, across her abdomen, onto the softness of her rounded belly and then retrace their lambent path back to her straining breasts. She arched her back and he felt her legs under him opening, yawning, beckoning, and he answered, moving softly, gently.

He was with her, locked in the embrace of her legs, when his ears, always alert, like those of a cat, heard a sound, a faint movement on the deck. He tensed, holding himself still, listening, and he heard it again, a slurred footstep, and then he felt the girl grab at him.

"Don't stop," she gasped. "Damn it, don't stop now!" She pushed her belly upward against him frantically, intent only on pursuing the ecstacy nearly within her grasp. But Logan heard the step on the stairs and, in one swift motion, he pressed himself against the girl, grabbed her and rolled off the bed with her. They came apart only as they hit the floor and at the same instant the three shots resounded, crashing into the bed. Julie's scream was muffled against Logan's bare chest as he reached up under the mattress and yanked out the big Colt Python .357 magnum.

"¡Viva Camacho!" he heard the would-be killer shout as he appeared, framed in the doorway. The big-bore Colt Python erupted, firing two shots almost as one, and Logan saw the figure arch backward, seeming to leap into the air as the heavy slugs slammed into it. Logan, on his feet instantly, crossed the cabin in one lithe bound to stare down at the dead man sprawled across the two bottom steps of the companionway, "¡Viva Camacho!," he had yelled. Who the hell's Camacho? Logan asked himself. He stepped over the crumpled figure, grasped the man's shirt collar and pulled him onto the deck, taking care to keep him on his back so that the fast-spreading red stain wouldn't spill onto the deckboards. He looked up to see the girl, red satin blouse pulled over her, black skirt wrapped crookedly around her waist, edging out the companionway. She looked down at the dead man and up at Logan, her eyes round with fear.

"Wait," Logan said to her, but she shook her head as she edged past.

"No," she said. "Oh, no. I'm sorry but you got too many funny friends."

He watched her as she stumbled up onto the gangway, shot an apologetic glance back at him, and hurried on, pulling her skirt straight with one hand. Logan kicked the dead man in the head. "Bastard!" he said. 'Whoever the hell you are!"

He lifted the man by the back of his shirt and pushed him overboard, lowering the body over the side so it wouldn't land with a noisy splash. It would, he knew, float around the cove until someone discovered it in the morning. He went below, put his clothes back on and hurried onto the quay. It was just past midnight, his watch told him, and he went to the phone booth at the end of the quay. He called the number Alvarez had given him and heard the man's voice snap awake as he identified himself.

"What happened?" Alvarez asked.

"That's what I'd like to know. This more of your stuff?" he finished.

"No, no, not at all," Alvarez said. "They had me watched, I know, but I thought we took care of that. Apparently, they sent someone else who saw me go aboard your boat. I suggest you sail for the red buoy at once and wait there. The man you killed may have had others with him."

"Who the hell is Camacho?" Logan asked. "I thought you said their leader was Panico."

"I do not know any Camacho," Alvarez said but Logan caught a small pause in the man's voice. He's lying, Logan told himself. He hung up. He was getting more curious himself, now. He'd had his ass beaten in a crummy little cell, and just missed getting three slugs in the back, and he hadn't even begun the job yet. The ten thousand's beginning to look like bargain rates, he told himself. Back aboard the *Sea Urchin* he started the engine and let the twin V-12 diesels purr quietly while he cast off bow and stern lines. Then, nosing the boat out into the cove, he headed for the wide mouth of the harbor in the blackness of the hot, humid, thick-aired night.

"Let's go, honey," he said, quietly. "Let's find the little red buoy. Like the girl said, I've got too many funny friends around here."

CHAPTER FOUR

Logan heard the steady clang of the red buoy as he neared it, and he used his flashlight to study the chart in his hand. The reefs were to the right of the buoy he noted on the chart, where the harbor curved in a slow arc. The chart told him he had more then enough spare water around the buoy and, cutting his engine speed, he began to execute lazy circles around the clanging signal. His body once more seethed with restlessness as he thought of the girl's soft breasts. He felt like a starving man who'd sat down to a banquet only to have it yanked away. He shifted in the seat and patted the big Colt Python he'd stuck into his belt. He'd hoped for a moon but instead a steady, fine rain began to fall about three o'clock, which added to the blackness of the night. He was running without lights, and that was always dangerous. Coastal patrol cruisers were his main concern. These waters were a haven for smuggling contraband of all kinds and the police coastal cruisers had a habit of running without fights, too, as they searched for smugglers. A boat with running lights circling the red buoy for three hours would surely attract attention, probably from shore patrols, too. So he had opted for no lights, and now he peered into the moonless night searching for any black bulks that might loom up.

It was nearly four when he stopped circling and headed upwind of the buoy, cut the powerful engines and let the boat slowly drift back toward the buoy. His eyes swept the blackness and his ears were turned for the faintest sound. Only the soft slap of the sea against the hull broke the silence. He leaned his head out of the pilot house window and let the soft rain cool his face. Then, suddenly, he heard another sound, the faint scrape of an oar against the metal side of a boat. He slowed his sweep of the inky blackness and then, to the right, saw the flash, followed by three more. He waited and let the light flash four times again before answering. Then he blinked his flash twice, and twice again, in the answering signal. He'd just switched off his flash when he heard the dull, ominous sound, a powerful engine running at low speed. He spun around and, squinting through the fine rain, was able to pick out the black bulk of another vessel off the port bow. He traced the line of the high prow, high forward cabin and low stem, and knew at once the vessel was a coastal patrol boat. It was also plain that they'd seen the *Urchin's* bulk and were heading for her.

Logan peered to the other side and saw the rowboat materializing through the rain, the lone occupant rowing furiously, having also heard the patrol boat's engines. He moved fast, tossing a line over the side of the *Sea Urchin* and then, racing back to the wheel, kicked over the port engine. It sent the boat skittering a few feet sideways through the water as he yanked at the wheel, bringing it closer to the frantic oarsman. Logan heard the night come alive with the deep, throaty sound of the patrol cruiser's horn and he saw the boat's running lights snap on. But the rower had reached the side of the *Urchin* and grasped the line. With Logan pulling on it, the figure clambered up the side of the boat. Logan glimpsed a loose jacket, trousers and a floppy oilskin hat pulled low over the face. But he also saw smooth cheeks, an unlined face. It was no more than a kid, a small canvas bag slung over his shoulder.

"Get down," Logan commanded. He left the crouched figure with the big oilskin hat and raced below into the forward cabin. He had to work fast. The patrol boat would switch its searchlight on any second, he knew. He reached up to the top edge of what seemed the plain wall siding of the cabin and, running his fingers along the top, pulled down hard. The side of the wall opened up to reveal a hidden alcove, six feet long by nearly three feet wide. He left it open and raced back onto the deck.

"Inside the forward cabin," he said to the figure crouched at the rail. "Climb into the wall and pull the side back up with you."

He went to the wheel, a plan already formed in his mind. He didn't want any trouble with the coastal patrol, no dawn chases that he might or might not win. He'd let them come aboard, look around and then tell them he had been running without lights because he'd had generator trouble. Maybe they'd give him a jaundiced eye, but they would have to take his word for it. He'd get a reprimand, or possibly a summons, and that would be it. He had started to swing the *Urchin* around when the powerful searchlight beam opened up the night, a wide, blue-white finger probing the dark. It caught the pilot house at once and Logan waved and throttled the engine. He followed the beam of light as it swung down to the forward deck, moved slowly, then stopped as it illumined the small figure crouched at the gunwale.

"*Sonofabitch!*" Logan exploded, surprise and fury matching each other. "Dammit to hell!" He had just ended his second oath when the shots erupted, cracking the night and shattering the patrol boat's searchlight. Logan's hands clenched in helpless rage and he heard the angry voices from the cruiser as the light went out.

"That did it!" Logan swore, and he gunned the engines at once. Had it not been necessary for him to handle the *Urchin*, he'd have been on deck, strangling the crouching figure by the rail. There was no chance of playing it cool, now, and he knew that aboard the coastal patrol boat they were yanking the cover from their deck gun, probably a 20 mm machine gun. Logan saw them swinging around to bring their aft light into play, and as the light came on, he heard another fusillade of shots and the light went dark at once. A burst of machine gun fire whistled over the roof of the pilot house. He opened the throttle to full and kicked the rudder to port. The *Urchin* turned and leaped forward like a skittish sea horse, the powerful propellers grabbing at the water below. He assumed the coastal patrol was radioing for help, figuring he'd try to put in at one of the nearby coves. He straightened out the wheel and sent the *Urchin* surging forward in a shower of salt spray. The clouds and rain were holding off the first early streaks of dawn, and he was grateful for that. They sent another spray of shots after him but he had opened water between them, and until they closed it, he wasn't worried about the gunfire. The *Urchin* moved with surprising speed, surprising to anyone watching her, that was. The plowhorse was running like a thoroughbred. But to Logan there was little surprise. He knew what she could do. But he also knew that, given enough time, the coastal patrol boat would probably eat its way up to her if only because its streamlined prow offered less water resistance.

He opened the throttle a few notches more, just about all she had, and he glanced forward at the deck. His passenger had gone below and Logan's lips tightened in a surge of fury. Light was beginning to tint the sky, gray, murky light, but still fight. If they were able to get his name and number, they'd have every harbor master in every stinking cove alerted. Logan leaned his head out the window, peering forward, and suddenly he swung the *Urchin* to starboard. A fogbank was spreading across the water, low and wide, plenty wide enough in which to get lost. He couldn't tell how long it was. He took a fast bearing, threw a glance at the chart, veered back to port a little, and went into the fogbank at full speed, hoping no one else was hiding inside it. The fog closed around the boat at once and muffled the deep roar of its engines. He was sitting alone in a disembodied pilot house, with no bow and stern to his boat as the fog closed its pink-gray blanket around him. Logan cut the engines to half-speed and put on the autopilot. He couldn't see anything so he turned on the radar and watched the scope for a few moments.

Everything seemed to be clear ahead. He slipped from the pilot's seat and headed for the companionway, the fury within taking a renewed lease with each step. The youth was bent over inside the cabin, rummaging through the canvas bag, his back to the door. Logan's foot lashed into his behind and the figure flew headlong across the small cabin.

"On my boat you do as I say," Logan roared. The youth hit the bunk, went sprawling across it, and the oilskin hat flew off. Logan, crossing after the figure quickly, halted as a cascade of jet black hair came tumbling down and the figure turned around.

"I'll be damned!" Logan cursed. "A girl!" He saw her eyes, as black as her hair, lose some of their fury as she looked up at him. She was not only a girl but a beautiful one, with long black hair framing a heart-shaped face, straight nose and full, sensuous lips. Lying on her back half-across the bunk, her breasts swelled and she pushed herself upright.

"They didn't tell you?" she asked.

"Not a goddamn word."

"Does it make so much difference?" He felt his blood starting to boil over.

"Yes, it makes a difference. I agreed to get someone to a village, not to be a wetnurse to some crazy chickie."

"You won't be a wetnurse to me," she snapped. "Or didn't you see me take care of that coastal patrol boat?"

"I saw you almost get us both arrested. Why didn't you get the hell down?"

"I thought I'd be more help on deck."

"On my boat I do the thinking. You give me a hard time and I'll kick your little ass right over the side."

Logan turned and strode from the cabin. On deck, he checked the radar screen. He cut off the engines. There was no sound but the sound of her following him. She stood at the rail.

"They're waiting back there for us to come out," she said.

"Yes, but we're going on through and out the other end."

He watched her face closely but saw only a small, enigmatic smile.

"You're supposed to tell me where we go from here."

"Down the coast of Peru, just above the Río Huarmey, we'll come to a small inlet, the mouth of the Tinina River. We go up the Tinina, far upriver, to a little village called Quechayo."

Logan pulled a chart from the compartment just below the wheel and studied it for a moment. "No problem getting to the Tinina," he said. "You know the country from there?"

"Not really," she answered. "We'll be on our own once we start upriver."

They were starting to come out of the bank and he switched off the radar, turned on the engines and peered through the now patchy wisps of vapor. The sun was out and the yellowness of it fought through the fog and then, suddenly, they were out of the fog into morning sun.

'What's your name?" Logan thought to ask.

"Ariana," she said. "Ariana dos Vayez. You, I know, are called Logan."

Logan saw that they were in clear waters and he headed due south through the long swells of the Pacific. He set a course that would take him far enough off shore to skirt the bulge where Ecuador jutted out into the Pacific. He watched the girl at the rail. Her figure was long, slender, and the blue-jeans clung to her narrow hips. Finishing school, Logan muttered to himself. Then some fancy girl's college. It always showed in the way they moved, in a certain arrogance of the body. She was used to money, to good things. He put on the autopilot and went down to the deck.

"Where'd you learn English?"

"In America," she said. "I went to school there, finishing school. And in Switzerland."

"I don't like being tricked," he said. "And I don't like operating in the dark. How do you fit into this bit?"

"I dated Panico when we were in college," she said. 'I'm one of the few people who know him well enough to identify him. Among those on our side, that is."

"What's your side?"

"I work for the Peruvian Government. Like *Señor* Alvarez. Normally, I work in the Diplomatic offices. They asked me to do this and I agreed."

Logan tinned her answers over in his mind. He wasn't at all sure he believed her. There were soft spots, just as there had been with Alvarez. South American governments didn't go in for using women in sensitive areas. He tabled her answers for the time being and turned to her. A sea wind blew the red jersey against her breasts, outlining the round undersides of them and the rising, upturned tips. Logan felt the unsatisfied hunger inside himself rise like a dull ache.

"I'm going below for some sleep," he said, gruffly. They were in open waters and any vessels would be able to see them. The autopilot would hold their course well enough till he came back. And he was tired. But, as he went below, he knew it was not tiredness alone that sent him to the forward cabin.

"You have the aft cabin," he called back to the girl. He felt her eyes watching him as he disappeared below decks. He undressed and stretched out on the bunk. A slow smile moved across his lips. Maybe the trip would have its own rewards. If she wanted to play games he'd play, too. Only she'd find out he played for keeps. Ariana. The name moved across his mind. An unusual name. An unusual girl. He went to sleep.

CHAPTER FIVE

The midday sun was hot and Ariana was on the foredeck when Logan emerged from the cabin. In deep pink shorts and a turquoise blouse, she rose on one elbow as he appeared. Her legs, he saw at once, were long, lithe and slowly curving, and they moved lazily as she stirred. Her jet-black hair hung loosely, almost to the middle of her back, and her onyx eyes reflected amusement as she saw the open admiration in his eyes. Logan caught the note of anticipation in her eyes as he came toward her. She was used to being admired and had the honesty to openly enjoy it. Logan walked past her, glanced again at her, and gazed out across the sea. They were going before a good current and making time, he noted.

"No comment?" he heard the girl say mockingly. He turned and looked down at her, his face impassive.

"Do you need one?" he asked.

"No, but it's always nice to get one."

"All right, you're beautiful," he said, flatly.

"I've never heard a compliment sound less like one."

"It was a statement of fact. Someone said beauty is its own excuse. It doesn't need compliments."

"Maybe beauty doesn't but girls do."

He went up the side of the deck, pulled himself onto the small ledge surrounding the pilot house and went to the wheel. He was checking out his instruments, engine synchrometer, fuel oil pressure, tachometer when she appeared in the doorway.

"Who are you, Logan?" she asked, watching the slow smile crease the man's face as he continued to check the gauges in front of him.

"Nobody. Everybody," he said. "A sea-going bum. Arms and legs for hire."

"A sea-going bum who can quote the poets." She moved up and sat down on the narrow seat beside the port window.

"You're no sea-going bum," she said. "You're running away from something."

He laughed. "Sorry, honey," he said. "I hate to disappoint you but I'm not on anybody's wanted list. Nobody's after me. No cops, no governments, nobody."

"Maybe just yourself."

"How are you at making lunch?" he changed the subject.

"Pretty good."

"The galley is forward," he said. "The refrigerator and the freezer are well stocked. You're on your own."

"Lunch coming up," she said and hurried out of the pilot house. He watched her go, her small, compact rear moving gracefully with every step. He checked the course, made a few corrections, reset the autopilot and went below. He came up with a tray, ice, glasses and bourbon just as Ariana emerged from the galley. She had made bacon and lettuce sandwiches on toast and not even burned the bread. They sat on the deck, under the bright Pacific sun, and ate and he saw that she could enjoy the good warmth of the best bourbon and he found himself wondering again about her. Maybe she did work for the Peruvian Government in the Diplomatic offices but she was no office girl, no earnest little file clerk. She was a girl used to having what she wanted, used to looking down, not up, to people. It was in every gesture of her, in the way she tossed her head, in the way her eyes flashed with that touch of controlled arrogance. She caught the speculative look of his eyes as he watched her and smiled.

"What are you thinking, Logan?"

"That you dress up the *Urchin*," he lied, blandly. She laughed and the laugh said that she knew he had merely tossed her a bone and not his thoughts.

"You are like your boat," she said. "Deceptive. The inside is very different from the outside. And you hide the inside purposely. What do you think about when you're sailing alone?"

"Nothing I just stare out at the ocean," Logan said, annoyance coloring his voice. "Don't keep making something out of me that I'm not. I'm a drifter. I like to do nothing and do it slowly. I leave thinking to other people."

She made a face. "Baloney. You think all the time, too much, probably."

Logan felt his temper rise. Her perception and intuition were a disturbing combination and her fast, sharp probes were more than merely annoying. In fact, he decided, she was very bothersome all the way through.

"How'd you like to be locked in your cabin?" he growled.

"I wouldn't. Give me some work to do," she said, suddenly, eagerly. Logan seized the thought at once. It would keep her busy and out of his way while he checked out the sluggishness of the bilge pumps.

"There are rags and there is polish in the aft port closet," he said. "You can do the deck fittings."

She hurried down to get her equipment. Logan went below and pulled up the engine hatch cover. He'd keep plenty busy with the pumps...

But by the day's end, the good idea was still good, only it hadn't really worked. He had fixed the pumps quickly, too quickly, and with too much time left to watch Ariana. She polished and cleaned with the carefree joy of someone who doesn't normally have to work and who can afford to make work a fun game. And every curve and bend of her body was a delight to watch. By dinner time she was back in the galley, broiling steaks from the freezer, and Logan's angry restlessness had grown worse. His calculations told him they'd passed Colombia and were proceeding along the coast of Ecuador. He went into his cabin, showered and put on a fresh, white shirt. When he returned to the deck she had the small trays out, the steaks ready, and had changed into deep blue slacks and a white halter top, bare-midriffed. Logan's lips pressed together in a tight line.

He brought up a bottle of bourbon and made Logan Specials to go with the steaks. Dinner was fun and her vitality and wit were on a par with her beauty. She was having too much fun to notice the determined decision in the lean man's eyes. Darkness came over the Pacific and Logan switched on the running lights. They cast a low glow over the deck. The half-moon did the rest and the more he watched and listened to her, the more convinced he became that there was more to her being there, on his boat, then he'd been told. Her ability to describe a place, an event, an occurrence with complete detail seemed to disappear whenever he brought up anything concerning her mission. Her reaction to his questions about Panico stayed in his mind.

"What did this character Panico look like when you dated him?" he had asked.

"Very ordinary looking," she'd answered and started onto something else. But he'd pressed further.

"Was he blond, red-haired, dark?"

"His hair was just an everyday color," she said, a small, nervous frown crossing her face. She was being purposely evasive, unwilling to be pinned down about the man. Why? he asked himself, and came up with no answers.

"What if he had all his hair cut off and raised a mustache?" Logan probed. "Would you still be able to identify him?"

"I'll be able to make the identification," she said and closed off the subject. It had gone the same way when he tried to get her to talk about her work at the Embassy. She gave more fast, evasive answers that left his mind completely unsatisfied. She was a beautiful girl playing games. How many games, and what they were about, he didn't know. He only knew he was about to put a stop to one of them. He got up, drained his drink, and went over to her. He saw her eyes maintain their veiled, amused confidence. That was just as well, he knew, because there would be no stopping, no turning aside. His body would refuse to obey. The need that had been denied him twice now focused on this lovely, raven-haired creature in front of him. He put a hand on the back of her neck and felt the soft, wispy hairs there. He ran his hand partially down her back, and then lifted her to her feet. She rose to meet his lips, her mouth opening just a little. But his own hunger had burst loose and he pressed his mouth on hers, forcing his tongue into the warm, wetness of her mouth, darting, circling, anticipating further pleasures. She managed to pull away and tried to slip from his arms but he held her still. He yanked her head around and again pressed into the open, red invitation, this time feeling her own tongue answer in short, quick motions, like a bird taking flight.

"No, Logan!" she gasped as his hand fell on her breast and she clasped her own hand over his. But she didn't pull his away and her eyes were searching his, troubled, uncertain. Conflicting desires, were raging inside Ariana, he knew, and he gave some of them a little helpful push. He pulled the string of her halter and it fell from her and his hand was against her breast, pressing into the warm, vibrant flesh. Her body stiffened as she tried to hold back the pleasure she felt at his touch. But it was a useless gesture and suddenly her body pressed forward, her breast pushing itself into his palm. Her lips were hungry against his. He lifted her up and the halter fell off completely and he gazed down at the softly rounded breasts, cream-white gifts waiting for his lips. Ariana's head lay against his shoulder and she was making small sounds of protest but they were meant to be disregarded. He carried her to the cabin below and on the fold-out bed his lips fastened on the smooth tips of her breasts, caressing them with his tongue until the small, pink tips lifted in gratification and he moved his lips around the firm softness, the deep fullness of her chest. He let his hands pull down the slacks and move over the rise of her hips, across her flat belly, down to the exciting little mound of softness that waited for his touch.

As he moved across her, Ariana gave a cry of release that sprang from some hidden place and she threw herself upon him, rubbing herself against him, her hands clutching, caressing, stroking, and he matched her wild abandon, touching the wellsprings of passion she cried out for him to touch. Her lips sought every part of his body and she moved up and down the strong, oak-tree muscles of his frame, crying little cries of ecstasy and desire and when he pressed her back and thrust himself fully into her, she tossed her head from side to side and her fingers dug into him with a rapture more than she could contain. Higher and higher she reached with her body, half-crying, half-laughing, her little fists pounding against the bed as the tall, lean man carried her beyond being, beyond thinking, beyond feeling, to a place where there was only knowing.

"*Logan!*" she screamed the word. "*Oh, God, Logan!*" and as her body went steel-wire taut he went deeply into her and her neck arched backward, her mouth opened and the scream that came was one of total surrender. He fell back onto the bed, keeping him with her until the world became real again. Logan gently massaged her breast until her regular breathing indicated she had relaxed. Only then did he pull away and lay beside her, feeling the accusation in her black eyes.

"I didn't want this," she said quietly, almost hesitantly.

"Didn't you?"

"Not tonight, not so soon."

"You wanted to play some more," Logan said, his voice cold. "Till you could decide when or if. You're used to having things your way. But I'm not one of the crowd."

"I know that," she said. "I saw that the first minute we met. You're different."

"And you liked that," he said. "But different things are often dangerous."

"I just found that out."

"Are you sorry?" He got to his feet and looked down at her, letting her drink in his nakedness. She turned away. "I don't know," she said quietly.

Logan's laugh was hard and short. "Tell me when you find out," he said, biting the words. He took his clothes and dressed on deck and his smile was thin. There were games she still had to play, he was certain. But there'd be one less now. He took the wheel of the boat and turned toward shore to find an inlet to anchor for the night. In a mile or so he spotted a small pocket and fitted the *Urchin* inside it. He dropped anchor, waited to make sure it was holding, and then turned off all but the white fight on the forward mast. He went to his cabin and stretched out, letting the sea wind through the porthole move across his naked body. He would sleep well, he knew. The hunger within him had been satisfied. Though Ariana had been so much more of everything then he'd expected that, in a strange way, she'd sharpened as well as satisfied his hunger. He thought of her cream-white body and the blackness of her hair. She could be everything to someone, sometime. But he was beyond those things, and as sleep drew a curtain over his mind, he wondered if he would ever care again about anyone. Nothing was impossible. But some things were highly improbable.

CHAPTER SIX

B right hot sun made bearable by the sea winds, the deep blue of the Pacific a rolling carpet. That was morning and Logan made coffee and got under way early, once again staying far offshore. By noon, according to his charts, they'd be moving along the coast of Peru. He settled himself at the wheel. A helmsman, playing the wheel, could always make better time than the automatic pilot, and time had become important again to him. He wanted to do the job, get finished with it, and be on his way. Ariana was staying in her cabin, and that was good. Whatever had brought her into this strange and dirty business, were hers to wrestle with. He wouldn't get involved beyond the needs of his agreement. Involvements were something he'd ended long ago. He turned on the ship's radio, picked up a station, and settled down to concentrate on his job.

Ariana dos Vayez heard the man on the deck above and held her arms tightly across her breasts. She had put on a loose, rayon blouse and the pink shorts, and she could still feel the touch of his hands on her, the tingling of her body as he moved his lips across it. She had asked herself over and over all day why it had happened the way it had. It wasn't enough to blame the commonplace things, the soft Pacific night, the cool wind, the lulling swell of the waters. It wasn't even honest to blame the compelling looks of the man, the dangerous hardness about him that reached out and grabbed at you. She had wanted him, with a kind of wanting she had never experienced before. And when he had taken her, it was something she had never known could exist in just that way. She was on this boat to do something that had to be done, because she was the only one that could be trusted. She wasn't here to become involved with a strange and distant man. She had met many men, in her own country and in those lands where she had gone to school, but none like Logan. She had known men who refused to compromise and those who did nothing else. She had known men who were cold and men who were warm. She had known men who believed in honor and those who didn't even know the word. Honor, the word moved across her mind. It was a big word in her country, in most places, probably. But she wasn't sure anymore if it meant the same thing to all men. She wasn't even sure where honor really began, and ended, any longer. Very often it seemed that honor was really no more than which was best for you. She wasn't really sure of much anymore, except that you did what you did because you had to do it. You were brought up a certain way. You got used to certain things. You became part of a particular world, and it all decided what you did from there on.

The past really owns the future, Ariana told herself, at least for most of the world. Perhaps that was what was so intriguing about this lean, hard man and his deceptively funny little boat. He owned himself. He was one of the few who refused to let the past own the future. Of course there had been a past, that was clear, and it had left its mark. But only its mark, not its franchise. Ariana heard him go into the galley for coffee. He went back to the wheel as she traced his footsteps and fought down the urge to rush up on deck. It would be worth it if she could make him a part of her world, worth it for them both. A man like that could bring not only strength to her life but give her world a definition it needed. And she could give him material pleasures and comforts. Maybe, she mused idly, maybe. She would have to get over wanting him as much as she did. That made her position much weaker. But, she asked herself quickly, could she meet this man on his own terms? Was that the impossible thing about him that gave him the strangely compelling strength he had, the fact that his terms were his and his alone? She gazed out of the porthole. The sea flowed past, the sun-speckled surface somehow reflecting the terrible strength below, very much like the man at the wheel over her head.

Logan watched the coast of Peru grow larger as he piloted the *Sea Urchin* inshore. The afternoon sun had moved across the horizon and he scanned his chart closely. The mouth of the Tinina River was poorly marked and he estimated they would near it just before nightfall. It was time the girl started doing her job, which included the decisions on entering the river. He called to her, his voice flat, emotionless.

"Ariana. Get out here. We have to talk," he said, and heard the sounds of her moving about, then coming up the companionway. He watched the cascade of jet-black hair emerge and her eyes, and there were resentment, hostility and uncertainty in them. He could almost feel the turbulence of her and once again he found his eyes on the thrusting mounds of her breasts. They seemed to rise and swell as she walked up the few steps to the pilot house. He took his eyes from them and the girl's face and gazed out over the water as he spoke to her

"By night we'll be at the mouth of the Tinina," he said. "It's your show from there. I'm only the chauffeur. Do we start upriver or anchor and wait for morning?"

"Anchor," Ariana said. "The Tinina is tricky and winding. I don't know it that well. I only know it'll be hard enough by day "

"All right," Logan said "You can go back down below."

"No!" the girl said the one word with enough vehemence to surprise herself. "I … I want to talk about last night I want to explain."

Logan kept his eyes straight ahead, peering over the long blue swells. "There's nothing to explain," he said, flatly. "You wanted it to happen and it happened. That's all."

"No, that's not all," she said, angrily. "I'm no tramp."

"Anyone say you were?" he countered. "You want to explain to yourself," he said.

He saw the black fire shoot from her eyes, saw her swing in fury and he caught her wrist with one hand. He bent her body backward and she gasped. The buttons of the blouse came open and the rounds swell of her breasts emerged. She had nothing on beneath the blouse. He pressed his mouth on hers and felt her quiver and then she was kissing him back, lips open, tongue searching for his. He let go of her wrist and her hand flew against his chest, clutching his shirt, her fingers working on the muscled hardness of his skin. Suddenly, angrily, she tore away from him and stood back, her eyes boring into his.

"God, what is it about you?" she said, a question that was more of a statement than a question. "I don't want this, not this way, and yet I want you so bad it hurts."

"An unsolicited testimonial," Logan said, his grin hard, his eyes narrowed. She had gathered herself together and the anger in her had taken command.

"You never let up, do you?" she said.

"It's your comer. You put yourself in it."

"And you had nothing to do with it, I suppose," she snapped.

"Only a little," he said. "I just held up a mirror."

"That's how you get your kicks," she bit out.

Logan shrugged. "People shouldn't have hiding places," he said. "It makes them dishonest with themselves and then with each other. I make them face themselves. And that's important, even if they refuse to admit it."

She wanted to hit out at him to avoid the truth of what he was saying. She wanted to find a vulnerable spot and in so doing only exposed her own vulnerability.

"Why don't you try facing yourself?" she cast out, almost desperately. He caught her wrist again and pulled her to him.

"No problem, honey," he said through clenched teeth. "I want you again, tonight, before we start up that damned river. I want you and you want me. You don't want to want me but you do. You still want to play games." He thrust a hand up under the loose blouse and closed it over her round breast and she lifted her head and closed her eyes.

"Tonight, later," he said. "You'll be waiting for me and I'll come." He withdrew his hand and Ariana stepped backward, her eyes troubled, almost frightened. She turned and ran out of the pilot house and she heard the man's short, angry laugh.

Logan put his thoughts on following the curves of the Peruvian coastline. He passed a few fishing boats, mostly one and two-man operations. The full, lush foliage of the coastline told him of the country he'd be pushing through, heavy, over-grown, hot. He had slowed to half-throttle and he kept one eye on the lowering sun, one on the chart. The sun had just touched the distant line of the horizon and started to flatten out behind it when he reached the mouth of the Tinina River, a crack in the green wall of the coastline. He cruised past it, swung around and came by again. A small village graced the mouth of the river, mostly shacks, a few somewhat sturdier wooden houses. Canoes, small hand-rowed fishing craft, a few with outboard motors, and a shallow river barge made up the villlage waterfront. He found a spot just outside the mouth of the river and dropped anchor. By the time he'd made the *Urchin* secure for the night, darkness had closed down on the boat. He went below and made himself a Logan Special, took it on the deck and sipped it. He was taking his time, but he knew it was a double-edged sword, for his groin ached for the luscious creature in the cabin. He drained the drink and went down below, pushing open the cabin door. Ariana was still in the blouse and deep pink shorts, looking at him as he filled the doorway, legs curled up beneath her on the fold-out bed. He walked toward her, taking in the absolute beauty of the raven hair framing her cream-white skin. She waited till he was standing in front of her.

"I looked into one of those mirrors of yours," she said. "And I don't want what you want."

"Look again," Logan growled. "You'll see a damned liar."

He grabbed her by the back of the neck and yanked her head up. Her eyes grew blacker and her breath was deep, hard. He saw her lips move, her tongue flick out to wet them, and her mouth open before she said the one word.

"Bastard," she gasped and flew against him, her arms wrapping around his neck in a fervent grip. He forced her back onto the bed and felt the blouse come undone and his lips were on her breasts, moving on them, rapturously massaging their small, pink tips. Her hands were pushing against his trousers, taking them down over his hips so she could clutch him to her and she cried out in small, animal sounds of pure desire.

Dimly, she heard the sound of a mirror shattering.

Once more, he found the wild passion that was part of this gorgeous girl, but this time, she was more eager to make love to him. Her hand holding him stroked and smoothed and pressed and she moved her mouth across his body like a hungry little bird. The tall, lean man's face relaxed under the pleasures of her mouth, her circling, caressing tongue and he knew she was trying to say something with her body that words could not say. He reached down, lifted her head up to his and moved atop her. He would be less savage with her tonight, less savage but just as complete. The boat moved up and down slowly in the rhythm of the waves and Logan, tuning his own movements to it, brought Ariana to that wild moment when it seemed the world must explode. But still he delayed the explosion and once again she knew that feeling of transport, of pure and utter unbearable ecstacy. Her lovely breasts rose and fell and her gasping cries grew more and more intense. Once again he saw her pound her fists into the bed, saw her black hair fly as she tossed her head from side to side, and she cried out in her own tongue and in English. Then, with a tremendous thrust of her hips, there was no more time to delay, and the inner explosion of rapture tore through her body and she clutched at Logan, half-moaning, half-sobbing until slowly she relaxed. He lay down, half-atop her, resting his head on her breasts and she cradled him there. Finally, her even, steady breathing told him she'd fallen asleep and he moved his head from the wonderful softness of her breasts. He gazed at her. Sleep revealed more clearly the delicate lines of her heart-shaped face, her small wrists and fine-boned body, a body used to the best. And once again he had to wonder why this girl had taken on this strange task. It didn't add up.

He got to his feet and went on deck. He didn't know why but a strange sadness had gripped him, as if their lovemaking had been more of an end than a beginning. Somehow, he had the strangest feeling that, for all his having reached her so completely, he and this raven-haired girl would part bitterly. A small smile crossed his face. With a few it hadn't been bitter, he recalled, only bitter-sweet. But this girl, this creature of evasions and hidden pieces, still had to fit the pieces into a whole and he had the feeling that when she did, they wouldn't fit right, not for him. He lay down on the hardness of the deck and slept there.

CHAPTER SEVEN

Logan didn't know which hit him first, the thick, heavy-aired heat as he nosed the *Urchin* into the Tinina or the narrowness of the winding ribbon that stretched out ahead of him. The minute he'd entered the mouth of the river the heat had fallen onto them like an invisible curtain. The cooling winds of the Pacific swept by the river's mouth, refusing to extend even a probing finger of air into it. Logan moved the *Urchin* slowly past the ramshackle buildings that were clustered on both banks. He saw a man in a peaked and braided cap set out in a craft with a small outboard and a tillerman and he slowed the *Urchin* still further. The man was a town official, perhaps out to make his usual show of status for the people. Perhaps not. Ariana was below decks but watching through the porthole, he knew. It had already been decided that she would stay strictly out of sight. He had shown her how to pull down the wall siding and climb into the alcove at the first sound of anyone coming aboard. The little craft swung alongside the *Urchin* and the man in the cap called to Logan.

"*Buenos días*" Logan saw the notepad and pencil in his hand. "I am the river traffic master. May I have the name of your boat and your destination?"

A river traffic master on a stinkin' little river like this? Logan asked himself the question silently. Yet it was possible, he knew. These minor officials invented titles for themselves and duties for which they could collect extra pay.

"*Sea Urchin*," Logan said. "I'm going upriver as far as I can go."

"Your business?" the man asked and Logan saw his eyes move up and down the length of the *Urchin's* paint-chipped hull.

"Hides and bark, and anything I can buy for a good price and sell for a better one."

The official touched his cap and pushed away. Logan gunned the *Urchin* and the boat responded at once. He grinned back at the craft, rocking precariously in the sudden rush of his wake. He had been gone from the village for almost a half hour before he slid open the small hatch in the floor of the pilot house. It let him look down into the passageway between the forward and aft sections of the boat and he saw Ariana appear at once, stepping up on the ladder to poke her head out of the hatch opening in the floor.

"What did you think, back there?" she asked.

"I think he was legitimate," Logan said. "But I wish I knew for sure." The girl's lovely face was passive and told him nothing. "These guerrillas," he said. "You think they'll really be watching for us? ... for someone?"

"Three of our people have been killed trying to get into Quechayo by land," she said quietly, and Logan's left eyebrow rose.

"Then you be sure and keep your ass out of sight during daylight," he said. "Then they can watch all they want and all they'll see is the *Urchin* and me moving upriver."

"I'll get lunch for us soon," she said. "This is fun in a way, isn't it?" She flashed him a little-girl smile of enthusiasm and disappeared. She didn't appear again till she came up with sandwiches and a can of beer. He steered with one hand and ate with the other. She stood on the ladder, her head and shoulders through the hatchway opening, her plate on the floor of the pilot house. Logan took off his shirt and sat at the wheel stripped to the waist. The heavy air lay like a blanket, oppressive, cloying, stealing energy in huge handfuls. The Tinina River was not only shallow, with shifting sandbars, but dotted with small islands in the center which necessitated skirting them along a needle-thin channel. His only clue to the channel was the color of the water and, sometimes, the speed of it. His sonar worked for a short while and then he shut it off. It kept bouncing back erratic signals from the bottom just beneath their keel. He watched as the *Urchin* nosed her way through swarms of water beetles that covered the surface of a spot near a bend like a moving, squirming mass of paint. On shore, the brilliant flash of a gold and blue macaw cut the endless green of the heavy vegetation. They passed two more small native villages, hardly more than a cluster of huts crowding the bank of the river. "Damn," Logan swore aloud as he wiped the perspiration from his chest only to have it trickle down his back. His hands on the wheel were wet from the intense concentration of guiding the *Urchin* through the shallow spots, the tricky currents at the turns of the river. A large island loomed up in midriver, about the size of a football field in length and about half as wide. Logan steered to the right of it and felt the sound of the *Urchin's* propellers tipping the mud, stirring up the murky water. He gunned the engines and the boat shot forward and he held her close as he dared to the shore, keeping away from the edge of the island. The islands, he noted, were nothing much more than small collections of trees on a base of earth rising up like so many humps on the back of an endless caterpillar. Golden marmosets and squirrel monkeys were scampering among the trees.

Except for the occasional small village they passed, there was only the unending lush green foliage of the banks. And yet he knew a thousand eyes were watching the *Urchin* as she slowly made her way upriver. Somewhere, someplace, there were hostile, prying eyes. He could feel it in his bones. For him and the *Urchin* this lush, burning land was a place of potential danger and that fact brought out the steel-wire hardness in him. Threats from outside always did. He had always made threats into a simple decision of win or lose and he didn't like losing, ever. There was danger here, he knew. It hung in the air like the heavy scent of the dense foliage and it made him think about Ariana and the unanswered questions about her. And then, with surprising suddenness, it was night. There was no slow sinking of the sun over the ocean water, no gradual disappearance over the horizon. There was heat, and then a grayness and dark, falling like a curtain. With the night came a chorus of new sounds from the thick foliage on both sides of the river. Logan dropped anchor quickly, felt it catch into sand and finally hold. Below decks, Ariana had turned on the cabin light and had dinner ready. Once more, he saw the little-girl enthusiasm of her, the eager wanting to please. It was nice to be near her again, he admitted to himself. He'd almost forgotten what it was like. The tiredness in him started to fade. The tension only retreated a little. He was pouring himself a jigger of warm Tennessee "sippin' whiskey" when Ariana came back into the cabin. Her fingers were smooth on the back of his neck. He reached up to pull her down on his lap when he saw her eyes widen as she looked past his shoulder. He cut off her scream with his hand and whirled.

"A face," she gasped, tearing his hand away. "At the porthole window. I saw it."

"Dammit!" Logan swore and raced up the companionway just in time to hear the sounds of someone swimming frantically away. He switched on the *Urchin's* searchlight beam over the top of the pilot house. He swept the water and halted, holding the fight on a man swimming furiously for shore. Ariana was beside him.

"Keep the light on him," he growled. "Don't lose him."

He didn't dare risk a dive in these shallow waters. He dropped over the side and went after the swimmer. The big Colt Python was still in his belt but he didn't want to use it. Shooting would only bring others and trouble. The man lost time by trying to dodge from the beam of the searchlight but Ariana kept it on him. Logan clambered ashore only seconds after him and saw him disappear into the thickness of the brush and the trees. Moving at a crouch, Logan followed and once inside the tangled foliage, he stopped and listened. There was silence and he rose on the balls of his feet, ready to move fast in any direction. The man was near, staying still. Logan moved, slowly, now, his eyes trying to make out shapes in the blackness of the forest. He moved behind the thick trunk of a tree, leaned against it and waited. Slowly, he bent down and felt along the base of the tree with his hands. He came up with three small twigs and a rock. One by one, he tossed them to the left, into the denseness. They landed with small, cracking sounds, as though someone was carefully moving off in that direction. In but a few moments, he heard the man start to move away and, stepping from behind the tree, he saw the black bulk of his figure. Logan moved with the speed of a panther pouncing, stealth disregarded for swiftness. The man whirled and Logan glimpsed a young face, brown-skinned with long black hair, one of the Indian natives of the region, and then he was on him, carrying him backward to the ground. Logan smashed a short, chopping right to the man's jaw as he landed on top of him. His knee sunk deep into the man's abdomen and he felt his quarry's legs draw up in pain. But the man managed to get an arm up and Logan saw the dull glint of steel. He grabbed the wrist as the knife started to come down and pressed the arm backward while his own elbow slammed into the man's throat. The arm went limp for an instant as the man gasped in pain, the knife falling to the ground. Logan had it in hand and slashed once with it, backward across the man's throat. There was a shuddered gasp and the lean, hard-eyed man sprang to his feet. He dropped the knife on the lifeless form and quickly moved out of the forest. Ariana, he saw as he hit the water, had had sense enough to douse the light. He swam quickly with long, powerful strokes and covered the short distance to the *Urchin* in seconds. The girl tossed him a line and he clambered aboard.

"He won't tell anyone he saw you," Logan said flatly. Ariana's eyes were round, troubled as she studied his face.

"What if he were just looking in?" she asked. "The people in these regions are very curious."

"A local Peeping Tom?" Logan snorted. "Then his career is over."

"Didn't you ask him, or try to find out?" she said.

"Why? I wouldn't have believed him anyway," Logan answered. "So trying to find out would only be something to help your conscience and I haven't got time for that crap."

"No time or no conscience?" she flared at him.

"You pick whichever you like," he said, his eyes hard.

"Logan," she said, her voice softening, "I'm sorry. I guess we're both a little on edge since starting upriver."

"I guess so," he said, his voice cold, flat. "I know I'm tired. I'm going to turn in."

He left her there and went to his cabin, pausing only to shower off the river water before climbing into the bunk. As he lay there, waiting for sleep, feeling the tense fatigue of his body, he thought of the girl's words about his lack of time or conscience and his eyes burned with a terrible coldness. Once he had indulged in both and paid a price beyond all the wealth in the world. He would never do it again. He turned over and went to sleep with never another thought of the lifeless form in the forest.

The day dawned hot and humid and as Logan rose, he looked out the porthole of the cabin to see a gray blanket of mist still over the river. He put on only trousers, tucking the big Colt Python into his belt again, and went to the aft cabin to wake the girl. She lay with a sheet half over her, breasts exposed, hair a black halo on the pillow. He went into the cabin and touched her breast, running his hand over its soft firmness and then put his fingers upon her cheek. He had only come to waken her but as she stirred, opened her eyes slid her arms around his neck, he put his lips to the delicate pink of her left breast. Her legs raised and moved languorously, like long stalks waving in a slow wind, and he went to her, moving his body onto hers, and once again she became his.

The sun had ripped the gray blanket of mist from the river when he finally slid from the bed to stand beside it.

"What a way to wake up," Ariana purred, stretching her long, lithe body. Logan went to the pilot house, angered in a way at himself. Not that he hadn't enjoyed, or wanted her. He just had decided it might be better without it now. There were still too many unanswered things about her role in this, too many small uncertainties that kept bothering him. And yet, she was so guileless sometimes, so little-girl in her openness. He opened the *Urchin's* engines as soon as the anchor came up and headed into midriver, still wondering about the girl. She popped up in the open hatch, handing him coffee, wearing only the pink shorts, looking like she had stepped to his boat from the marbled palace of a Roman emperor.

"You make it hard to concentrate on this damned river," he growled. She laughed, a very female little laugh.

"I'll put something on," she said. "The faster we get there, the sooner we can start back and that's what I really want."

It was not an unpleasant thought and Logan felt the small stirrings of anticipation inside himself. A week with Ariana would be something else, he knew. Now, their lovemaking had an unhappy aftertaste, at least to him, as though he had made love to a girl who was essentially a stranger. He corrected himself. Essentially a fraud. She was two or three people, separate and compartmented—a warm, enthusiastic girl who liked playing house and a wild, abandoned hedonist in bed. As he was thinking of her, she poked her head up through the hatchway with a map in her hand, no doubt extracted from the small canvas bag she'd brought aboard with her.

"We ought to be coming to two islands almost touching each other," she said. "That means we're making good time."

"I see them up ahead," Logan said. "Let's have a look at that map."

"Quechayo doesn't appear on it," she said, handing it to him. "But it'll be on our left and we ought to reach it by tomorrow night."

Logan looked at the map quickly. She was right, the village of Quechayo was unmarked. He gave the map back to her and started to edge the *Urchin* to starboard to skirt the two islands which lay almost end to end. Reaching the village tomorrow night was more than fine with him. He'd had enough of this damned river. Even now the sweat was coating his body as he played Russian roulette with sandbars, underwater roots and uncertain depths. Getting by the two islands took slow, careful going. The Tinina River was made for flatboats and rafts. They rounded a sharp bend and he saw a small native village, the first they'd passed in a good while, grass- and leaf-roofed huts, small, brownskinned naked children and women with loose, bright garments. The village disappeared from sight as they went on and only the walls of the unending green looked out at them. He wanted to watch the brilliant slashes of color that were the parrots and toucans, but always the river demanded his attention as the narrow channel meandered from side to side, first near one bank, then the other. He was glad to see the grayness descend which heralded night and he edged out of the channel and dropped anchor. Ariana came on deck as the blackness closed around them, sandwiches on a tray. He ate and stretched out on a deck chair. The clicking, clacking, chirping and buzzing of a thousand different kinds of insects filled the thick air, echoing across the river from bank to bank. He went below, fixed two stiff bourbons and brought them back on deck.

"A nightcap," he said. "I'm finishing this and going to sleep. The earlier we get started in the morning the happier I'll be."

The bourbon was good going down and it even gave him a lift to stay on deck longer. But he fought it down and went below. He stripped to his shorts and lay down on the bunk, stretching out on his stomach. He heard Ariana's footsteps and started to get up on one elbow but she was in the cabin and beside the bunk in an instant, her hands massaging his back, rubbing, kneading, working out the tensions of his neck and shoulder muscles.

"Mmmmm, nice," he murmured. Her fingers, which could stroke and caress, could also press with surprising strength, he found.

"When we get back, you and the *Urchin* are coming with me," she said. "I'll show you a new world, Logan, a world you'll like."

"I have a world and I like it," he murmured.

"You'll like mine better," she said. He didn't answer. He just fell asleep under the relaxing touch of her hands.

He was alone when he woke and he didn't know how long he'd slept. He just suddenly awoke, his subconscious alarm ringing loudly inside his head. It wasn't the feel of danger so much as the feel of something gone, something missing. He went out onto the deck softly, on cat feet, moving like a panther on the prowl. He saw the pink shorts and the white halter top lying on the deck and he crouched down beside the rail, his eyes scanning the water, trying to pierce the darkness. Suddenly, on the nearest bank, he saw a light blink on and off. He watched and his eyes made out the figure on the shore, ghost-white. He went to the pilot house, got his field glasses and returned to the rail. Through the glasses he could see, not well, but better. Ariana was on the bank, in bra and bikini panties, and she was blinking the light on and off again. She did it every half minute or so, flashing to the opposite shore. Logan watched in silence and then he heard the soft sound of water being disturbed. He swung the glasses to the opposite shore and saw the dark figure of a man poling a small raft into the river. Ariana's flashing light went out and Logan watched the man move toward her, poling the raft against the slow current. As he reached the shore, Ariana moved toward him and stretched out a hand. The man handed her something and immediately started to pole away downriver. Logan saw the girl wait for a moment, watching him go, and then walk into the water and strike out for the boat. Field glasses resting on the top of the rail, he watched her approach, saw her white arms rising and falling in the darkness as she swam toward him. He stayed as long as he dared and saw that in one hand she held something rolled up, scroll-like. Grim-lipped, he retreated to his cabin and lay back on the bunk, face-down. He heard her climb aboard, pause at the door of his cabin, and then go on. She's doing a good job, he admitted to himself, silent, smooth, efficient. He lay still and let an hour go by before he rose. This time, it was his tall figure that moved silently and paused at a cabin door, listening to the sounds of her even, steady breathing. He went into the cabin and his eyes immediately found the small, canvas bag on the ledge beside the bed. He reached inside it, felt a hairbrush, a rolled-up blouse, comb, extra sandals and then the small, wet, rolled object. He pulled it out and went up on deck. In the pilot house, he turned on the soft green of the instrument lights and unrolled the object. It was a photostat, plasticized to make it waterproof. He felt the frown creasing his brow as he looked at it. It was a dental chart and in the upper right-hand corner was the name of one Charles Panico. Logan found himself whistling silently as he studied the chart. It was an ordinary enough dental chart, except that five of the teeth were marked with an X, two lateral incisors, two anterior molars and one upper canine. The X, of course, could mean anything. It could mean simply that those teeth had fillings, or needed work or any number of things. But then, it could also have a special meaning. It was a special chart, special in importance, it seemed, and he asked himself what the hell did she need with a dead man's dental chart? He rolled the chart up again, tiptoed back into the cabin with the sleeping girl and put it back into the little canvas bag. Then he went on deck to think, starting at the beginning. This is almost like old times, he told himself grimly.

First, the man Alvarez had lied to him. He had known that when Alvarez had caught himself at mention of the name Camacho. Then there was Ariana, the girl of obvious breeding and background who didn't fit into this kind of role. Yet she was here and ready with evasions and deft turn-away answers to any probing about Panico. Logan's eyes were narrowed and he felt the icy coldness stirring inside him. He didn't like being lied to or played for a fool. And Ariana was holding to her role, keeping it separate from what she felt for him. He knew she had come to want him for more than a toy. It was in her eyes, it was in the flaring anger that came out when she thought of her job. She was feeling the inner turmoil, the pain, of keeping separate accounts. But whether she wanted to or not, she was lying to him, and her games were more intricate than he'd suspected, which brought him back to the dental chart. It was plain that it had been arranged that she be given the dental chart only when they neared their objective. She obviously wasn't to risk carrying it around, in case something went wrong. That made it a rather special dental chart. His mind raced on. Dental charts were often used for identification purposes. Nothing wrong there. But then anyone could have taken it and done this job. Ariana was here because she was one of the few people able to identify Panico the guerrilla leader on sight. That's what they'd told him, anyway, and it brought back the question of questions. Why, if she knew him would she need a dental chart in her hot little hands? And what of the X-marked teeth? Did they mean anything special?

Nothing really fitted, he realized. He had only questions and no answers. All he knew about Panico was what he'd been told. He did know one thing. He was mad as hell and getting madder. He'd been beaten and shot at, blackmailed into being here, been lied to by a smooth operator and now by a beautiful girl, a girl who was, herself, still a big question mark. Inside that gorgeous wrapping there existed hard-steel determination. Only because of it could that kind of girl come from her background into this kind of task. Only because of it could that kind of girl make love the way she did. But, Logan promised himself, he'd get at the truth before too much time went by. He decided to say nothing about what he'd seen. Maybe she'd open up to him before they reached Quechayo. He closed his eyes and dropped off to sleep.

The smell of scrambled eggs woke him and he slipped on his trousers in the gray dawn light, pushing the Colt Python into his belt. Ariana came in with a tray and plates of eggs and toast.

"How is our supply holding out?" he asked.

"Fine," she said. "You've a big freezer on this boat."

"Specially built for me," he commented. Ariana seemed happy and chattery with uncontained excitement. "Mostly I'm thinking about going back home with you," she said, and he wished he didn't doubt her. She obviously expected everything would go smoothly.

"I'll show you an inlet, Logan," Ariana said, her eyes taking on a soft, dreamy quality, "where the sea comes in through a narrow rocky bridge and the house goes down to the water. It's your own ocean pool, clear and cool and calm even on rough days."

"Your place?" he asked casually.

"Maybe someday," she answered. He waited till she had put the plates on the tray and picked up the tray to go to the galley. "Who's Camacho?" he asked mildly.

He saw the moment's pause, the twitch of her jaw and the way her hand tightened on the tray. He smiled, inwardly, with admiration, at how quickly she recovered and looked at him with round, big eyes.

"Camacho?" she repeated. "Where'd you get that name?"

"Heard it around," he answered.

"I haven't," she said. She went on into the galley and Logan's smile was thin as he pulled up anchor and kicked over the engines. He found that the Tinina had narrowed still farther and each island left less room to skirt around it.

"How are we doing?" Ariana asked, popping her head through the hatch near midday.

"You could swim upriver faster than we're going."

"Not this far inland," she said, a grimness in her voice that made him look at her. "Piranhas," she explained. "Up here the river is full of them. Nobody swims here for very long."

Logan's eyes automatically scanned the water. The piranha moved in schools, he knew, and were probably the most vicious of all underwater river life. He had once seen them strip a cow to bare bones in less then five minutes, and that was something you didn't forget.

"Okay, no swimming," he said. They were skirting a small island that turned out to be wider than he'd realized. Suddenly he heard the *Urchin's* keel dig in deeply, her headway grind to a halt and he quickly switched off the engines. Ariana's head popped up.

"We're hung up," he said angrily. "We really dug in this time. I don't know if it's sand or mud. More important, I don't know if the screws are in it. I've got to go down and take a look. It's not deep, that much we know."

He read the question in her eyes. It wasn't deep but the piranhas weren't concerned about that, either. He took out his keys and opened a tall, thin locker in the side of the pilot house. Six highly polished rifles gleamed in it, each in their own stand. Taking a Browning Double Automatic shotgun, he handed it to Ariana.

"You'll have to go on deck. Try and stay behind the rail," he said. "You'll be able to see them coming, if they come. Fire a blast into them. The rest will be kept busy chewing up their schoolmates for a while."

He went on deck, stripped to his shorts and lowered himself over the side. Submerged, he struck out for the stem of the vessel and saw that things were not as bad as he'd feared. A high ridge cut across the channel and the *Urchin* had cut into it all the way to the start of the aft cabin. But her screws were free and the ridge was sand, not mud. He knew what had to be done and it wouldn't be difficult. Just to make certain, he surfaced and swam around to the shore side of the boat, in case there was anything he'd missed on the other side. Ariana had crossed the deck to keep watch on him and as he surfaced he heard her short cry of terror.

"Behind you!" she gasped. He whirled just as the snake struck and he felt the fangs sink into his thigh. He saw the snake's head, lance-shaped, and the blue-gray marks on its hide as it swam quickly away, pointed like the tip of an arrowhead, and he knew he was in trouble. Ariana had tossed him a line and he grabbed it and pulled himself up. Her eyes, full of fear, told him his guess was right.

"Goddamn," he cursed and started for the cabin. "There's a snake-bite kit in the bathroom cabinet and serum in the refrigerator." She didn't have to be told to move fast and Logan felt the numbness in his thigh as he stretched out on the bunk. Damn my stinking luck, he swore silently. Though not a water snake, the fer-de-lance took to the water occasionally. Logan had had to be around on one of those occasions. The fer-de-lance was deadlier than the rattler, its poison swifter. He watched as Ariana ran back into the cabin with the serum in the hypodermic. She injected it quickly, making a face of her own as she did so. Then she made a tourniquet, put a suction cup on the small wound and began to suck out the blood. He let her, saying nothing. His life depended on two things, neither of which he nor anyone else could do a damn about. One was the serum. It either took, proved potent enough, or it didn't. The other was the possibility that being in the water had immediately washed out some of the venom. If that had happened, he might make it. Otherwise, the world population would go down by one. The water and the serum, one or the other or both. He closed his eyes. His leg was beginning to hurt.

The girl made two small razor-blade cuts in his leg and moved the tourniquet up and put the suction cup on the incisions. There is no need to worry about anchoring, Logan told himself. They were wedged into the sandbar and very secure. He lay still. The less movement the better. Ariana stood beside him, looking down at him.

"Maybe I can get help," she said. "I'll try to find a village."

He managed a grin. "Maybe something from a local witch doctor," he said.

"I can't just stand here," Ariana exploded.

"You can sit down," he said. "And that's about all you can do, now. The serum bottle says I can get another dose in eight hours. If I'm around to take it, that is. Don't worry. I'm not easy to kill."

His head was suddenly feeling very light and the cabin was doing funny things, moving around, getting smaller and larger and then smaller again. He closed his eyes. It didn't make much difference. He got a sharp stabbing pain in the abdomen and his legs drew up involuntarily. Drawing a deep breath, he relaxed his body and stretched out again. He wanted a drink of good bourbon but he was still conscious enough to know better. He snapped his eyes open with a determined effort and saw Ariana at the side of the bunk. She had brought a high stool over and was perched on it. Again he managed a reassuring smile. He hadn't been exactly kidding her. He was a hard man to kill. He was a hard man to do anything with. But it was that very hardness that would help him now, he knew. It took over and fought for him as his body began to pour perspiration and his breath grow shallow and labored. For a while he could hear himself breathing hard and then he lost contact with himself. A strange darkness settled over him that was neither death nor life but some nether world suspended in between. It was a funny world made up of shadows and names without voices, faces without bodies. He heard himself talking, calling out, but it was as if he were inside some giant bottle and everyone else was outside staring in at him. He saw faces from the past pressed against the glass, there for a moment and then vanishing before his eyes. He saw Willie the Beaver and Henny D'Angelo. He saw the big sign that said *Private* and he saw feet chasing, running, and guns that fired soundlessly. And then the faces and names all faded away and he heard himself calling out again, calling into emptiness.

Is that me shaking? he wondered. Is that my body that feels so cold? How could he be hot and cold all at once? Then suddenly, or it seemed suddenly, he was burning up, his body afire, his throat aflame and he lay still while the fire consumed him. It went on consuming him, and on and on until finally there was nothing and he was falling, falling. Darkness had been his, and now it wrapped itself even tighter around him, squeezing him into nothingness. Silence, utter silence, his mind turned off and he lay still.

It was far into the night, turning toward dawn, when the tall, lean man stirred and his eyes fluttered, then opened. The girl sitting curled up on the bunk opposite him was asleep, no more than a blurred outline at first. It was perhaps a half hour before his eyes could focus enough to see her as a person. He tried to lift his head but it wouldn't lift. He felt as though he had been turned inside out, was drained of every drop of blood, the limpest of limp rags. But as his eyes took in the cabin, every corner familiar to him, he smiled and there was a line of triumph in the smile. He was alive and now, consciously, he put together again what had happened. It had been the snake, of course, the goddamned snake in the water. Ariana had given him the serum and it had worked. Probably the venom had partially washed out in the water, too. Whatever had done it, he was alive and all the things that still waited to be done still lay ahead. But not now, not till morning. He managed to turn his head and go to sleep.

He woke first, in the morning, and saw Ariana in the bunk across from him, still asleep where she'd curled up. He felt less limp. As he struggled up on one elbow, he realized that he was in

something less than championship shape. The noise of his movement woke the girl and she jumped from the bed and was at his
side, her arms cradling his head against the white halter top, her
breasts pressed into his face. He had to admit it was a nice way
to be greeted.

"Oh, God, you're alive," she said, looking down at him. "I
didn't think you'd make it."

"I told you I'm hard to kill," he grinned, sitting up and letting
the dizziness go away.

"Did I put cold compresses on you!" she said. "All night, one
after another." He let his eyes search hers. The relief he saw there
was genuine enough. But all the deceits and lies and unanswered
questions flooded back into his mind and he knew that nothing
had really changed. He was alive and they were still heading for
the village of Quechayo and she was still playing it her way. And
he was going to get at the truth his way.

"I'll make tea," Ariana said. "It's what you need this morning."

Logan waited till she went to the galley, then he slid from the
bunk and tried his legs. They, wavered a while, then straightened
out. He stretched them, moved, put on trousers, and began to feel
alive. Ariana returned with the tea and it felt good, invigorating.

"You were delirious, you know," she said casually.

"I didn't know," he commented dryly.

"And you talked a lot."

He felt his jaw set and an invisible mask descend over his
face.

"Were you ever a private investigator, Logan?" she asked. He
chose his spare, terse answers carefully and let the smile stay on
his face.

"I sounded like that?" he said.

"Yes."

"As you said, I was delirious. God knows what I said. It could
have been anything."

She was looking at him out of the corner of her eyes, studying his impassive face, the smile that masked rather then revealed.

"Who was Nancy?" she asked casually.

It was hard keeping the smile but he managed it.

"Did I talk about a Nancy?" he asked.

"Not exactly talk," the girl said. "More like calling. In fact you called for a Nancy one and a Nancy two. Very confusing, I must say."

He shrugged. "To me, too," he said.

"You're lying, Logan," she said flatly.

"I'm just not remembering," he said. He got up. "I'm going to get us off this sandbar."

"You're not well enough," she said, quickly. "You need more rest."

"I'm all right," he said, almost angrily. He didn't tell her that her questions had sent cold determination and anger and pain through him like a shot of adrenalin. He had remembered, all right, with a memory that seared and burned. It was funny-sad how it always happened at the dark times, the times when he needed help. Her face or her name, it was always there. He climbed onto the seat before the wheel, switched on the engines, let them run for a moment and then put them into reverse at full throttle. The *Urchin* shuddered only a moment, then pulled back out of the sandbar. He reversed engines immediately, before he backed into some other ridge hidden in the murky water. He sent the boat forward at full speed, feeling her bite into the shallow water, protesting that there wasn't enough for her to grab. But she hit the sandbar and went right on through, spewing sand up into the water as the twin screws churned through it, and they were in free water again. He slowed down and proceeded at the deliberate pace they'd used all along. Ariana stayed below once again and he heard her pacing the cabin. The closer they came to Quechayo, the more she paced, and Logan's grin grew grimmer.

She refused to level with him. Her plans, whatever they were, stayed set, and so would his.

But progress was slow in the narrowness of the river. He saw four schools of piranha. He knew there were a lot more that he hadn't seen. It was still light but a gray hint of night was coloring the sky when they came into sight of the village, on their left, where she said it would be.

"Quechayo," he called to her and knew she'd be glued to a porthole. As they drew abreast of the village he saw four wharves jutting out from the bank and then the wooden houses amid the thatched leaf huts stretching back from the shoreline. Quechayo was larger than it appeared from the river bank. He glimpsed a half-dozen men wearing cartridge belts slung over their shoulders, carbines in their hands, watching him move by. Children waved and he waved back. He was past the village in a minute and he continued on, maintaining the slow, steady speed. About three-quarters of a mile ahead he saw another small island. It would be perfect for his plans. It was dark when he nosed around it and dropped anchor in midriver, off the far tip of the island. He moved around the *Urchin* in the dark, gathering bits and pieces of equipment from fore and aft. From the aft locker, he pulled out a small rubber raft and inflated it on the deck. Ariana had come out and offered to help. He cheerfully let her finish inflating it. While she was doing that, he took some canned food, a tin of biscuits and filled a plastic bottle with fresh water. He put all that into a plastic bag.

"What on earth is all that for?" Ariana asked, a small furrow creasing her smooth forehead.

"It's a CARE package," he said, cheerfully, and watched her frown deepen. He lowered the raft into the water and tossed a piece of dried meat he'd taken from the freezer into the river. The water boiled furiously for a minute and then subsided.

"The river is sure filled with them," he said to Ariana, and watched her shudder.

"I still don't understand what your 'CARE package' is for," she said.

"I might run into trouble in Quechayo," he said. "One never knows. I might have to lay low for a whole day. Meantime, you might get hungry on that island."

He saw her frown really deepen and her eyes darken.

"Just what do you mean by that?" she asked, her voice ominous.

"I mean that you've been lying to me from the start, you and Alvarez," Logan said. "Now I'm going to find out a few things for myself while you stay on that island. I know you won't be swimming off and I don't want you to get hungry."

"You'll do no such thing," she said, flaring. "And I haven't lied to you."

"That a girl, keep pitching," Logan said. "But you're going on that island unless you start leveling with me. Let's try the dental chart for openers.

He saw her eyes widen in surprise and his grin was cold. "Still want to play games?" he asked.

"Logan," she began, moving toward him, her eyes wide and deep. "Trust me. Please. I can't tell you more than that. Not now, anyway." Her hands were against his chest, her eyes imploring. She could be meaning every word, he knew. Or she could be a damned good little actress. It was natural to most women, anyway. But she'd forgotten that man at the porthole. He didn't take chances, not anymore.

"Sorry, doll," he said, his voice hard, unyielding. "I'm very poor at trusting, especially when I've been played along. The game is over. Talk or I take it alone."

The girl was going to try to reach the tall, stone-faced man again but the expression in his eyes told her it would be a waste of time. She stepped back, paused, and then made a flying dive for the bunk, reaching her hand under the mattress. But Logan had her wrist as her fingers closed over the snub-nosed Smith and Wesson .38 Police special. She had had the gun when she had come aboard and shot out the lights of the patrol boat, but he'd quite forgotten about it. She clawed at him with her other hand and he spun her around, turned her wrist backward and pressed. She cried out in pain and the gun fell from her grip. He caught it, spun her around and slammed her into the wall. She aimed a kick at his groin and he half-turned to take it on the leg. Eyes blazing fury, her voice half-sobbing in anger, she tried to duck under his arm. He brought a short, chopping right up that caught the very point of her lovely chin and she went down in a heap, rag doll fashion. He lifted her over his shoulder, took the plastic bag of food and went on deck. He lowered her into the raft and paddled to the island. She was still out as he dumped her on the sand and put the: bag of food beside her. He returned to the *Urchin*, got a large burlap bag from a closet, and took another look at the dental chart before he heard her call. Burlap sack in hand, the big Colt Python in his belt, he swung down onto the raft.

"Damn you, Logan," he heard Ariana call. "You don't know what you're doing. Take me with you." She could see him moving past on the little raft, paddling silently. He waved an arm to her and went on. She was right, of course. He wouldn't know if the body was really the guerrilla leader's or not. He'd find out when he returned with it to the boat. He took the raft downriver, almost to the very edge of the village of Quechayo, before he paddled into shore and pulled it up into the thick foliage. He didn't want to have to lug his grisly burden far. He'd never dug up a grave before. Hell, he wasn't even a member of the Gravediggers' Union.

CHAPTER EIGHT

The village of Quechayo, as he'd glimpsed when he and the *Urchin* passed by it, ran far deeper than it appeared to go. Making his way along the edge, he saw a number of well-built wooden houses and one clay structure surrounded by a cluster of smaller ones. The cemetery was the last thing in the village, almost outside it at the very far end and, when he reached it, he realized that neither he nor the girl had thought of the one thing needed for gravedigging, a shovel. But he was glad to see that the cemetery was a fairly large one with a tool shack to the side. He crept to the shack, found a shovel, and began to move silently among the small mounds. All had some sort of headstone or marking, in many cases merely a stick of wood with a name cut into it. Off to the right, at the very edge of the cemetery, he found the one he thought he wanted, marked with a wooden post and the initial *P.* dug into it. He was surprised that it was marked it at all. He pushed the shovel into the ground and tossed aside a clump of earth. The ground was soft and he could dig silently. Soon he had a sizable amount dug up and he saw the one end of a plain, pine box. He paused to wipe the perspiration from his hands and face. He wanted to get the hell away from this damn spot. The whole thing was giving him a very funny feeling. Dammit, he told himself angrily. Stop being a kid on Halloween and get on with it.

He got on with it but the feeling wouldn't go away. Good, small-town upbringing never really shook itself loose. The Golden Rule, church every Sunday, honor thy father and mother, respect for the dead and all the rest of the traditional virtues. He'd shot holes in most of them long ago and this made one more. The pine box was uncovered, now, and he put down the shovel. On his hands and knees, he reached down and lifted the cover of the crude casket. The corpse lay there, naked, looking more like some waxen figure than anything else. Logan saw the three small bullet holes in the chest, the discolored tissues surrounding each hole. He had expected more stench, and there was the smell of death, but it wasn't as bad as he'd feared. Formaldehyde had apparently been used in massive doses on the body and the interior of the pine casket and it had so far succeeded in keeping the hordes of creeping, crawling creatures to a minimum. Logan let his eyes rove over the body. Panico had been fairly tall but slender, his face thin and drawn, more so now, of course. The skin had started to pull together, making the body seem older then it actually was. He surveyed his prize, distastefully but with some satisfaction. He'd learned a little. There was a body buried under the marking *P*. And it had three bullet holes in it. That much tied in with the story of the guerrilla leader's possible death during the battle with the government forces. But was this really Panico? He'd hoped the man would have been clothed, with something on him to provide a clue. He decided he'd have a look at those teeth. He remembered which had been marked with the *X* on the chart. Maybe he'd find out that all the marks meant were that the teeth were missing.

He spread the burlap sack out and lay flat on the ground to reach down into the coffin. He got his hand onto an arm, cold, wax fruit, a brittle feel as though a little too much pressure would tear away the skin. He lifted, slowly, and the body started to rise, stiffly, and then with a dry, cracking sound, bent in two. Logan kept his mouth tightly closed. The body rose further. He had it almost sitting up when the voice cut through the night, a deep, clear voice.

"That will be enough, *amigo*," the voice said. "Put him back."

Logan didn't look up but just opened his hand and let the body slide from his grasp. It fell back into the coffin with a small thump.

"Now we will have a little talk, whoever you are," the voice said. Logan's eyes cast around and he saw boots, at least six pairs, with more coming to stand on the other side of the grave. He raised himself just enough to look behind him and see the big man standing there, a heavy, jowled face with a big nose and a drooping mustache under a white, floppy hat. The man wore a cartridge belt slung across his chest and two guns in a gunbelt. Behind him, in ragged, tattered clothes, three men waited, two with carbines. Logan turned his head to see the three standing on the other side of the open grave. Just past them was the forest.

"On your feet, *pronto!*" the big man with the floppy white hat commanded, impatience suddenly in his voice. Logan drew up one knee as if he were starting to rise and then, with one motion, he had the Colt Python in his hand and was firing in a sweeping arc. He didn't aim, he just let go a blast of lead in all directions. The big man and the others dived away as the heavy Colt slugs tore through the air. He heard two voices cry out in pain as he leaped forward, across the open grave, and streaked for the woods.

"*¡VIVO!*" he heard the big man yell. *Alive!* They didn't want him dead, not yet, anyway. He crashed into the thickness of the forest only to find it was filled with a reception committee. They had been there, in hiding, he realized at once, watching the gravesight. Two men tried a tackle and he kicked the first one in the face and heard him scream. The second one got his leg and Logan brought the heavy butt of the Colt down on the back of his head. The man dropped off like a fly. There was still a shot in the Colt and he fired pointblank at a wild-eyed character leaping at him. The figure spun in midair, kicking his legs out in a last protest against death, and fell at his feet. He whirled, swinging the butt end of the Colt in a wide arc as he heard others crashing up behind him. He saw the gun split the face of one man, sending a geyser of blood spurting from it and his attacker dropped to his knees, both hands clutched at his face. Logan kicked him hard and he went over backward. Logan ducked the vicious swing of a carbine and felt it graze his hair. He sunk his arm almost to the elbow into the riflewielding man's stomach and the figure doubled over. Logan grabbed the carbine just as someone slammed into him with a flying tackle, catching him around the middle. He brought the rifle down on the back of the man's neck but another figure leaped on his back He fell forward, twisting so that he landed atop the man on his back. He saw the butt of a rifle descending on him and he turned his head. The blow landed too high on his head and though he felt the sharp pain of it he was very much conscious. He grabbed at the legs nearest and yanked. Their owner fell in a tangled heap and Logan pulled free of the man under him. He came up swinging, felt his fists strike flesh and blood, felt figures giving way, falling, and then the blow hit hard against his temple, the stock of a carbine swung flat. He fell sideways to his knees. A kick sent him sprawling to the ground. He tried rolling over to catapult to his feet but they were on him, rifle butts and feet slamming into him. The lights began to go out. He shook his head, tried to grab at something, anything, and then blackness swept over him and he felt himself falling as if through a deep tunnel.

When he woke it was with light seeping through his fluttering eyelids, bright light, and the shapes swimming in front of him slowly took form. The first form was the big man, still wearing the floppy white hat. His drooping mustache materialized first and then the rest of his face, like an out-of-focus movie screen being brought into focus. Logan looked around. He was in a room with unpainted clay walls, some wooden chairs and a table. The big man was watching him and two others with rifles stood by the door. Logan saw that his hands were tied in front of him and he was lying in a corner of the room. At a signal from the big man, one of the guards came over and lifted Logan onto a chair. Head cleared, Logan's eyes narrowed as he noted the small window of the room, the one door. It opened as he looked at it and a girl came with black hair came into the room. She wore a low-necked peasant blouse and a green wool skirt. Large, heavy breasts swung pendulously as she leaned against the big man.

"That's him?" she asked, gesturing toward Logan, contempt in her eyes. "He does not look like so much."

"That's because you are a woman and a poor judge of fighting men," the man answered. "He has the body of a jaguar. And the disposition, too, I think."

Logan let a thin smile cross his face. The big man's eyes were serious.

"Who are you?" he said, suddenly. "How did they get you into this?"

"I was hired," Logan said. "The name is Logan."

"You are the fourth one to try to get to Panico," the big man said. "You are the only one to get through to the cemetery. Later you must tell me how you managed to get by our sentries. Unfortunately, the others were all shot and killed before we could question them. But you are alive."

He smiled, a not unpleasant smile. Only the glitter of his dark eyes revealed its real meaning. "If you want to stay alive, you will answer my questions," he said. "It is lucky we had men posted at the grave, watching from the trees, no?" He had turned to the woman and she nodded, her eyes still on Logan.

"I still cannot understand how he did so much damage," she muttered. "Jorge dead. Aquito dead. Morales, too. Poor Costallacho so badly hurt he cannot see to walk. Quinachi, too."

"Believe me, he did it," the man said. "But if we can get the truth from him it will have been worth it." He turned to Logan and his voice dropped a few notches as he spoke.

"You say you were hired," he began. "Who hired you?"

"A man named Alvarez," Logan answered.

"To bring back Panico's body, yes?"

Logan nodded. It was as good a story as any he could come up with at the moment.

"Why is Panico so valuable to them?" the big man shot out, quickly, pounding his fist into his palm. "Why must they have him?"

Logan studied the intensity in the man's eyes. It was an odd question, he thought. This big man had obviously taken over upon the death of the guerrilla leader.

"You ought to know the answer to that one," Logan said. The big man's eyes flickered for a moment.

"You tell me the answer," he said. "Maybe I am stupid." This man might be a lot of things but stupid wasn't one of them, Logan was convinced. His eyes were too bright, too quick, too canny. But he felt his own temper rising. What the hell kind of a cat and mouse game were they playing with him?

"They want him for the same reason you buried him here in this stinking little hole and put a guard around his grave," Logan said.

"We buried him here and put the guard out because we realized he was so valuable to Alvarez and his group," the man said.

"You're full of shit," Logan answered, his temper flaring. "You don't want it known that your great guerrilla leader, the spirit of your crummy revolution, is dead. No big leader, no big revolution."

"Ay!" it was the girl's voice. "He is *loco*, this one. Maybe he fights good but he is *loco*."

The big man held out a hand and she fell silent at once. "Wait a minute," he said. "Say that again, *amigo*. We have buried our dead leader, yes? And we don't want the people to know he is dead, eh?"

"That's right," Logan said, and suddenly he had a very funny feeling. The man seemed to be leading him along and suddenly he wasn't sure where the road was going.

"And our dead leader's name? Come, come, *amigo*. His name?"

"Maybe you are stupid," Logan said. "Panico."

He saw the big man shoot a glance at the girl, his lips open up in a soundless laugh. And then the sound followed, a deep-chested roaring laugh that started slowly and built up into a hurricane of bellowing. The girl has joined in and had buried her head in his wide chest. Logan watched with a strange uneasy feeling. Suddenly the big man stopped his roaring laughter and lashed out with one foot. His boot caught the front leg of the chair and, as he yanked, Logan went sprawling onto the floor. The boot lashed out again and he felt the sharp, stabbing pain as it landed in his ribs, rolling him over and into the wall. The big man was standing over him and Logan tried a kick of his own. He was in a poor position and the kick only grazed the man's kneecap.

"You know who is stupid, *amigo*?" Logan saw the drooping mustache quiver. "You are stupid, that is who."

He turned to the girl and the two guards, including them all in his bellow. "Who leads the movement?" he yelled.

"Camacho!" they said as one. "¡*Viva* Camacho!" The big man turned to Logan and pounded his chest with one huge fist.

"Me, Camacho," he roared. "I lead the people's movement. I lead the revolution."

A few things were snapping into place while an icy fury gathered inside Logan at the same time, things such as a figure in the cabin door yelling ¡*Viva* Camacho!, and Alvarez's pause at the name. Ariana, too.

"You are Camacho," Logan said, his voice flat. "And you lead the movement. Then who the hell is Panico?"

"One of Alvarez's men," Camacho said.

Camacho reached down, picked Logan up like a child and put him back on the chair. He was grinning broadly and Logan felt his temper rocket. He didn't like being taken. He didn't like being laughed at, either. A few things were falling into place, but only a few and not nearly enough.

"So that's what they told you, eh?" Camacho laughed again. "You were going to bring back the body of the big leader of the revolutionary movement so they could be sure he was dead."

"That's what they told me," Logan said flatly. Camacho laughed again and leaned into Logan's face.

"Tell me, do I look dead to you?" he roared, grinning.

"Not near dead enough."

"Watch your tongue," Camacho snarled. "I'm not sure I believe this crazy story of yours."

"Believe whatever you want," Logan said. "It happens to be the truth."

"And you do not know why this Panico is so valuable to Alvarez?" Camacho barked. Logan shook his head.

"I told you what they told me about him," he answered. *That* wasn't really a lie. He didn't know what made the corpse so damned important. He had a few new ideas, but he didn't really know.

"Take him away," Camacho suddenly barked at the guards. "I want to think about this a little bit more."

Logan was pulled to his feet and led outside. He saw he had been inside the largest of the clay structures he'd noted when he skirted the village. They led him to one of the smaller ones that half-encircled it, opened a door and threw him in. He landed on a dirt floor in a pitch-black room. Well, almost pitch-black, he noted, as a sliver of the outside night came in through an air hole about a foot long and three inches wide. His hands still bound in front of him, he crawled to one of the walls and sat down with his back to it. Alone in the dark, he tried to sort out what he had learned this far. The story he'd been given by Alvarez, and carried on by Ariana, had been simple, logical, easy to swallow. And he'd swallowed it, hook, line and sinker. He had had some misgivings and suspicions, finally, but he'd never really suspected the truth about Panico. And just what was the truth about the man? As Camacho had said, he was very important to Alvarez and his group. Logan wondered who the hell the group was if not the Peruvian Government. He wished he had the girl here and could wring some answers from her gorgeous lying little throat. But he brought his mind back to Panico. Alvarez and Ariana wanted to get to him and wanted it very badly, enough to hire him, make up a phony story and risk their own necks, or hers, anyway. Suddenly that dental chart began to make real sense. Panico was important, all right, and it had something to do with what was in his mouth. He was dead but he had plenty to say. Ariana had known that right along, of course. Her job had been to get at the body and those teeth. Identification was never even in the picture. If Alvarez had a group, what kind of a group was it? Were they in the Peruvian Government? Ariana was part of it, that was certain. Camacho's opinions couldn't be taken seriously, he knew. If they were really the Peruvian Government force, and had seen fit to tell him a story for their own reasons, Camacho would castigate them too. The man was a revolutionary, an antigovernment leader. Damn, Logan swore. He had to find a way out of this place. He could almost sympathize with Camacho's frustration. He was feeling pretty damned frustrated himself. They were all frustrated, Ariana, Camacho and himself, for different reasons. Camacho had a prize, a valuable corpse, and he didn't know why it was so damned valuable. Ariana had an island to herself and nothing more and he had a dark hole and the prospects of being killed before he ever really learned the truth. Damn, Logan muttered again. He started to crawl around the little cubicle in the dark, feeling with his hands for a sharp rock, a pointed stick, anything that might be used to cut the wrist ropes. But there was only loose soil on the ground and he got to his feet and ran his hands along the walls. The clay was rough but not rough enough. He scraped the ropes against one part, only to finally realize that all he was doing was making his wrists bleed. He slumped down on the ground again. They'd taken the Colt Python from him, of course, and searched him thoroughly. As yet, they hadn't tied him in with the little boat that had chugged past their stinkin' village earlier. He was sitting there, the night drifting toward dawn, and wondering why he hadn't just let Ariana do her bit and ignore the fact that she was lying to him. But if he had—he realized with a mirthless smile— they'd both be here together, now. Camacho's men, watching the grave, would have nabbed them both, and by now they'd have gotten the truth from Ariana or killed her. So maybe it was best this way, after all. He wanted to get back to her and choke her himself.

Time lost itself in the silent blackness of the little clay cubicle and Logan concluded that escape could only come through some break when he was taken outside. There was a small wooden door and he heard the sound of a guard on the other side of it. He sat there, still trying to piece together what Ariana had been after in Panico's mouth, and why. She still didn't fit into this kind of thing. But she was in it. Very much in it. Suddenly he heard the bolt of the door being pulled back. He got up and saw the door open. It was a woman, and he glimpsed the white, cotton scoop-necked blouse and skirt. He thought it was the woman who'd been with Camacho, until he heard the voice.

"There you are, you bastard," she said. She closed the door behind her and came toward him.

"I'll be damned," Logan said. "How the hell did you do it?"

"The guard? He was easy. I took these clothes from one of the women and just walked up to him. He thought I was one of the village belles coming over to be friendly. I got him to put down the gun and then I hit him with it."

"I was thinking about the piranhas," he admitted.

"Oh, that," she sniffed. "I got lucky. A big, fat piece of drift-wood came downriver and landed against the island. I just laid down on it and paddled to shore with my hands. Now, what did you do with Panico?"

"Nothing. Get these damned ropes off me," he said.

He saw her pull a knife from her belt and hold it in her hand, motionless. "Not until you tell me what you did with Panico," she said. "I saw the grave dug up and empty. Where did you hide the body?"

"Noplace," he repeated. "They nabbed me red-handed, or maybe it's dead-handed. Anyway, I was pulling him out when they came out of the woods. They must have decided to put him someplace else for a while."

She cut down on the wrist bonds with the knife and Logan felt his arms come free.

"Courtesy of the guard," she said, waving the knife.

"How did you know I was here?" Logan asked, rubbing his wrists.

"Your burlap sack was still by the grave. I thought, first, you'd had to make a quick exit with the body. Then I saw the guard stand-ing in front of this place, the only one with a guard in front of it. I figured it had to hold either you or Panico. Or maybe both of you."

"Disappointed?" he asked, grimly. He felt her hand on his arm. There was contriteness in her voice.

"I told you I'd explain it all to you in time. You refused to wait," she said. "Please give me a chance to make you understand."

"Oh, you'll get a chance at that, you can count on it," he answered. "And it better be good. But first I'm getting your pal, Panico, and find out what he has to say. Let's see, now, it was the two lateral incisors, two anterior molars and one upper canine. How's that for a quick read?"

"Logan," she said, a catch in her voice. "Please don't interfere. Just let me do what I have to do and we can get out of here."

"Interfere? Come on, baby, you must be kidding. It's my way from here on in. Either that or I'm taking the first, last and only boat leaving this glamour spot tonight."

He waited as she hesitated. Even in the blackness he thought he could see the set of her jaw and her eyes, dark, reflecting the way her mind was clicking off the possibilities. She needed him. She couldn't lug the corpse back alone. Or, probably even find it on her own. There was no telling what she might run into, now. He gave her twenty seconds. She took fifteen.

"All right, we do it your way," she said. Logan grinned in the dark.

"Smart girl," he said. "Let's move."

He opened the door a crack and looked out into a semicircle of clay huts. The guard's body lay on the ground, alongside the rifle. Logan picked up the gun and smashed him on the temple again with the butt. "Insurance," he grunted. He gazed up at the sky. It told him that in less than an hour it would be dawn.

"I don't think they'd stash Panico in anyone's parlor," he said. "Let's try these huts."

They moved on silent feet to the nearest hut, opening the door carefully, only to find it empty. So was the next, and the next. They were only two from the end when they found the naked corpse lying on the ground inside the hut. Logan cast another look at the lightening sky.

"No time for any dentistry now," he said. "We take him with us. I wish to hell you'd brought my burlap sack."

Making a face, the tall, lean man scooped up the naked corpse. He slung it over one shoulder and started out with it. It wasn't heavy, just strangely slippery, as though it were made of a poor grade of plastic. When they reached the woods he dropped the corpse to the ground and, holding one arm, pulled it along after him.

"Can't you carry it?" Ariana asked. "It seems so, well, indecent this way, dragging it along like a piece of beef."

"Don't flatter him," Logan said. "You want to carry him?"

That ended the conversation and they were silent till they reached the raft at the edge of the river. Logan cast another anxious look at the sky. He knew all hell would break loose when dawn came and he wanted to be aboard the *Urchin*. "You hold and I'll paddle?" he said, but Ariana had the paddle in hand already. He shrugged and laid the corpse over his lap as he sat, yoga-fashion, in the raft. It was a tight fit.

"Get going," he said tersely. "This place is going to be alive with Camacho's boys within the hour."

"You think they'll suspect us of heading for the river?"

"I think they'll look everywhere. They'll cover all the bases. Besides, this row in the moonlight does nothing for me. Your friend here is a lousy conversationalist."

She paddled steadily and the sky grew lighter steadily. They reached the *Sea Urchin* just as the dawn came up in its first, misty-gray light. Carrying Panico under one arm, he pulled himself aboard the *Urchin*, tossed the corpse on the deck and took in the little raft as Ariana came up. He saw something metal glint in her hand as she knelt down beside the corpse. He turned to watch her and saw it was a dentist's pliers. She forced the jaws open on the corpse and Logan could see the grimace around her mouth, her lips drawn tight, and the strained tension of her face as she fought to control her feelings. He knelt down a few paces from her and watched as she extracted first one tooth, then another, then another, checking with the dental chart each time. Finally she was done and she had the five teeth clenched in her fist. She got up and Logan noticed the dry paleness of her face, her hard breathing.

"I'll take those," he said quietly.

"No," she said. "Please, Logan. Stay out of this. I have what I came for. Let's just go."

"Let's have them." His voice was colder, deeper.

"Why, Logan?" she asked, despair in her voice. "We can go now, so let's go. It's not your concern."

"Maybe it wasn't, once. It is now. The five choppers, Ariana. Give."

"They don't matter, now, Logan," she said. Her eyes were begging him, her voice imploring. "Let's just leave while we can."

"They do matter to me," he said. "What I'm doing matters. Why I'm doing it matters. Truth matters. Give, doll, or I'll knock yours out to go with the five you have."

He held out his hand. As she dropped the five teeth into it he saw her eyes turning from despair to anger. Logan took the teeth and went down into the cabin and pulled down the fold-out table. He knew that by now the village of Quechayo was erupting. He ought to get under way. But he also knew that once he did so it would take every bit of his concentration to get them back downriver alive. There could be no sandbars, no hang-ups, and there'd have to be speed. Once under way there'd not be another chance for him to get at the truth, not until they'd reached the wide-open waters of the Pacific and that was at best an even-money bet, now. So he had to take the time now to learn the truth. It wouldn't be there to take later, Camacho or no Camacho.

He laid the five teeth out on tire little table, took out his small fishing box and picked up a good, strong three-inch marlin hook. Working quickly, he dug at the filling in the center of the first tooth. He dug hard, casting a look at Ariana. She stood against the bunk, arms folded across her lovely breasts, glowering at him. The filling crumbled and came loose under the sharp point of the hook. He got the hook into a corner, pulled, and the whole thing came out and with it a tiny, rolled piece of material. He picked it up and smoothed it out. It was a tiny piece of microfilm.

"Interesting fillings your friend Panico has," he commented as he took a magnifying glass from the chart drawer. The message on the microfilm leaped in legibility under the magnifying glass and he read it aloud.

"Bechano: 776-654-00G," he read, frowning. He laid the little piece of microfilm aside and dug the fishhook into the filling inside the next tooth, certain of what he'd find. The filling came out and with it a second piece of microfilm. Once more he read it aloud and this time a slow smile spread over his face as he did so.

"Alvarez: 45533-22G," he intoned and cast Ariana a glance.

"Logan, let's get away from here. Please," she said.

"One more," he said, picking up the third tooth, the molar. "This won't hurt a bit. Or will it?"

But the third one did hurt. He saw it in her black eyes as he read from the tiny bit of film that came out with the filling.

"dos Vayez: 881-00-343G," he read. He saw the pain deep inside her eyes as, his face stem, hard, he took the piece of microfilm and held it up to her.

"Your father?" he said and Ariana nodded.

"My brother, too," she added. Logan held up the last two of the teeth.

"In one of these?" he asked and she nodded. Her eyes blinked, slowly, carefully.

"These are microfilm records of numbered accounts in a Swiss bank, aren't they?" he said quietly. He didn't need an answer. Her silence was more then enough, her pain-filled eyes an exclamation point to it.

"What is your father in the Peruvian Government?"

"He is minister of Economic Development."

"Your brother?"

"Purchasing agent for the Defense Department." She anticipated his question. "Alvarez is head of internal security forces. The others are both cabinet ministers."

Logan dropped the two remaining teeth and the three tiny bits of microfilm into a small plastic bag he took out of the fishing box. He gazed at the girl as he did so. The pieces were all finally falling into place and, as he'd feared, they were falling into the wrong places for him, ugly places, sordid, corrupt places.

"Your father and brother, Alvarez, the others, they've been using their position to play in graft and corruption and stealing," he said. "And they've been putting a bundle away in numbered accounts in Swiss banks. Nice going."

Ariana was opening her mouth to say something, a denial, probably, but she ended up saying nothing.

"Where did old Panico fit in?" Logan asked.

"He was a cousin of Alvarez," she answered. "He took the monies to Switzerland for deposit. This way, if he were caught, there'd be nothing on him to implicate anyone, no instructions, no deposit slips, no account numbers, nothing."

"No wonder you wanted him back so badly," Logan mused aloud. "And who says the dead can't talk? And what about you, Ariana? Where do you come into this?"

"I never knew anything about it until a month ago, after Panico was killed, quite by accident, when the guerrillas attacked a government force he was with. My father told me everything then. I was the only one they could trust to try and get the teeth. All efforts to get at the body had failed."

"Blood being thicker than water and all that sort of thing," Logan added. "So you agreed to go right in with their little plan. That makes you no damn better than they are, just one more crook and lying thief."

He saw Ariana's eyes lose their hurt look and a fire flare in them. "Try something else, like human, or weak," she said. "I'll admit to that. I grew up in my world and I want to keep it. In my country, people's worlds are further apart than in yours. When I learned that my world, or some of it, anyway, had been bought by stolen money, I was shocked and hurt. I couldn't believe it. They convinced me how true it was. Being hurt and shocked and disillusioned is one thing. Loving your father and brother is something else. You don't turn your back on your family. You don't turn your back on all the things you've grown up to enjoy and want and believe in."

"Why not?" Logan heard the harshness of his voice. "Didn't you learn that corruption is corruption, that stealing is stealing, that wrong is wrong? Didn't they teach you that in all those fancy schools?"

"You can't understand at all, can you?" she asked, her eyes wide, sad, now.

"Sure I can. It happens all the time," he said. "It's more important to be comfortable than honest. But a crook is still a crook, no matter how comfortable he is."

"And who gave you the right to be so moral, to judge so?"

"I'm not being moral. I'm just mad at being sold a bill of goods. I don't like being swindled on anything. You said you were the good guys, against the Commie revolutionaries trying to wreck your country. Hell, all you're after is protecting your own racket. Maybe Camacho ought to have these choppers. Maybe they're the good guys."

"They're swine," Ariana blazed. "They'd use that evidence to bring down the government. They'd use it to take over and turn the country into a dictatorship run by Camacho."

He half-smiled to himself. In her own, crazy way she was terribly upset at that thought. The idea of her father and brother stealing the government blind, of five highly placed officials being part of a corrupt regime, didn't phase her. That wasn't all that unusual, he concluded. We're never as bothered by our own misdeeds as we are by those of others. And corruption was a built-in part of the political scene. It became almost acceptable. Revolutionary movements were an outside threat. Hell, he reminded himself, he didn't know Camacho or what he stood for anymore than he really knew the make-up of the Peruvian Government. He wasn't going to make political decisions. There was an established government and there was Camacho and they could fight their differences out with each other. He kept remembering a certain character once called an idealist on a little island called Cuba. Maybe Camacho was another Castro. Maybe he was something better. All maybes. The only real thing he had was evidence of five corrupt thieves and he knew that he would act on that. He wasn't sure yet just how, but he knew he would find a way. He put the little plastic packet into his pocket.

Ariana's eyes met his and he felt sorry for this beautiful and headstrong girl. She'd been torn by this. He was even sorrier she hadn't come up with a better answer to it.

"What now, Logan?" he heard her ask, quietly. "Now that you know everything, what are you going to do?"

A rifle shot supplied his answer.

"Get the hell out of here, first," he said, racing up to the deck. He stayed low, crouching, as he made the pilot house. There were three of Camacho's men on the shore and as he looked over at them he saw two disappear into the woods. Ariana had followed him on deck.

"Stay low and get the anchor up," he said, kicking the engine over. The Diesel coughed, then roared into life. The man on shore sent another shot at the boat and he heard the slug whistle past the pilot house. Ariana had crawled into the pilot house now and stood beside him. The *Sea Urchin* started moving forward and Logan steered around the far side of the island, away from the shore where Camacho's men waited. It was the wrong side of the island to take but the Tinina was hardly crowded with river traffic.

"Here, take this key and open that locker," Logan said to the girl. He watched as she pulled open the gun locker and gave him back the key. She took out one of the rifles, the Mossberg 640-K with the telescopic sight.

"You get behind the rail and shoot at anything that heads for us or shoots at us," he said. "I'm going to keep us moving. If they really try to rush us I'll join you. Other than that, I want to stay at the wheel. There's extra ammo on the floor of the closet."

"All right," she said. "But first, I want that little package back."

Logan looked around to see the Mossberg aimed at his chest, Ariana's face behind it calm, immobile.

"Go to hell," he said and turned away. He'd call her bluff. Without him, she wouldn't get more than a few miles downriver. The Mossberg's roar was deafening inside the pilot house and Logan felt the bullet crease his belly as it tore by him and imbedded itself into the wood. He jumped back from the wheel in reflex action.

"You're crazy," he said. "How far do you think you'd get without me?"

"I don't know," she said, her voice tight. "Just give me the package. Now."

He had thought to reason with her, or that she'd see for herself she needed him but he realized that she wasn't reasoning any longer. She was reacting only to what she'd done, the pressures that had been on her, to the things he'd said that had struck deep. It was in the wild-frightened look of her eyes, all of it, the inner turmoil, the panic, the emotional torture. Just then, the *Urchin's* nose came around the end of the island and three shots rang out. Logan dropped down, automatically, and he saw Ariana do the same. Staying low, he moved across the floor of the pilot house almost to her side. But the Mossberg was still pointed at him.

"Let's do our fighting later or neither of us will get back," he said and suddenly she was against him, trembling in his arms, her face buried in his shoulder.

"Logan, I don't want to fight with you," she said. "I want you to come with me. Please."

"We'll see," he said, letting a smile cross his face. Her deep eyes were searching his, now, looking for some sign of reassurance and compassion. He put a hand against her cheek, tenderly.

"We'll talk more, later," he said. "We'll find time. Right now you better get down to that rail."

She nodded, her eyes suddenly misty, and crawled away, moving outside to the rail of the *Urchin*. He could see her from the pilot-house window as he took the wheel. The shots had come from the shore and he saw the same figure ducking back into the

ALAN JOSEPH

trees as the boat swung out into midriver. Logan increased speed
as another shot rang out, passing harmlessly over the top of the
pilot house. A few more shots whistled past them as they moved
downriver and he saw Ariana looking up at him.

"What are they doing?" she called.

"Keeping pace with us," he said. "They probably have two
or three men moving along with us just at the line of the trees.
They're making sure we don't ditch the boat and take off."

"And the others?"

"Preparing a surprise for us, I'm sure." He slowed the engines
as he saw the water curling up on the surface, indicating a sandbar beneath. He moved the *Urchin* across it carefully, feeling the
churning of her propellers in the shallowness of the water. Then
he gunned her again and they moved forward. But he knew,
grimly, that real speed was impossible. On shore, even moving
through the jungle trails, Camacho and his men could make better time. And they were there, someplace behind the green wall.
He stepped to the gun closet and took out two more of the rifles.
He put one beside the wheel and handed the other out the window to Ariana.

"Stay low," he cautioned as she moved over to take it. "Keep
it with you just in case they try a sudden rush. It'll save time
reloading."

She had returned to the rail and sat on the deck, looking up
at him at the wheel.

"Logan," she called to him. "I would have told you everything. Later. I would have. Please believe me."

"I believe you," he said, and he wasn't lying. She would have
told him the truth, he knew. After she'd shown him all the things
of her world, after she felt she'd softened him up enough so he
could no longer reject what she offered. It wouldn't have worked.
He knew that and he knew that was something she couldn't make
herself believe. She'd lived all her young life in a world where
having what you wanted was taken for granted, where pleasure

was the most important thing in it. In that kind of world, all the principles and the teachings are nothing more than pleasant abstractions.

"Logan," he heard her call again and he peered out the window at her. "What about him?" She was pointing a finger at the corpse on the other side of the deck. He'd forgotten about Panico in their hurry to move on and the hot sun was beginning to make him something less then fragrant. He locked the wheel in place and scurried down to the deck.

"Let's make a show of it," he said. "It'll keep them busy a while."

He dragged the corpse to the side facing Camacho's men and heaved it into the river, watching for a moment as the current immediately seized it and started to push it toward shore. He knew he wasn't the only one watching and he smiled, grimly, as he went back to the wheel. Another dammed island was coming up and he began to steer around it. He would be on the far side when the body hit shore but he knew there'd be a scramble of arms waiting to pull it in. He turned his attention back to making the best time they could. Camacho had apparently faded away with his main force. Logan knew better. He had one girl, six rifles, a boat and a lousy little river between himself and Camacho. He felt the little plastic package in his pocket. Maybe bargaining would be a lot smarter than fighting. Their fives against the microfilm and the two teeth. Maybe Camacho ought to have it, anyway. But Logan tossed away the thought as quickly as it had entered his mind. That would be taking sides and he had no right to do that. He looked down at Ariana on the deck, at the long-stemmed beauty of her and he doubted whether she'd let him even bargain with the guerrilla leader. Perhaps her idea of principles was vague and undefined but her loyalties were firm and clear. What the hell, he wasn't much for bargaining, anyway. Not unless there was no other way, and that remained to be seen.

CHAPTER NINE

I t was late afternoon and they'd only had an occasional stray
shot from the shore. Ariana felt the tension inside her building up to almost unbearable heights. Only the presence of the
tall, lean, hard-faced man at the wheel kept her from diving
overboard and fleeing, running from all of it, from her decisions, her loyalties, her desires. Why did they always have to
conflict so? She glanced up at Logan, at the hard handsomeness
of his face and she wanted so to be in his arms again, and to
feel his hands caressing her body. It was all right, then, when
he made love to her. Everything wrong disappeared. It would
be night, soon. Maybe she could have that world once more.
She shook her head angrily. The night wouldn't bring safety. It
would only bring increased danger. His eyes would not be for
her but for the dark shadows of the shore. His arms would hold
the cold steel of a rifle and not the soft warmth of her breasts.
Dammit, she swore, silently. Somehow, she had to find a way
to reach this uncompromising man. She couldn't lose him. She
needed the strength he had to give, the courage that could make
her do what was right, not what was best. If she could wrap
herself around his magnificent body once more, perhaps he'd
realize he could not turn away from her. She suddenly laughed,
silently. She'd often talked of love, with the girls in college, her
friends, the usual social chatter of and around the subject. But
she'd never come up with a definition that really satisfied her
and now, here on this horrible little river, with her life in danger, she'd come up with as good a one as any she'd ever heard.

Love is someone you can't turn away from, no matter what. She looked up at Logan, his deep, probing eyes shifting from side to side, and she knew he could always turn away. Yet, he must have loved once, terribly deeply. No matter, she could bring enough for two and in time, he'd love again as he had once.

It was getting dark and they were rounding a bend in the river. She moved from the rail and went up to the pilot house, just in time to see Logan cut the engines.

"Look at what they've rigged up for us," he commented and she gazed ahead to see the double row of rowboats and canoes stretched across the river from shore to shore. Six guerrillas with rifles were spaced across the double row of boats. Each boat had a burlap sack or blanket stretched across it and Logan brought the *Urchin* to a halt. It was nearly dark and he dropped a small hand anchor in midriver, just heavy enough to hold them still.

"Why are you stopping?" Ariana asked. "If you got up speed, we could crash right through those little boats."

"It would seem so," Logan said. Ariana searched his eyes.

"What are you thinking?" she asked.

"That Camacho isn't stupid," he answered. "That would occur to him, too."

"But he put them there?"

"He probably figures we'll wait till dark and then slam through. I think his little boats are some sort of booby trap and I'm going to find out."

"Meanwhile?"

"Meanwhile we sit tight till it's dark."

"And while we're sitting here they can swim out to board us."

"No, not now, anyway. They've set up this one and they'll go with it. They'll wait for us to make the next move."

He felt the girl's head against his shoulder as he moved back against the wall. He slid down to the floor to rest and she came with him, her body pressed against his. He turned to her and found her lips as the blackness closed over them and her tongue was eager as ever, searching, probing, asking. She took his hand and thrust it against her breast and gasped as he let his thumb gently caress her pink tip. Finally, he pulled back.

"Easy, honey," he murmured. "This is not the time."

"I know," she said. "I just wanted you for a moment, anyway. I needed that. We will talk again, when this is over, you promised."

"I promised," he said, getting to his feet and pulling her with him. "Think we're downriver enough to be out of piranha waters?" he asked.

"Oh, yes," she said, quickly. Logan pointed to a switch on the instrument panel.

"This puts on the searchlight. You can make it revolve and direct it from these two little levers alongside. Give me two minutes and then put on the light. Keep it pointed down into the water and revolving around the boat. That way you can catch anyone trying a sneak approach. When I come back, I'll swim under the boat and rap three times against the port side. Turn off the light, then."

"Where are you going?"

"To have a look at those boats," he said, starting down to the deck. He moved over the rail and lowered himself quietly into the water. It was warm and thick. He swam downriver with slow, measured strokes, noiselessly. As he neared the line of rowboats that had been stretched across the river he saw the outlines of the two nearest men sitting on the boats. He dived and swam underwater, passing under the double-row of boats and surfacing on the other side. Treading water, he moved to the two rowboats in between the first and second sentry. Grasping the gunwale lightly, he hung there for a moment, watching the sentries, ready to submerge in an instant But the two men peered steadily ahead toward the *Urchin* a half-mile up river. Slowly, he reached one arm up and pulled back the blanket inside the boat. There were two clusters of dynamite sticks, one at each end of the boat, with the fuse string running across into the next boat.

He put back the cover and slipped below the surface of the water again, swimming back beneath the boats, staying underwater till he was a safe distance from them before surfacing. He hadn't looked into the other boats. There was no need to do so. He knew they'd have the same cargo, more dynamite. He saw the *Urchin's* searchlight revolving around her and he swam toward it, surface diving when he neared the swiftly moving circle of light. He came up under the port side and rapped three times against the hull. The light went out and he surfaced, drawing a deep breath. He took the line Ariana tossed out and climbed aboard to rest on the deck, catching his breath.

"Dynamite inside the boats," he said. "As soon as we began a run to smash through, one of those six jokers they put there as fake sentries would light the fuse and they'd all take off. It'd blow up in our faces as we reached the boats."

Ariana's face was set, frightened. "So what do we do now?" she questioned.

"Beat them at their own game," he said. "That's why I came back. I want my cigarette lighter in the drawer beneath the wheel. You'll find a fish-bait knife there, too." She was back in moments with both things.

"Give me another five minutes then switch the light back on and keep it revolving," Logan said. "It'll keep them thinking we're both on board."

He kissed her, taking her by surprise, and grinned at her. "That's for luck," he said and disappeared over the side. Once again in the tepid water, he swam silently, using long, deliberate strokes, grateful for the inky blackness of the night. Nearing the line of rowboats and canoes, he surface dived again to come out behind them. He stayed near the end of the line of boats and came up behind the first of the six waiting guerrillas. This would be tricky, he knew. One wrong move, one sound on the man's part, and the whole idea would go up in smoke. But he had to be fast and being fast would cause problems of its own. If the man toppled into the water, one of the others would hear it, peer over and find him gone. He was almost directly behind the guerrilla, now, and he drew the razor-sharp bait knife from his belt. The man was sitting crosslegged in the boat. Logan, moving noiselessly, rested his left hand lightly on the gunwale of the boat and then, with one motion, pulled himself half-out of the water and brought the knife around in a fast, vicious slash. It almost severed the man's head and at the same instant, Logan had his other arm around the guerrilla's body and was pulling him from the boat and into the water, lowering him silently into the river. He submerged with the man, keeping him underwater just to be sure. Finally, he let the limp body go and pushed it away, letting the river current carry it downstream. Holding onto the boat, he reached in and severed the fuse on both clusters of dynamite sticks. He hung there a moment, pausing for breath, drying his hands by rubbing them along the inside of the rowboat. Then he took the fuse, tied it together and bypassed the dynamite in the first boat. He made his way to the second and cut those fuses also. Then he spliced the cut fuse onto the other and bypassed the dynamite on the second boat. He now had a long fuse running to the dynamite in the third boat where the second sentry sat.

Once more he submerged to come up again directly behind the man. He was about to draw the knife from his belt when something made the man turn, perhaps instinct. He saw Logan, half-out of the water, and his eyes widened. There was only time to clasp a hand over the man's mouth and pull. The sentry came off the boat and into the water with Logan's hand still over his mouth. Logan submerged and felt the man's hands clawing at his eyes. He released his hold on the man's mouth and grabbed him by the throat. He held tightly as the man thrashed and kicked and swallowed more of the river. With the desperate strength of the dying, he twisted and tore free of Logan's grip. He started for the surface but Logan got his ankle and pulled hard. The man came down and suddenly Logan felt his struggles turn off, almost the way a wind-up toy turns off with a sudden cessation, a last, feeble shudder. Logan's lungs were searing. He hadn't had time to take a proper breath before diving and he struck out for the surface, seeing blackness before his eyes, his head starting to pound dangerously. He broke the surface and gasped in the life-giving air and saw he'd drifted down some twenty yards from the boats. He trod water for a few minutes to regain his breath and then returned to the third boat. Once again he cut the fuses to the two dynamite clusters and spliced the cut pieces onto the long fuse that now ran across three boats to the fourth one. Enough, he decided.

He swam, underwater, back to the first of the rowboats and surfaced again. Taking out the cigarette lighter, he lit the fuse and waited to make certain it had caught properly. Then he dived beneath the boats and struck out for the *Urchin*. The long fuse would give him time to reach the *Urchin* before it burned down to the dynamite in the fourth boat. This time he paid no attention to the revolving fight and called out to Ariana as he swam into it. He saw her put down the Mossberg and douse the beam. He clambered aboard, rested for a moment on one knee, and then hurried to the wheelhouse. He turned the engines on to full and the *Urchin* roared into life. There was no time to pull the hand anchor. As the boat roared forward, her prow sending up sprays of the murky river water, the night suddenly exploded in a gigantic fireworks display as the dynamite went up. Against the red-orange flames he saw bits and pieces of rowboat and canoe sail into the air, silhouetted against the brilliance of the flash. In seconds, a barrage of rifle fire erupted from both shores, most of it wild, whistling harmlessly around the *Urchin* as she sped through the water. He kept the throttle wide open and the brilliant night-lighting flash of the explosion disappeared as the *Urchin* hit the debris of the rowboats and sailed on through.

"Put on the light," Logan shouted at the girt "I can't see where the hell I'm going!"

The searchlight came on, sending its blue-white eye ahead, lighting a path for them, and the rifle fire came to a halt. Ariana's arms were around his neck, her soft breasts pressing into his back as she came up behind him.

"We've made it," she exclaimed happily.

"They'll try again."

He felt his eyes growing heavy-lidded, and fatigue was wrapping itself around him like a too-tight suit. He held on till they skirted another of the islands and then he pulled into midriver and dropped the regular anchor.

"I've got to get some sleep," he said. "Or I won't be worth a damn come morning. You too."

Ariana nodded. "We'll take turns standing watch," Logan said. "Two-hour shifts. I have a feeling they'll let us alone for tonight."

He lay down on the floor of the pilot house and in seconds he was asleep. Ariana sat on the seat by the ship's wheel, the Mossberg in her hands. Despite what the lean man had said, she felt confident. About a lot of things.

CHAPTER TEN

L ogan took over in two hours and watched the girl's sleeping form on the floor beside him, the regular rise and fall of her breasts, the soft, long curve of her thighs and, despite his fatigue, he felt himself wanting to move down on top of her. She was a strange girl, this Ariana dos Vayez, so maturely determined in some things, so much of a little girl in others. And she got to you. With her beauty she got to you. With her wild, passionate body she got to you. Yes, even with her wrong-headed loyalties, she got to you. But he knew that if they got down the Tinina, if they got away from the infuriated guerrilla leader, they'd still part bitterly. He wouldn't walk her side of the street and she still hoped he would. He knew that. He could see it in her eyes, that and something more. He'd seen it in the eyes of many women. They had learned that he couldn't give all that they wanted. Some he had told beforehand, and they didn't believe him. Others he only told after, and they didn't believe him. But they all came to accept it, some with anger, some with bitterness, some with sadness. Yes, there'd been a few who managed some form of understanding, but only a few. He wondered how it would be with Ariana. Furious anger, he told himself. Her passion and her temper would see to that. And so he contented himself with watching her lovely body stir in its sleep and remembering the warm feel of her legs around him, her lips on his. She woke some three hours later and he caught a few more hours, finally waking refreshed enough to go on. The sun was out in full and Ariana made coffee.

"See anything during the night?" he asked.

"Nothing," she said. "Not a sign. Do you think they've given up?"

His eyes answered her. "Didn't you say Camacho's people control most of this area down to the coast?" he asked.

"Yes," she said. "But we made good time yesterday. We could reach the coast by midnight, couldn't we?"

"If we can keep going steadily," he answered. "But they've gone ahead of us again, you can bet on it. They've got to. It's their only way to get at us, to set up something and wait."

He pulled up anchor and started the *Urchin* downriver, faster than he should, his eyes once again glued to the water ahead, watching for current changes, churning whirlpools, all the signs of shallow bottom. But they made good time and he was beginning to think that perhaps he'd been overly pessimistic. Maybe Camacho had retired after the *Urchin* had got through his elaborate booby trap. Yet it was not like the man. He had seen too much pride in those eyes and the guerrilla knew that whatever it was Panico had that made him valuable was now in their possession. No, he wouldn't quit till they reached the Pacific. The afternoon sun came, paused high in the heavens and started to slip down toward evening, and still there was no sign of the guerrilla force. It was too quiet, and as they nosed around one of the sharper bends, his fears were confirmed. Camacho he saw, had gathered every one of his crummy little group. Across the river, stretched from tree to tree, they had put a rope bridge. It would just clear the *Urchin's* pilot-house roof, and it was sagging with the weight of the guerrillas clinging to it. He slowed the boat and surveyed the scene. Beyond the bridge—in rowboats, canoes, dugouts and rafts—the rest of his men waited on both sides. He slowed the *Urchin* further, barely moving forward, as his mind raced. He couldn't see the guerrilla leader who had probably stayed on shore. His guess was confirmed as he heard Camacho's voice, amplified by a megaphone.

"You out there," he heard the man's voice. "You, Logan. Listen to me." The guerrilla paused for a moment and then went on. "Give us what you took from Panico and we will let you go," he called. "We saw from his body that you took five teeth from him. We want what was in those teeth."

He lapsed into silence and waited for a reply. He didn't get one. Logan was too busy trying to figure out their best chance to get through and he decided there was no best chance. The forward mast would hit the rope bridge. It would probably snap off, but whether it did or didn't, it'd knock a few of them off into the water. The rest figured to drop down aboard the boat as it passed under them. Then the others in their little craft would swarm in from both sides to board them. Logan looked at Ariana. There was fear in her eyes and angry determination in the set of her jaw. He asked himself why the hell he didn't just give Camacho what he wanted and he knew the answer at once. Stubbornness.

Logan reached into the gun closet and took out another of the rifles, leaning it against the wood near the wheel.

"You stay in here," he told the girl. "It's as good a spot as any. Get up against the side and just keep shooting."

He glanced at her again. "Want to change your mind and give up?" he asked. Her head shook impatiently. "I'll be right back," he said. He jumped down to the deck, moving quickly, and down into the large hatchway to the engines. He took only a few moments and when he returned to the pilot house he no longer had the little plastic package with him. He took the wheel, reversed engines to gain more headway, and pulled the throttle to full speed ahead. He pointed the *Urchin* for the right-hand end of the rope bridge as she sent river water spraying up from her prow. Just beyond the bridge, where the boats were gathered on either side, the river was just wide enough for a tight circle. If he timed it right, and had a little luck, he'd make the boarding party work for their dinner.

The *Urchin's* mast slammed into the rope bridge, bent, and snapped. But guerrillas were dropping into the river on all sides as they passed under the bridge. He saw three of them come down on the forward deck. Ariana's Mossberg was firing and they never got a chance to get up. He heard the thump of two more landing, one on the starboard deck amidship, the other aft. Ariana poked the rifle out the right window and fired. He heard the man topple overboard. They'd passed the rope bridge, now, and he swung the wheel hard to port and locked it in place. The *Urchin,* moving at full speed, started to wheel in a tight circle, slamming into rowboats and canoes, scattering them in all directions. The circling vessel made boarding much harder and almost eliminated any attempts from the port side inside the circle. The door of the pilot house flew open but Logan had been expecting it and his rifle barked first. The guerrilla arched backward and fell to the deck.

"He was from the bridge," Logan commented. "You cover the port side. I'll take the starboard."

He ran on deck, a rifle in each hand. Three of them had managed to get a hold forward and were climbing up the side. He fired three times and they were gone. A bullet slammed into the wood a half-inch from his head. He dived flat on to the deck, whirled and fired at the figure climbing over the stern rail. The guerrilla fell heavily, landing in a crumpled heap on the deck. He heard Ariana's rifle firing on the port side and then he saw more clambering up over the stern. He moved aft, firing as he went, and more figures toppled back into the river. Then he heard the thump of boats against the bow, whirled and saw another cluster of figures climbing over the rail. He fired and the rifle barked once and fell silent. He threw it at a black-haired figure climbing aboard amidship and saw it smash into his temple. He slid back into the river. Logan ran forward, firing with the other rifle. Two figures fell to lie across the rail, half-in and half-out of the boat. A shot grazed his head and he felt the trickle of wet across his scalp.

He dropped to one knee and whirled, firing at the figure on the aft deck. The guerrilla dived to safety behind the pilot house. They were coming over the starboard rail now, leaping up and hanging on, and though he was firing as fast as he could, there was always another one clambering aboard. More shots were coming his way and he dropped to the deck and started to crawl toward the pilot house. He heard Ariana scream, and the sound of glass shattering. He got to his feet, firing furiously, racing up the few steps to the pilot house. His rifle went dead just as he reached the pilot-house door. Ariana was gone, and he saw the broken glass window at the port side where she'd been dragged through. Then he heard Camacho's voice through the megaphone.

"¡Parer!" he called to his men and the firing stopped. Logan shut off the *Urchin's* engines and the vessel slowed at once. He stood by the instrument board, one hand on a switch lever.

"We have the girl, Logan," Camacho called. "Look out your left window. There is a gun at her temple."

Logan edged forward just enough to see the port deck. One of the guerrillas had his arm around Ariana's neck, his other hand holding a revolver against her temple.

"Now do we get what we want?" Camacho called out. Obviously, the man was watching through binoculars from the shore. Logan had a bull horn along the top edge of the pilot house and he turned it on.

"Camacho," he called, "I have my finger on a switch. If I press it what you want will disappear out of the bilge pump and into the river. It will never be seen again. Harm the girl and I'll press it."

There was silence. "All I have to do is press my finger and the information I have, all the evidence, is gone," Logan repeated. There was a long moment of silence and then Camacho replied.

"You would risk the girl for this evidence?" he asked.

"No," Logan said. "I just tell you if she is harmed, I press this switch."

"Then it appears we have a stalemate, *amigo,* no? And I don't like stalemates."

"I have a proposition," Logan called. "But I want the girl up here where I can see her, first."

Another moment of silence and then Camacho spoke to his man. "Take the girl to the pilot-house door where he can see her," he ordered. "But don't let go of her."

Logan waited and the smell of gunpowder, acrid and heavy, hung in the thick, humid air. Hand on the bilge pump switch, he watched as the guerrilla brought Ariana to the pilot-house doorway and stepped inside with her. He held the revolver to her temple.

"Now you see the girl, Logan," Camacho called. "What is your proposition? What are you getting out of this? Money?"

"Not that much," Logan answered. "The evidence I have will be put in the hands of the proper authorities. I promise you that. Alvarez and his group of thieves will be ousted from their posts in the government and punished."

'We will do the same thing if you give it to us."

"No. You will use it to further your revolution and I don't know if your revolution will be a good thing or not for the people of Peru. I don't know if you will be a friend or an enemy of democracy. I won't take sides."

"And if I don't believe you?" Camacho queried. Logan's lips tightened. The guerrilla leader had most of his people here, looking on, and certainly many of the uncommitted natives.

"Then we will both lose," Logan said. "This is your chance to show if you are really interested in the people, in a good government, or only in the glory of Camacho. Let me go and Alvarez and his group will be in jail in forty-eight hours. Camacho will have helped rid the people of Peru of five thieves. Force me to press this switch and there will be no evidence to prevent Alvarez and the others from continuing."

What happened next, Logan blamed himself for later. If he hadn't spelled it out so plainly maybe she wouldn't have acted. Ariana twisted, suddenly, and leaped across the pilot house, hands outstretched for the pump switch. The guerrilla fired and Logan saw her body shudder, twist and fall to the floor. She landed at his feet and the guerrilla stepped back, out of the wheelhouse, fear in his eyes. Logan was cradling the beautiful head in his arms and the black hair fell in cascades onto his chest.

"You little fool," he muttered and watched the red stain spreading, seeping. She opened her eyes and her hand made little motions. He lifted it and held it against his broad chest, and she smiled.

"You wouldn't have come with me, would you?" she asked.

"No," he said. She didn't deserve being lied to. "But I would have thought about it."

"It's better this way, then."

"No it isn't, dammit," he said. "Why did you have to play heroine?"

"I couldn't have done anything else. The past owns the future, or didn't I tell you that?"

His hand was stroking her cheek and he was shaking his head in disagreement when she half-rose, fighting down the pain, and he held her to him.

"Don't leave me here, Logan," she said. "Take me with you. Take me to where we first made love."

"I will," he said, quietly, and suddenly she was slumped in his arms and he stroked her hair for the last time. He got up and he heard Camacho's voice through the megaphone.

"I am sorry about the girl," the guerrilla leader said. "Was she your woman?"

"No," Logan answered slowly. "She was just someone I liked."

"You will do what you promised?" Camacho asked. "You will see that Alvarez and the others are jailed?"

"You can be goddamn sure of it," Logan said, cold fury in his voice. His eyes were not on the shore but on the lovely girl at his feet. "You can be goddammed sure."

"All right, I believe you," the guerrilla leader said. "Only a man who means what he says would be so determined."

Camacho gave crisp orders to his men and they dropped from the *Urchin* like so many flies. Logan started the engines, turned the nose of the boat downriver and moved forward. He saw the river widening and he knew that the blue waters of the Pacific were not far away. His eyes stared ahead, deep, and only those who knew him very well would have been able to see the pain inside them. He didn't want to think about the girl who lay at his feet but that was impossible. The past owns the future, she had said and he wondered whether she really believed that. Maybe for her it did. Maybe it did for a lot of people. But he couldn't help thinking that if he'd lied to her, if he'd made her believe he would go into her world with her, she would not have leaped for the pump switch. And so it was not the past that owned the future, that governed her action, but fear of having to live in a shadowed world. She'd been told she had to fight for that world, when she didn't have to fight for it at all. In a very real way, she had been used, sold a bill of goods just the way they'd sold him a bill of goods. Their lies to him were merely about the real purpose of a job. They'd lied to her about the real purpose of her life.

And so now she lay dead and there was the real crime. They would pay only for stealing monies, not for stealing a life. Logan glanced down at the girl. One of them would pay the full price. He'd see to that. The steel-cold hardness crept over him and he knew exactly what to do.

It was dark when he steered the boat into the waters of the Pacific and at once the cool winds swirled about him in a kind of welcome. He sailed back along the route they had taken and, at a certain spot, he stopped the boat. Reaching down, he picked up the girl, carefully, tenderly, and carried her down to the deck.

He'd known prayers as a boy but they'd long been pushed back into the dim recesses of his mind. He remembered only something about the Lord giving and the Lord taking away.

When he returned to the pilot house he was alone.

CHAPTER ELEVEN

I t was late afternoon when he sailed into the little cove in Panama. He found a spot and tied up at the wharf. He took the number Alvarez had given him from the chart drawer and went to the phone booth at the end of the quay. The man's voice almost leaped in excitement as Logan identified himself.

"I have a package for you," Logan said flatly. "I'll come right over with it. What is the address?"

Alvarez gave him a number on Campanile Street and Logan hailed a taxi. The house turned out to be large, stucco, and Alvarez was waiting at the door.

"Where's Ariana?" the man asked as he admitted Logan, his smooth urbanity unable to cloak his excitement.

"She couldn't come," Logan answered. He took the plastic package from his pocket and held it up for Alvarez to see. He wanted to make sure the man saw he had it, to bait him into the wrong move.

"This is going to be turned over to the President of your country," Logan said. "If I were you I'd resign now."

He saw the man's face darken and Alvarez was out of his chair. "What are you talking about?" he growled. His smooth, urbane exterior was disappearing fast.

"Your little racket," Logan said. "It's over, done with. I'm going to expose you, all of you."

Alvarez fought with himself a moment and managed one of his charming, controlled smiles.

"I understand," he said. "And perhaps I should have expected it. You want more money. All right, how much more?"

Logan's temper was nearing the boiling point. He didn't want conversation. He wanted action.

"Nothing, you bastard," he said. "I want you, behind bars, or dead. I'd like that even better."

He saw Alvarez's jaw tighten and the man's eyes bored into his.

"Give me that package," the man said. Logan started for the door. "Go screw yourself," he said. Out of the corner of his eye he saw Alvarez dart toward a desk in the corner of the room. A thin smile crossed the tall, mean man's face. This was it, what Logan wanted. He whirled and reached the desk at the same time that Alvarez yanked open the drawer and brought out a snub-barreled revolver. Logan's hand closed around Alvarez's wrist and he used his weight to slam the man's body back across the desk. He heard the revolver drop to the floor as Alvarez's arm bent backward. Logan was smiling, a cold, mirthless smile, as he smashed his fist into the man's jaw and watched him skid across the desk and into the wall.

"Now, you bastard," Logan said. "I'm going to save your country the expense of a trial."

He reached for the man but Alvarez, with the instinctive knowledge of every animal facing death, erupted in desperate strength. He kicked out and Logan managed to half-turn aside and take the blow on his arm. But it sent him skittering back a few feet. Alvarez leaped, landing atop him, his hands finding Logan's throat. Logan hit the man in the belly with all his strength. The hands left his throat and Alvarez doubled over in pain. A looping right sent the man somersaulting backward across the room and Logan felt the crack of his jawbone as the blow landed. Only the desperation of the cornered animal kept Alvarez fighting. He lunged across the floor for the revolver lying beside the desk. Logan's foot reached it first and kicked it away. Then he reached down and hit the man again. Alvarez landed half-across the desk. But his hand closed around a steel letter opener, as sharply pointed as any knife. He rolled from the end of the desk and landed on his feet. As the big man came at him again, he lunged. Logan shifted his body a fraction and the letter opener tore through the folds of his shirt. He sent a short, hard right into Alvarez's stomach and the man tottered backward. But the weapon was still in his hand and he swung again with it as Logan moved in. Logan stepped back and avoided the blow, and his right flashed out like a bullwhip being snapped. It landed on Alvarez's shattered jaw and spun the man into the wall. He heard Alvarez's gasp of pain.

"That's for that beating I took in that stinkin' jail," Logan hissed. Alvarez collapsed against the wall, crumpling to the floor. Somehow, he still held onto the letter opener. Logan lifted him to his feet with one hand and rammed his fist into his face. Alvarez arched backward, half-turned in the air, and fell to the floor.

"That one was for Ariana," Logan said bitterly. He went over to the still, crumpled form and turned it over. The letter opener was deep into the man's abdomen. His hand still held the handle.

Logan straightened up and walked to the desk. He picked up the telephone and dialed long distance, Washington, D.C. He asked for Ted Russell, State Department, and went through a succession of secretaries. Finally the phone was picked up and a voice from the not-too-dim past spoke in his ear.

"I don't believe it," the voice said. "Say something so I know it's you."

"It's me, Ted," Logan answered. "I have something for you. You'll know what to do with it and how."

Logan spoke quickly, leaving out only a few details, and the two men exchanged brief comments with the quiet respect of friends. When he'd finished, Logan drew a deep breath and waited.

"Christ, what a story," Russell commented. "It'll sure help us with the top level of the Peruvian Government. Can you get the evidence and a statement to our Consul there?"

"I can be there in an hour."

"Great. I'll call him and they'll be ready and waiting for you. We'll take it from there. You say you've got names, account numbers, everything, eh?"

"Everything."

"Five of them, eh?"

"Five. But one's dead. Alvarez."

"You wouldn't like to tell me how he got dead, I suppose."

"You suppose right," Logan said flatly. He heard Russell chuckle, and then the man's voice grew serious again.

"Everything all right with you and the *Urchin*?" Russell asked gently.

"Fine," Logan said. "No help needed."

"Good. Anyway, you know what to do if there ever is." The man's voice paused for a moment and then went on. "Logan," he said. "Thanks. Take care of yourself."

"I will," the tall, lean man answered quietly. He put down the phone and thought of how a few words could say a lot. He stepped over the crumpled form on the floor and walked out of the house into the gathering dusk. He moved quickly, anxious to finish with this business.

It was night when a tubby little vessel sailed out of Panama Harbor. She wasn't going anywhere in particular, just out into the night and the sea, where the world couldn't crowd in on you so.